Chevalier Coqdor
vs. The Zodiac

FROM THE SAME AUTHOR

Mephista

Chevalier Coqdor
vs. The Zodiac

The Thirteenth Sign of the Zodiac
by
Maurice Limat

The Fourteenth Sign of the Zodiac
by
**Jean-Marc Lofficier
& Jean-Michel Archaimbault**

translated by
Michael Shreve

A Black Coat Press Book

Visit our website at www.blackcoatpress.com

ISBN 978-1-64932-340-8. First Printing.: December 2024. Published by Black Coat Press, an imprint of Hollywood Comics.com, 18321 Ventura Blvd. Suite 915, Tarzana, CA 91356. All rights reserved. Except for review purposes, no part of this book may be reproduced or transmitted in any form or by any means, electronic or mechanical, including photocopying, recording, or by any information storage and retrieval system, without permission in writing from the publisher. The stories and characters depicted in this novel are entirely fictional. Printed in the United States of America.

TABLE OF CONTENTS

Maurice Limat
(photo by Philippe Marlin)

Introduction

When an author dies, his characters go with him, but when a science fiction author dies, planets, galaxies and entire universes can sink into oblivion.

This is particularly true of Maurice Limat, whose death on January 21, 2002 at the age of 88 could have been the equivalent of an apocalyptic black hole engulfing a universe unique in the history of French science fiction.

French critic Igor B. Maslowski wrote of *Monsieur Cosmos*, one of Limat's favorite works, that his hero's adventures "sometimes achieved greatness and raised many questions beyond those of the usual SF potboilers."

Renowned Belgian critic and essayist Jacques Van Herp described Limat's novel *Le Sang Vert* [The Green Blood] as "beautiful."

Other critics, such as Georges Nahon, emphasized the "spellbinding atmosphere" of Limat's *Angoisse* novels[1] and Tina Sol, a novelist herself, described *Moissons du futur* [Future Harvests] as "an exciting and entertaining novel written in a pleasant style."

If Limat's style was deemed slack by some, entertaining or unpretentious for others, his themes were always captivating, spellbinding, and even grandiose. What reviewers lacked was a historical point of view, which, instead of examining each novel separately, could have looked at his entire oeuvre.

One could then have come to the conclusion that Maurice Limat, far from being a minor author, was, on the contrary, a true creator of universes. If he was not the only one, he was undoubtedly one of the best in the entire history of French science fiction.

What is a *creator of universes*? It is an author who, over and above his individual novels, has created a fictional superstructure that brings them together, historically and geographically. That author has built a unique work that is more than the sum of its parts, a world that extends the novels, a backdrop that serves as their setting. In short, a universe.

---

[1] See *Mephista*, a three-novels collection, Black Coat Press, ISBN 978-1-61227-434-8.

One can mention here a number of great American writers: E.E. Doc Smith and his Lensmen, H.P. Lovecraft and Cthulhu, Robert E. Howard and Conan, Robert Heinlein's History of the Future, Jack Vance's Oecumene, Cordwainer Smith's Instrumentality, Larry Niven's Known Space, C.J. Cherryh's Union-Alliance, etc.

In France, there are the Enquêtes Galactiques by J. & D. Le May, Laurent Genefort's Omale, G.-J. Arnaud's Ice Company,[2] Michel Demuth's Galaxiales, Roland C. Wagner's Futurs Mystères de Paris and Christia Sylf's Kobor Tigan't.[3]

And then there is Maurice Limat's Martervenux universe.

For just over thirty years and a little over fifty novels, Limat depicted the epic story of a human race that left its native Earth, allied itself with the neighboring races of Mars and Venus, and from there, set out to discover the galaxy, finally proudly taking its place alongside the natives of Altair and Perseus.

Like *Star Trek* creator Gene Roddenberry's Federation, to which Limat's universe bears a strong resemblance, the stellar odyssey of the Terrans from the Martervenux is, above all, peaceful, and turned towards the discovery of the Other. Conflicts, when they arise, are resolved with the author's characteristic humanism.

It is true that Limat's fast-paced writing—due mostly to his publisher's demands—introduced some plot inconsistencies, contradictions and dating errors in some of his books, but they are all minimal and more than made up for by the majestic cosmic fresco unfolding before our eyes. One can only dream of what Limat, with a publisher more motivated by quality than speed and quantity, could have produced; what a publisher who knew how to inspire an author of undeniable talent and imagination could have drawn from him.

Limat's universe is surprisingly rich. The flora and fauna of its planets, from Eridan unicorns to Aquarian spiders, have no need to envy Jack Vance in terms of strangeness. Alien races abound, be they three-eyed, luminescent or even two-dimensional. Cosmic phenomena, undeniably poetic and defying the known laws of science, are plentiful: ice suns, negative stars, the Great Livid Ray... In a universe where physicists believe in the existence of eleven dimensions, supragravity and string

---

[2] *The Ice Company*, Black Coat Press, ISBN 978-1-935558-31-6.
[3] *Kobor Tigan't*, Black Coat Press ISBN 978-1-64932-225-8; *The Reign of Ta*, Black Coat Press, ISBN 978-1-64932-308-8.

theory, Limat's fantastic imagination may one day prove more predictive than that of more rigorous authors.

Finally, it's worth noting that, at that time, publishers forced their authors, when writing *space opera,* to give their heroes American names. From Richard Bessière's "Sydney Gordon" and "Dan Seymour" to Germany's "Perry Rhodan", we look in vain for a leading French hero in a galactic future. Yet, Limat uniquely didn't hesitate to use names like Robin Muscat and Bruno Coqdor. This isn't a sign of chauvisnism as the nation-states of the 20th century have been absorbed into the Martervenux entity, and France as such is hardly ever mentioned in the books, but a simple recognition that our descendants won't just be selling Beaujolais wine across the galaxy, but, like Roddenberry's Jean-Luc Picard, will be traveling among the stars.

Jean-Marc Lofficier

Chevalier Coqdor & Râx
by Gaston de Sainte-Croix

Bibliography of the Martervenux Universe

Chevalier Coqdor

1. *L'Étoile de Satan* [Satan's Star] (Anticipation 241, 1964)
2. *Particule zéro* [Particle Zero] (Anticipation 252, 1964)
3. *Ici finit le monde* [Here Ends the Universe] (Anticipation 257, 1964)
4. *Les Soleils noirs* [The Black Suns] (Anticipation 262, 1965)
5. *Le Flambeau du monde* [The Universal Torch] (Anticipation 274, 1965)
6. *La Terre n'est pas ronde* [Earth is not round] (Anticipation 296, 1966)
7. *Le Soleil de glace* [The Ice Sun] (Anticipation 302, 1966)
8. *Le Dieu couleur de nuit* [The Night-Colored God] (Anticipation 308, 1967)
9. *Les Portes de l'aurore* [The Gates of Dawn] (Anticipation 325, 1967)
10. *La Planète de feu* [Planet of fire] (Anticipation 341, 1968)
11. *Le Treizième signe du Zodiaque* [The Thirteenth Sign of the Zodiac] (Anticipation 379, 1969)
12. *Flammes sur Titan* [Flames Over Titan] (Anticipation 391, 1969)
13. *Tempête sur Goxxi* [Storms Over Goxxi] (Anticipation 398, 1969)
14. *Le Voleur de rêves* [The Dream-Thief] (Anticipation 411, 1970)
15. *Les Cosmatelots de Lupus* [The Spacers of Lupus] (Anticipation 430, 1970)
16. *Et la comète passa* [And the Comet Went by] (Anticipation 441, 1970)
17. *Un Astronef nommé Péril* [A Spaceship Named Danger] (Anticipation 453, 1971)
18. *Un de la galaxie* [One from the Galaxy] (Anticipation 464, 1971)
19. *Moissons du futur* [Future Harvests] (Anticipation 474, 1971)
20. *Quand le ciel s'embrase* [When the Sky Lights up] (Anticipation 497, 1972)
21. *L'Empereur de métal* [The Metal Emperor] (Anticipation 526, 1972)
22. *SOS.... Ici, Nulle Part !* [SOS From Nowhere!] (Anticipation 556, 1973)
23. *L'Étoile du silence* [The Silent Star] (Anticipation 574, 1973)
24. *Où Finissent les étoiles ?* [Where Do the Stars End?] (Anticipation 676, 1975)

25. *Le Maëlström de Kjor* [The Maelstrom of Kjor] (Anticipation 689, 1975)
26. *Les Incréés* [The Uncreated Ones] (Anticipation 749, 1976)
27. *Mortels Horizons* [Deadly Horizons] (Anticipation 821, 1977)
28. *Les Fontaines du Ciel* [The Fountains of the Sky] (Anticipation 857, 1978)
29. *Moi, le feu* [I, Fire] (Anticipation 971, 1980)
30. *Coup dur sur Deneb* [Real Blow on Deneb] (Anticipation 1143, 1982)
31. *Les Esclaves de Xicor* [The Slaves of Xicor] (Anticipation 1164, 1982)
32. *Le Mécaniquosmos* [The Mechanicosmos] (Anticipation 1184, 1982)
33. *Comme un vol de chimères* [Like a Flight of Chimerae] (Anticipation 1231, 1983)
34. *Les Vikings de Sirius* [The Vikings From Sirius] (Anticipation 1279, 1984)
35. *L'Élixir pourpre* [The Purple Elixir] (Anticipation 1314, 1984)
36. *Khéoba-la-Maudite* [Kheoba-the-Accursed] (Anticipation 1465, 1986)
37. *Et la Pluie tomba sur Mars* [And Rain Fell on Mars] (Anticipation 1497, 1986)
38. *Le Serpent de rubis* (The Ruby Snake] (Anticipation 1526, 1987)

Robin Muscat (solo)
1. *Les Foudroyants* [The Lightning Men] (Anticipation 164, 1960)
2. *Lumière qui tremble* [Shivering Light] (Anticipation 196, 1962)
3. *Les Créatures d'Hypnôs* [The Creatures from Hypnôs] (Anticipation 218, 1963)
4. *Fréquence ZZ* [ZZ Frequency] (Anticipation 266, 1965)
5. *Plus loin qu'Orion* [Farther than Orion] (Anticipation 417, 1970)
6. *La Lumière d'ombre* [The Shadowlight] (Anticipation 717, 1976)

Luc Delta (solo)
1. *Les Sirènes de Faô* [The Sirens of Faô] (Anticipation 351, 1968)
2. *Le Septième nuage* [The Seventh Cloud] (Anticipation 362, 1968)
3. *SOS.... Ici, Nulle Part !* [SOS From Nowhere!] (Anticipation 556, 1973)
4. *Le Zénith... et après ?* [Zenith... And After?] (Anticipation 1000, 1980)

Martinbras (solo)
1. *SOS Galaxie* [SOS Galaxy] (Editions Métal, Collection 2000, 18, 1956)
2. *J'écoute l'univers* [I Listen to the Universe] (Anticipation 154, 1960)

New Adventures
1. *Le Quatorzième Signe du Zodiaque* [The Fourteenth Sign of the Zodiac] (Rivière Blanche 2028, 2007)
2. *Là où s'ouvre l'Univers* [Where the Universe Opens] (Rivière Blanche 2041, 2008)
3. *Le Retour d'Hypnôs* [The Return of Hypnôs] (Rivière Blanche 2053, 2009)

Other novels which mention characters or concepts from the series
Les Enfants du chaos [The Children of Chaos] (Institut des Hautes Études Interplanétaires) (Anticipation 141, 1959)
Le Sang du Soleil [The Blood of the Sun] (Martervenux) (Anticipation 147, 1959)
Métro pour l'inconnu [Subway Into the Unknown] (Institut des Hautes Études Interplanétaires) (Anticipation 159, 1960)
Le Carnaval du cosmos [Cosmic Carnival] (Institut des Hautes Études Interplanétaires) (Anticipation 173, 1961)
Océan, mon *esclave* [Ocean, My Slave] (Interplan) (Anticipation 178, 1961)
Message des Vibrants [Message From the Vibrants] (Future of the Martervenux) (Anticipation 184, 1961)
Le Sang vert [The Green Blood] (Martervenux) (Anticipation 230, 1963)
Les Sortilèges *d'Altaïr* [The Spells of Altaïr] (Institut des Hautes Études Interplanétaires) (Anticipation 235, 1963)
Les Oiseaux de Véga [The Birds of Vega] (Institut des Hautes Études Interplanétaires ; alias used by Robin Muscat in *Le quatorzième signe du Zodiaque*) (Anticipation 317, 1967)
Métalikus (mentioned in *Le quatorzième signe du Zodiaque*) (Anticipation 374, 1969)
L'Espace d'un éclair [The Time of a Lightning Bolt] (Télé-Cosmos) (Anticipation 642, 1974)

Miroirs d'univers [Mirrors of Universes] (Télé-Cosmos) (Anticipation 758, 1976)

Les Diablesses de Qiwâm [The She-Devils of Qiwâm] (mentioned by Robin Muscat on *Le quatorzième signe du Zodiaque*) (Anticipation 789, 1977)

La Cloche de brume [The Fog Bell] (Interplan and Martervenux) (Anticipation 892, 1979)

Le Troubadour de minuit [The Midnight Troubadour] (Institut des Hautes Études Interplanétaires) (Anticipation 1097, 1981)

Les Presque dieux [The Almost Gods] (mentioned by Coqdor in *Et la pluie tomba sur Mars*) (Anticipation 1210, 1983)

Lointaine étoile [The Furthest Star] (Institut des Hautes Études Interplanétaires) (Anticipation 1545, 1987)

Timeline

The Martervenux Federation and Interplan were created in 2090.

Martinbras was born in 2140; Robin Muscat in 2158; Luc Delta in 2162; and Bruno Coqdor in 2168.

Coqdor visited Satan's Star and adopted Râx in 2193.

The novels take place from 2193 to 2203; the "new adventures" begin in 2206.

THE THIRTEENTH SIGN OF THE ZODIAC

CHAPTER I

Robin Muscat was in a terrible mood. It was raining on Paris-sur-Terre like on the rain planets he had visited near the star Algol.

And on the other hand, his direct boss, Mr. Lepinson, director of the huge Interplan organization, the interplanetary police force, had just entrusted him with a file that he already knew, before even opening it, and was stupefyingly dull.

He had left the documents on his desk and filled a pipe with tobacco from the plains of Mars, staring emptily out at the giant city, occasionally pressing his sturdy forehead against the window, with his hair pulled back high, while all the boredom of the world drifted through his gray-blue eyes.

He sighed, "I gotta get started... What a drag! Some obscure story of trafficking, no doubt... These so-called mysteries on board spaceships, always the same thing..."

The file was threefold and Inspector Robin Muscat already knew, roughly, what it was about. Three tragedies had played out in recent weeks on the same interstellar line, namely the Sol-Perseus trip. Three different tragedies, in fact. A crime, first of all. A case of dementia next. Each of them had had a man as a victim. Finally, the third case, a few weeks earlier (in Earth time), when the spaceship *Spica* was about to land at Paris-sur-Terre: a disappearance, this one. That of a young woman.

For Robin Muscat, this kind of case was commonplace.

On the long space trips, trafficking of all kinds (human flesh, drugs, unknown weapons, gems with uncanny powers) was frequent and the settling of scores was manifold. He who had experienced so many incredible adventures across the galaxy never failed to grumble when, on his return from some distant adventure, Lepinson gave him one of these

15

cases which he considered good for little terrestrial inspectors, the "crawlers" of Interplan, riveted to the ground of the home planet.

He took the three files, extracted the small strips and placed them in turn in the "dispensator." In front of him, on the white screen formed by the neutral wall, he saw animated or still images appear, in reliefcolor so perfect that the people and objects stood out in front of Muscat unbelievably real. They talked, they lived and, thus, he learned everything that his subordinates had gleaned either on board the *Spica* or in the immediate entourage of the three victims.

From the start, Robin Muscat was distracted. Lepinson had not hidden from him that in view of his extraordinary record of service, he was going to be promoted to commissioner—a position of huge importance which would give him control over the entire Interplan, a police force empowered to act on all civilized worlds. This pleased him, which was understandable, and the fact of having to go through a file considered tedious was hardly compatible with the carefree delight that would have been appropriate.

However, as the sequence went on and the various pictures clicked by, Robin Muscat began to take a keen interest, driven by his passionate professional self-awareness as a true policeman of the cosmos.

The crime, first. Yum Akatinor, a native of Perseus, was a strange character versed in the occult, particularly cosmomancy, which had long since replaced astrology due to the much wider scope of current clairvoyants. He had been found dead, but in a manner quite incomprehensible. Thunderstruck, one might have said. According to the autopsy, the man had been under tremendous stress, which had ended his life. All attempts at resuscitation were in vain.

Muscat reviewed certain elements of the file. He saw again the slightly greenish face, framed by a dark and smooth beard like those of the Assyrians of Ancient Earth. Then the report emphasized one detail. Muscat looked at the photographs from the medical examiner. A naked corpse. Zoom in on one part of the chest. A tattoo? It looked like it. A kind of sign, no doubt more or less esoteric, under the left breast.

Moving on. The *Spica* passenger who had gone mad was a Martian, one of the last representatives of alien life on the Red Planet, the majority of whom had already emigrated to Venus by the time of the first contacts with Earth, before the restoration of a world which had once had a rarefied atmosphere.

He was a highly esteemed financier throughout the Martervenux, respected not only on the six united planets of the Solar System, but also almost everywhere on other friendly worlds. Cladek Halstar led an orderly life. However, his wife, a pretty Earthwoman, had revealed that he was sometimes secretive, frequently leaving on long trips whose destination she did not know. But because of the billions in various currencies that he moved through space, she accepted this situation, saying only that she trusted in his fidelity.

Interplan had already determined that Cladek Halstar had had relationships with several individuals, including two other women, both of whom seemed a little unconventional and all of whom were involved in cosmomancy.

As for the third case, Giovanna Hi-Ling was a Chinese-Italian woman who had been missing for almost three months. Not much was known about her. Raised on Mars, she rarely returned to her home planet and was also deeply interested in the occult. Her real profession was unknown and, as she no longer had a family, it had been difficult to learn more about her.

Muscat sighed, "Too bad we don't have a nude photo."

He said this while staring at the image of Giovanna Hi-Ling in a swimsuit, a discreet, becoming outfit, but one that made it impossible for him to verify if, like Yum Akatinor and Cladek Halstar, the beautiful Giovanna bore the mysterious tattoo on her chest, below the heart.

Interplan had been able to examine the Martian at their leisure because Cladek Halstar was crazy, raving mad, and was currently locked up at the Sainte-Anne psychiatric hospital in Paris-sur-Terre, one of the oldest in the world and, without a doubt, the most modern of all.

But science was still making few inroads into curing insanity.

Muscat carefully reviewed the entire file and focused on the enlargement of the mysterious tattoo. He had grabbed an electro-pencil with inexhaustible lead, and scribbled while smoking, no longer listening to the film which continued to roll, no longer looking at the images.

He was drawing and redrawing the sign... A loop, two points... No, two lines in the shape of an upside-down V... One loop, two curves like circumflex accents...

What could it represent? A bird? Yes, possibly, relying on the hieroglyphic writings which, on Earth and elsewhere, were the origin of current writings, but which were all inspired by original drawings, having a precise visual meaning.

Let's say a bird. Two wings. But what are these lines that cross the wings? And the six little lines below?

Frustrated, Muscat pushed the drawings away and remained for a moment pondering.

Wings... wings... a bird... No, more like a beast, not a bird. A bird is always graceful, even when it is a bird of prey, a condor, a vulture, an algomaus of Wolf 424 or a pyrornithocus from the planets of Altaïr, a bird that spits electric fire, a feathered predator...

"I'm sure there's a symbol in there for something that flies. But it's not a bird..."

A machine? A spaceship?

The Quetzal, the feathered serpent of the ancient Incas... Wasn't it, as had been demonstrated in the 20th century, the memory of the first alien spaceship to come from Venus?

"It flies... No, it's not a machine, not a bird, it's..."

He frowned, got up, went to get a dictionary and put what corresponded to the letter Z in the dispensator from which he had previously removed the tapes from the *Spica* file.

Zeppelin... and there showed up an implausibly old-fashioned flying machine, but one which had been the origin of the jets that Robin Muscat knew. Zeus... and he saw the god of the Greeks, the lightning god... not the time to get into mythology. Zibeline... the sable, a charming little creature, pretty furs… Ziggurat... Mesopotamia… Zingaro... the bohemians who became legendary...

Wonderfully sharp images, a whispering voice.

Muscat pressed the "fast forward" button. Zircon...

"I don't care about precious stones."

Zodiac!

The soon-to-be commissioner examined the ancient representations of the celestial zone which always formed the ideal horizon for Earthlings.

"Yes! These kinds of signs... Now I'm getting somewhere. There's Virgo, Libra, Scorpio and Aries…"

He picked up the sheet where he had scribbled the same sign thirty times, the strange tattoo noted from the chest of two of the victims.

"Zodiac signs. Ah, there are also the symbols of the planets…"

The letter P in the dispensator replaced the letter Z and Muscat mused for a moment in front of this parade of esotericism.

"Oh!" he raged, "if only I knew if this Giovanna…"

Suddenly, the intercom rang. Grumpily, he answered, "Muscat. What's the matter?"

"Inspector, there's a visitor for you.

"Who is he ?"

"A citizen from Tycho-City, passing through Earth."

"What does he want?" Muscat growled, already determined to send this untimely Selenite away.

"He wants to tell you something about the *Spica* case."

"Ah? Well, well… Send him up!"

A moment later, Muscat pushed back the files. Standing at the window, he watched the rain fall on the immense spiral which dominated the city and around which the tramono lines wound up—the urban trains whose single tracks ran above the houses and streets, replacing the old metro of yesteryear, whose endless tunnels had long been converted into underground routes for electric cars and other kinds of individual transport.

"Inspector Muscat?"

"Yes. Please sit down."

Muscat had not seen the man enter. He turned around, took his seat and looked up, his eyes clear and hard, to probe his visitor. He was a young man in his early twenties. He had the special tan of people who lived on the Moon, in its weird lighting; that ashen complexion known as "earthlight." Skinny and brown, he probably originated from southern Europe.

"So, you have something to tell me?" Muscat said.

"I am Giovanna Hi-Ling's fiancé," the man began.

Suddenly, this boy warranted closer attention, thought the inspector.

"Go on! Tell me everything you know. She's disappeared and we think it was a kidnapping. Do you think so too?"

"Yes."

"You don't have any other theories?"

"No. She could never have left me. She didn't run away."

"Suicide?"

The young man laughed nervously, a little sadly.

"Oh no, she loved life. Passionately…"

He too seemed passionate, but was overwhelmed by the tragedy.

"One moment. Your identity?"

Muscat clicked on the camera which would record the man's statement, both in video and audio. The young man began:

"My name is Jean-Marie Spontini, born in Corsica, residing in Tycho-City."

Some professional and marital status information followed, then he stated that he had met Giovanna during a layover. She had told him that she was a student, and he had fallen madly in love with her. She planned to travel to Perseus... He wanted to go with her, but she'd told him that it was not possible.

It wasn't a very long trip, in fact, despite the enormous distances. It had taken only a few weeks. The *Spica* was about to bring her back when she had disappeared, inexplicably, on the spaceship as it had entered the the Solar System.

"Tell me, was she rich?" inquired Muscat.

"No, I don't think so."

"You don't think so, or you do not know?"

"No, I'm sure she wasn't."

"What about you? You just told me that you work in Tycho, as a wind tunnel technician.[4] It doesn't pay a lot of money. So, how could you have afforded a trip to Perseus?"

Spontini made an evasive, if somewhat distraught, gesture.

"There were some mysteries in your girlfriend's life, weren't they?"

The young Corsican nodded silently, then said:

"She wasn't really my girlfriend."

"But you just told me so implicitly. Don't worry. Miss Hi-Ling is very beautiful and you don't look so bad yourself. You're a nice-looking couple. Tell me, did she tell you about her past... about her experiences with the occult?"

The visitor became visibly uncomfortable.

"I see that she did," continued Muscat. "But again, don't worry. It's not a crime. We police officers understand what the study of parapsychology has contributed to humanity. And there are some truly fascinating cases... Only, you know about the *Spica*... Miss Hi-Ling is our third case."

"Yes. First, there was that guy from Perseus who died. And then, the banker who went crazy."

A cloud of horror passed over Spontini's face. Muscat stood up, and went to sit on the desk in front of him.

"We're amongst men here... So do you have anything to confess?"

---

[4] The oxygen blowers that feed the cities under the globe built on the Moon. (*Note from the Author*)

Spontini looked up in shock.

"What do you mean?"

"I'd like a small but intimate clarification concerning your girl-friend..."

Muscat noticed that his visitor was trembling slightly, very slightly.

"Have you ever seen... on her chest... a small tattoo? Oh, a trifle... Just below her left breast...?" he asked.

Spontini jumped but quickly restrained himself. He was visibly frightened.

"Well, what's the problem? You knew her well. So, tell yourself that I'm here to help you, that our role is to save her, to return her to you. Besides, you are so worried about it that you came here by yourself... spontaneously. So come on, spit it out, Spontini!"

He leaned over, pointed his finger at the young man's chest, towards the heart.

"There... Does Giovanna have something tattooed there?"

But Spontini pulled back so quickly that an idea flashed through Muscat's brain. For a moment, a very short moment, his eyes burned through this boy who seemed so spooked by his outstretched finger.

"Spontini, take off your shirt!"

"What? What do you mean?"

"You know very well what I mean."

Giovanna's fiancé jumped up in panic.

"Inspector!"

"You want us to help you get Giovanna back, right? Yes or no?"

Spontini took a step back. Muscat grabbed him by the arm.

"Then don't try to run away. It's a stupid move. You have to help us help her—if you love her."

Spontini's face tensed. He was on the verge of tears. Muscat said more gently:

"Show me. And afterwards, you'll tell me everything... everything you know."

And he was the one who undid the magnetic strips of the jacket. Spontini had given up; his teeth were chattering.

"Now the shirt," ordered Muscat.

The skinny boy was shivering, but he took off his shirt. Muscat leaned over the bare chest. He had not been wrong. The sign was there.

A tattoo? He wouldn't have sworn to it. It looked as if it was engraved under the epidermis itself, just under the left breast. And he recognizes the same mysterious symbol he had been tracing.

The central loop, the two wings in circumflex accents, the six small lower lines, also arranged in groups of three. The lines that crossed the wings, like lightning. It was about half an inch high, but inscribed in the flesh using a process that Muscat did not recognize.

"So I wasn't wrong. Now you will…"

A scream suddenly erupted in the office. Before his eyes, while he was still leaning towards Spontini, while he was lingering to better analyze the sign, Muscat saw it—this strange symbol—suddenly start blazing!

From a dark blue color, it changed to fluorescent crimson, dazzling the officer's eyes with a sudden point of fire. And Spontini's entire bare torso—and his entire body—in a split second, appeared enveloped in a fiery aura.

It was brief. And then, there was nothing left, at Robin Muscat's feet, but the body—the corpse—of Giovanna Hi-Ling's unfortunate fiancé. A thought passed quickly through the mind of the Interplan inspector:

"The dead man didn't talk. The crazy guy can't talk. But that one will talk!"

CHAPTER II

It was raining more and more and the beacons had been put in place. They were systems of rays and light beams, vertical and horizontal, emanating from projectors placed either on the top of buildings or on special pylons. Thus, in the sky of Paris-sur-Terre, new paths were traced by these dazzling beams which pierced the mist, these lines of colored infrared looking like huge quadrangles through which flew the helijets, the heliscooters, the gyroplanes, old archaic helicopters, and even a few saucers registered on different worlds.

Intersections, of course, had been planned here and there, following custom—traffic lights for stopping and starting with the orange intermediary.

A little below—on their single tracks launched from the Great Central Spiral which rose up on the site of what had once been Clichy—the countless tramonos set off in all directions, carrying crowds of travelers, never-ending traffic.

The Interplan helijet had absolute priority.

Robin Muscat wasted no time. The murdered man on the *Spica* had not talked. The madman wouldn't or couldn't. But this corpse that had fallen at his feet, he was determined to get its secrets out.

Quickly, in a few minutes, the building's lab had done what was necessary. Three chemicals had been injected into the body of the late Jean-Marie Spontini. He was dead, Muscat was sure of it. But with this process, he knew that he could hold off the chemical decomposition, halt the irremediable destruction which accompanies, in the minutes following death, the flight of the soul, after which there is no more anyone can do.

Certainly, Muscat had no expectations to resurrect Spontini. He was pretty sure that the criminals who had struck him down in front of him to prevent him from talking knew what they were doing, and that the "tattoo" was a powerful catalyst, quite useful on occasion to get rid of indiscreet people.

But while one of his assistants brought in the helijet and the other two treated the body, he called two very specific people by videophone and got an immediate appointment.

As his vehicle sped above Paris-sur-Terre through the big luminous squares which lined up to form a vast artery in the misty, rainy sky, while he passed the intersections where traffic was forced to a stop to allow him through, he knew that, on another route, another helijet was already en route, and the man who was aboard would meet him in a few moments.

Less than five minutes after leaving the Interplan tower in Montmartre, Muscat, and his special cargo arrived in Vincennes where a hospital tower overlooked the ancient, evergreen woods.

"Everything's ready," said a man in a white suit who barely took the time to shake Muscat's hand.

At record speed, Spontini's body was stripped naked and thrown into a kind of narrow pool where he would bathe in plasma. Probes and electrodes were stuck to various points on his body and needles dug into the flesh returning to necrosis. A flow of liquid hydrogen entered the pool. On the left, an artificial heart in the form of a pump was already starting the stimulation that would cause the resuscitation of the heart muscle.

A bald man with hard eyes behind rimless glasses watched what was still only a corpse pulsate and kept an eye on a dial that recorded the pulse rate.

Extremely impressed, Muscat saw the chest rising rhythmically under the impulse of the artificial lung already connected.

"What do you think, Stewe?" he asked in a slightly altered tone.

The dry voice of his old friend, Dr. Stewe, who had just arrived a minute before him, declared:

"He's dead. Obvious clinical signs. However, I believe that our friend Dusaule can do something about it and get you what you want."

Muscat made a move to pull out his pipe, but he changed his mind in time. It was neither the place nor the time to smoke.

The man who had welcomed him, Dr. Frank Dusaule, installed in a small glass cabin in front of a complicated console filled with dials, pressed buttons, turned wheels, lowered and raised levers. All the devices surrounding the miniature swimming pool where liquid hydrogen and plasma maintained the failing organism crackled and hummed with artificial but impressive life, trying to revive, as much as possible, this corpse that had to be asked important questions.

Frank Dusaule... Muscat had thought of him right from the start. The young and brilliant doctor who, very far from his homeworld, had realized—thanks to the inhabitants of the planet Mîo of Aquarius—a scientific dream that Earth had refused him.[5] Dusaule had probed death, forced open the doors of eternity.

It is true that the experience of the Necronauts had almost turned into a disaster, but since then, in the company of his wife Stella, he had returned to Earth and, taking advantage of his incredible discovery, had worked harder than ever to save human lives.

Stewe, who had been asked to witness the operation, spoke in a low voice:

"Thunderstruck, you tell me? And from this... this little spot at the level of the heart? Hmm... These people are powerful."

"And dangerous. But if Spontini could talk... He's really dead, isn't he, Stewe?" the inspector repeated angrily.

"No doubt about it. Still, I trust our friend Dusaule. You acted very quickly. It hasn't been twelve minutes since that spark struck down this man. In principle, the delay is not too long. Clinical death is obvious, but we all know that this fluid..."

"The soul... the spirit. Go on and say the word, you atheist!"

"I am not a metaphysician, like your friend Coqdor," Stewe sneered. "I only believe in science."

"You were about to admit just now that there's at least a fluid... something that escapes our understanding..."

"Oh, there's something we don't know yet, but that we shall discover one day. Basically, we know that, shortly after what is commonly called death, the body shows a certain loss of weight, which until now has been difficult to explain, even taking into account the halt of chemical functions and dehydration."

"And this something, this loss of weight—even if you don't want to admit that it's a departure of the soul—has not happened yet?"

"Right. A dial will indicate when it's ready. But it's still too early."

Muscat took a deep breath. He was counting on just that.

The two of them and Dusaule, from his cabin, observed the mysterious work of the machines which energized the corpse and gave it all the appearances of normal functions, which was truly extraordinary.

"If his soul is still there..." Muscat began.

"When it goes away, we'll see how much a soul weighs," mocked the incorrigible skeptic.

---

[5] See *Les Portes de l'Aurore.* (*Note from the Author*)

Muscat glared at him, but now was not the time for philosophical or scientific arguments.

Dusaule, for his part, was not only looking at the body but at the dials and, given the circumstances, he followed the development of the return to the living more carefully than his two friends.

Finally, after about six minutes, his voice rang out through a microphone:

"Inspector, Dr. Stewe, our subject is now ready. Would you like to take over for me, dear colleague?"

Stewe took Dusaule's place in the cabin and took over the monitoring of the machines that were making up for the deficiency of the patient's vital functions. Thus, although Spontini was dead, quite dead, still his heart beat, his blood circulated, and his lungs had resumed their rhythm.

Three assistants and two laboratory technicians, at Dusaule's call, entered at that very moment while, from the ceiling, which opened like a dome, Muscat saw an extraordinary device come down, which was placed silently just above the pool where the living dead man rested. It was a complicated interweaving of seven opalescent spheres, the smallest of which, in the middle, looked like one of those cosmonaut helmets so popular throughout the galaxy, and of which the other six were identical reproductions, but with increasing diameters.

The seven concentric spheres were lowered from the upper floor by a mechanism which unfolded like a crane arm. That same arm supported an energy generator, a dynamo engine bristling with very fine antennas connected to countless wires forming a graceful spider's web whose brilliance completed the illusion.

This whole ensemble was suspended above the pool of life, a synthesis of all the human inventions ever devoted to the search for survival. It was the latest discovery of Dr. Frank Dusaule, the enemy of death.

While Stewe was still leaning over the controls showing the movements of the synthetic organs, rectifying here, stimulating there, stopping or slowing down elsewhere, Dusaule, with a few hand movements and without a word, gave his instructions to the five assistants.

The two young women, with precise movements, almost mechanical but not devoid of grace, gently manipulated the spheres to bring them nearer the dead man. The three men were busy around various devices that they plugged into the generator whose purpose, this time, became very clear.

Cameras and microphones were set up.

The laboratory assistants delicately pushed sphere number one, the smallest, towards Spontini's head, which they framed like in a helmet. And the six other spheres, one after the other, resumed their proper position so that the general concentricity was again achieved.

Thus, the head of the corpse, slightly raised by a special support, occupied the absolute center of the whole. The largest sphere, more than three feet in diameter, stood over the pool and brought into the middle of the laboratory its huge translucent globe through which one had to imagine more than actually see the other spheres in which the dead man's head had completely disappeared.

Dusaule did not miss a detail, not a gesture from his collaborators. But the team must have been well trained because he didn't make the slightest correction. Everything was ready.

He turned to Robin who, with a dry throat, asked:

"If I understand correctly, everything is in order?"

"Whenever you're ready, inspector."

"Let's go!"

Dusaule made a gesture. One of the lab technicians walked over to the generator and pressed a simple button.

And they waited.

They could barely see the body of the dead man, but they could clearly hear the typical sound of breathing—his pseudo-breathing.

For a moment, Muscat, who had a bit of a headache, would have sworn that he also heard the beating of the heart, the heart of a dead man that human science was forcing to keep beating.

All this so that the brain be adequately irrigated, in an artificial way but regularly, so that from this organ, the seat of thought, they could extract, if not coherent sentences, at least clues, images, everything that forms a crazy conglomeration in the human neurons where everything that constitutes life is written on the mysterious seats of memory with their billions of different components.

Certainly, Muscat was fully aware that the will of the dead man was now absent. He couldn't count on the classification, the selection, the suitable juxtaposition of these elements to answer the questions he wanted to ask.

But the procedure was getting around the difficulty. Spontini was coming back to life, and it was better than someone permanently dead like Yum Akatinor; or better than a madman, like Cladek Halstar, whose interrogation had yielded nothing worthwhile, and whose brain probe would be useless since his weakened mind would give hardly any useful information, or might even fight it with that rigid stubbornness of the insane.

But in this captive organism of science, in this brain which they were trying—perhaps with a chance of success—to hold back for one more moment, preventing his soul from escaping forever, Robin Muscat hoped to read a word, a sentence, to glean some sign of what would allow him to find the trail of the mysterious evildoers.

And the interrogation of the dead man began.

CHAPTER III

The two assistants had taken their places on either side of the enormous installation. Both carried out their work methodically and, when the adjustment had been made, certain things started happening.

The light had dimmed considerably in the laboratory. Only the control cabin where Dr. Stewe was now sitting, leaving Dr. Dusaule to monitor the artificial resurrection, remained brightly lit.

So much so that Robin Muscat, now standing next to Frank Dusaule facing the apparatus, could see his friend in a glow that had something diabolical about it. This was due to his hairless features on a completely bald head, emphasized by the sparkle of rimless glasses. Leaning over the dials, which cast variegated reflections creating a nightmare rainbow, Stewe looked like one of those infernal scientists who performed the magical experiments of yesteryear. And yet, despite his fantastic appearance, Stewe remained pure, a relentless man in the service of science and humanity. There was a good reason why Muscat and Dusaule had asked him to come and help them in such delicate circumstances.

The three technicians prepared the complete recording of the revelations that they awaited and hoped for. Because, perhaps, it was too late and Spontini, definitely dead, would not talk, if one could use that verb.

The light dimmed again. All they saw, apart from Stewe leaning over the dials with sharp eyes, was the sphere that glowed in the semidarkness of the laboratory and, below, the weird reflections on the surface of the bath of plasma and liquid hydrogen in which was immersed the body of this dead man who they wanted for a few minutes, maybe just a few seconds, to make, if not a living man, but at least a zombie.

Muscat, impressed because it was the first time he had witnessed this type of experiment, even though Dusaule had often spoken to him about it, felt that the doctor at his side was no less tense than himself despite his apparent calm.

Slowly, the enormous sphere glowed ever more brightly. Muscat could not repress a sigh in which all his tense emotion was released.

A subtle play of mirrors reflected in the middle of the installation, and on a disproportionately magnified scale, the image of the subject's head. So, he saw the face of Giovanna Hi-Ling's poor fiancé as the head of a statue, almost two feet-tall. His rolled-up eyes, which were only partly veiled by the eyelids, the stiff lips, the atrociously pinched nose, all this further accentuated the impression of thinness of this face that would not have been ugly in its natural state.

This was what Frank Dusaule called effect No. 1, the simple photograph obtained by the first sphere.

After half a minute, they moved on to effects Nos. 2, 3, 4 and 5. Meaning Muscat was able to see the face decompose, show all the symptoms of fleshly necrosis and, as the image changed color and appearance, move on to the representation of a flayed head.

From this second stage, the muscular, they came to the third, that of the sole appearance of the nervous system outside the brain, then it was, by a subtle selection, the fourth, the cranium alone.

The pace of the parade of images sped up. There was no need to waste time. Moreover, through a microphone, Stewe's dry and unpleasant voice had just called the experimenters to order.

"Attention! Heart failure! Only a few minutes left!"

Muscat was sweating and guessed that Dusaule must have been experiencing the same thing. However, the chief of the laboratory said nothing. He was confident in his staff. He knew that no one would flinch, no one would lose a fraction of a second.

The image changed again. At the fifth stage, the brain appeared alone, an enormous, flattened, divided sphere, a double gray mass where, during the cosmic life of man, what is called intelligence is housed. The number one organ, the prodigious tool that the Creator of all things has placed at the disposal of man, who so often thinks that he himself is a god, thanks to the complicated scrolls of this prodigious device that he is quite incapable of creating himself.

But everything passed very quickly and effect No. 6 arrived—that of thought. Muscat held his breath.

Through the seven spheres, each originally responsible for photographing and filming the various stages of penetration of the strata constituting a human head, the waves radiated, were directed differently, and created the so strangely different visions.

Now they were moving beyond the physical stage itself. Already, what appeared on the outer sphere was the product of the sixth stage, the intermediary between the brain itself and the visions of this same brain. A kind of chaos, a feverish, tormented cosmos, crossed by dazzling beauties and horrifying abysses. Nothing definitive, clear-cut, no precision.

Everything was only suggested. It was thought in its raw state, spontaneous visions, reflex images that spring into the human mind under the impulse of external sensations.

No doubt, what was presented to the eyes of the experimenters, on the globoid screen, was not so much personal impressions, but the flash-representations of human sensations in general. From the tender blue of loving emotion to the red of anger, from the dizzying darkness of hatred to the gold of sublime love, from the green sweetness of spring hope to the intense mauve of passion, all shot through with flashes of fear or desire, or losing oneself in the whirlwinds and nebulae of despair, of morose delight, of melancholy and of long stagnation where thought unfolds without order.

"Hurry up," Stewe ordered. "Only a minute left, two at most..."

They had just passed the cerebral no-man's land. They arrived at effect No. 7, the last stage, the one which was the goal of the experiment, the one where, perhaps, if providence favored them, they would be able to glean the last reactions of the stricken man murdered by means of an incomprehensible symbol.

Shaken by his colleague's anxious comment, Dusaule murmured:

"It's finished."

The spheres relayed the seventh and final effect—the soul or consciousness.

For a very brief moment, Muscat saw an incredible conglomeration of images appear all at once. On the entire spherical surface of the enormous outer globe, human photos, visions born from the biological screen of thought, images projected into man by man according to his intrinsic nature and which vary from one individual to another, faces, monstrous forms and incomparable beauty, landscapes, scenes and things that one could not define, all this was born suddenly from who knows what genesis and it was only the reflection of the consciousness of a human, of the last fraction of a second in which Jean-Marie Spontini had lived, reliving his entire existence, but all superimposed by his final sensations.

Sensations born from his conversation with Robin Muscat and from which the interstellar detective hoped he would be able to glean elements that perhaps, when living, Spontini would have refused or at least hesitated to share with him.

Of course, Spontini had now been dead for almost half an hour, despite the great effort which had allowed the transfer of the body and the installation of the artificial resurrection device. But according to Dusaule's thesis, a thesis already corroborated by various experiments, one could obviously not read an evolving thought, even by probing a brain in a state of survival. The spark was no longer there.

At least, they could pick up what had been stagnant since the very moment of death, like what physiologists have demonstrated for a long time by searching for the image last seen by man on the sensitive plate of the retina.

Dusaule started from there, from the last retinal reflex, to build his entire system. The retina retains the single image, the vision. The brain remembers everything more or less nebulously, but more precisely what was the subject of its last thoughts.

During this very short moment when the multiple apparitions lasted, the cameras rolled, the flashes went off, the microphones picked up strange ultrasounds, inaudible to the human ear but that mysteriously accompanied the visions, and that sensitive microphones would later re-transmit.

Then everything faded away. There was nothing left but the vaguely opalescent sphere in the semi-darkness.

Stewe's voice stated:

"No need now. He's dead. The body is losing weight."

Dusaule sighed deeply and Muscat thought he detected a slight relaxation in him. The young doctor said:

"It doesn't matter! Thanks, Stewe, but we succeeded."

The light was coming back. The sevenfold sphere freed Spontini's head and rose towards the dome which engulfed him. The assistants, still silent and precise, delicately operated the controls and the three technicians were already bending over their devices, extracting the photos, films and magnetic tapes.

"Did you manage to see anything interesting, inspector?" Dusaule asked as Stewe came out of the cabin.

"Yes," said Muscat, overwhelmed by the sight-reading of the thoughts of a dead person, or rather of a dead person at the precise moment of his death. "The symbol I'm looking for—the symbol that's tattoed on this poor boy's chest that killed him."

"It's true. I saw it too. A sort of hieroglyph, an esoteric symbol..."

"Well, if you want to come to laboratory 3 where these gentlemen will give you the results of the experiment..."

Muscat, walked beside Dusaule and Stewe, following the three assistants.

The cameras, tape recorders, everything was able to immediately re-transmit films and recordings, developments being made on the spot.

On a screen, they saw the flat projection of all the images captured at the crucial moment on the outside sphere, meaning what was, in super-imposed vision, Spontini's last thought at the exact moment when death struck.

Muscat saw all kinds of things. But above all, dominating the whole, the fatal symbol: the loop and the two lines in circumflex accent, the lightning strikes crossing out the lines, the two groups of smaller lines below. But there were so many other things. Visions of space, spaceships—Muscat identified the *Spica*—a totally unknown world, a sort of bizarrely shaped temple, a vestibule, a rotunda or a forecourt sur-rounded by thirteen square doors, strange people obviously belonging to a planet he could not identify...

And more earthly, human things. Family scenes, visions of rooms, theaters, bars, cosmic ships. Several women, one of whom stood out, very beautiful. They could see her face and, from another angle, her na-ked, gorgeous body.

"Giovanna Hi-Ling! Can I have an enlargement of this area? Partic-ularly the chest."

It was quick. A technician adjusted the projection. The requested ar-ea grew bigger, filling the screen and, as he expected, Muscat, with a groan of satisfaction, saw the mysterious symbol under Giovanna's left breast.

And then, he saw several times, as if in a series of endlessly repeat-ed shots, a kind of disk or a rounded, maybe spiraled, surface. Here too, he asked for a blow-up. With Stewe, Dusaule and the assistants, he wondered aloud about its meaning.

"A plate," someone said, laughing a little.

"A dish, rather."

"No, it's a marine compass."

"Hmm! And there's a rotating, spiraling movement."

"Like a snail shell."

"Me, I see roulette," said an assistant, who was a fan of the game.

They shouted, booing him.

But the most varied, absurd and fanciful hypotheses came out. Mus-cat let them come, hoping that someone would put their finger on it, in the delirium that was possessing them all. Now it was becoming a little game. The technicians and assistants were young and Muscat was gambling on their enthusiasm. More or less valid suggestions were still being made.

Stewe, more realistic, piped up, "We can say at least one thing—it's a fairly circular and compartmentalized surface."

"Hold on," one of the young girls said. "The Zodiac, perhaps?"

There was some agreement but, right away the hypothesis fell flat.

"No, it would take twelve sections. Now, if I know how to count, there are thirteen here, right?"

Everyone agreed. Thirteen different sections. However, by zooming in, they found that the sections each contained a letter or a sign. It was imprecise but, little by little, they had to admit that the traditional representations of Aquarius, Sagittarius, Capricorn and the other signs were, if not represented in a traditional way, at least in a very similar way.

"But why thirteen signs?" Dusaule asked.

"Maybe we'll know when we hear the ultrasound. Prepare the audio transmuter."

They got ready to listen.

But while the specialized technician was adjusting the microphone, Muscat asked the two young girls, "Ladies, look closely at this symbol. What does it suggest to you? A bird? An animal? A spaceship? Or what?"

Bella Lesur, one of Dusaule's assistants, said ingenuously, "Yes... it flies... but it's not an ordinary bird. Not a machine, either. It's a beast—a scary beast. I see the wings, the lightning and these three little lines, three by three, are its claws..."

Muscat almost choked, "How did I not think of that sooner? Moron that I am. Ah, if only Coqdor was here..."

But a voice rose in the laboratory. A murmur, broken sentences, words, a jumble of words from which they would have to catch and classify, select, and finally find meaningful ones. After having "shown" his thoughts, Spontini was now speaking from beyond the grave.

CHAPTER IV

The children were very joyful. It must be admitted that the small class, during long, interminable interplanetary journeys, is quite difficult to entertain and to keep attentive.

Certainly, on the *Black Swan* like on any big cruise ship, everything was planned. The school was organized like workouts, swimming hours when the swimming pool was reserved for children, a lot of playtime, games, sessions of educational cinerelief, and so on. Except that the weird animals belonging to the passengers generally were the best part.

Râx was one of them. Half a dozen toddlers of both sexes were bustling around him, laughing and shouting, stroking his lustrous coat, a beautiful golden red, pulling his ears, with the light shiver that runs through all humans when they play with a little danger.

Indeed, the monster Râx, the pstôr from the planet Dzo,[6] although he played with the kids like a big dog, the body and head of which he had, he undoubtedly remained the most formidable fighter among the familiar demons of the people of the *Black Swan*.

The children preferred him to the hozz, the snarling parrot monkey that an old maid carried around everywhere, or to the vâr, the triple-bodied snake tamed by a former retired spaceship captain, who, unable to live without space, consoled himself by becoming a tourist after exploring the galaxy.

Impressive at first glance, Râx, thanks to his very keen intelligence and his innate love of humans, soon revealed himself as the most precious of playmates. With his elongated body like a big hare, under the skin of which knotted muscles protruded, its bulldog muzzle, its plumed tail that the urchins sometimes pulled, extracting a disapproving grunt, with its forelimbs which were immense bat wings on which he frolicked with surprising dexterity and especially with truly frightening claws and fangs, Râx, the flying dog was (everybody knew) a fearsome beast, something like a big cat armed like a large bird of prey.

But there was no one like him to fetch a ball that had fallen into the pool, to play horse on the ground or else fly a few dozen yards into the

---

[6] See *L'Etoile de Satan*. (*Note from the Author*)

35

large central room of the spaceship, carrying a little boy or girl on his back. And he held his place in the five- or six-a-side rugby games that the children organized. If a little boy went a little too far in bruising his paw, Râx reacted, gently cuffing him with his flattened muzzle and growling a little.

"Râx! Be nice!"

The clear, booming voice of his master called him to order while the real culprit, a little sheepish, blushed from ear to ear. On hearing Chevalier Coqdor, the pstôr broke away from the group of children, thus breaking up the game, and, walked clownishly on its winged limbs and on its hind legs, which looked like those of a young lion—he came asking to be petted.

"My beautiful monster... My Râx... Lie down. That's a good boy, Râx."

The kids, missing their best playmate, surrounded its master.

"He doesn't want to play anymore?"

"Râx is tired."

"What are we going to do?"

"Chevalier, tell us a space story!" A cute little one who was seven years old, with soft porcelain eyes and a mischievous little nose, asked this and, the others repeated the little girl's request.

"A story, Chevalier, a story!"

Bruno Coqdor's green eyes sparkled lightly and he smiled at all the beautiful youths that were taking seats, even climbing on his knees. With one hand rhythmically caressing the pstôr's spine, he began to recount his incredible adventure with the icy sun.[7]

Râx was calm while Coqdor held his young audience spellbound. But after a moment he began to sniff the air, to show signs of interest in something—or someone—that must have been nearby on the ship.

"Keep quiet, Râx." Coqdor kept telling his story...

And time passed as the *Black Swan* flew through the constellation Aquarius, a few light years from the worlds of Ozamara, Ulim and Opphet.

Suddenly, the huge bat rose up, let out a whistle, a long, joyful whistle and, gently shoving aside the circle of children, he soared up with three beats of his wings, crossing the vast room where the passengers were relaxing by the dozens, and he dropped in front of one of the doors where a young blonde girl with a delicate complexion and large clear

---

[7] See *Le Soleil de Glace*. (*Note from the Author*)

eyes appeared. And the monster, still hissing, rolled at the feet of the cute girl who, for her part, seemed very happy to see the pstôr coming towards her.

Then he stood up, spread his formidable wings, put his muzzle close to her face and began to lick it enthusiastically. The young girl laughed out loud, while trying to stop his friendly effusions.

"Yes, you are beautiful... How loyal you are... But where's your master? Where is Chevalier Coqdor?"

Jolted, the Chevalier stood up, leaving the disappointed children with a kind word, and rushed over to them. The young girl fell into his arms, and they kissed with obvious affection while Râx whistled with happiness around them.

"Monique! You! Here!"

Coqdor held the young lady's hands and stared at her with delight.

"Still beautiful! Even more beautiful, if that's possible!"

"Oh, Chevalier, but I'm so happy!"

"So you knew I was on board? But when did you get on?"

"Only yesterday, at the Opphet layover. And I only just learned that you, too, were on the *Black Swan*."

"Weren't you staying on Ozamara?"

"Yes, but my studies are over. Now I'm an interstellar psychology assistant and Jean has continued in our father's footsteps. He's a distinguished geologist."

"Jean? So where is he?"

"Here I am!"

A tall young man threw his arms around Coqdor's neck.

The Chevalier pulled the two of them close to him.

"What a joy to see you again! It's been two years already, in terrestrial duration..."

Two years earlier, in fact, they had shared a strange adventure. They had met on the *Grand Eclair* spaceship and, from there, had to begin a merciless fight against a god-like entity who had kidnapped Monique in an attempt to turn her into a goddess.[8]

That evening, they dined together, with Râx by their side. Monique and Jean had completed their studies and were to return to their home planet where they would get their space assignments. The brother and sister earnestly wanted to be sent on missions together, she as a contact

---

[8] See *Le Dieu Couleur de Nuit.* (*Note from the Author*)

agent with the unknown peoples of the galaxy, he as a specialist in geological detection, a science which had considerable importance.

They talked for a long time. Until Jean exclaimed:

"And you, Chevalier? Are you on holiday? On a mission?"

"Idiot," said Monique, "you know very well that the Chevalier never takes a vacation. Throughout the cosmic year, he is at the service of humanity, across the worlds where he saves the unfortunate, where he fights against demons!"

Coqdor's green eyes rested on the young girl.

"Thank you, Monique."

"It's not me who deserves the thanks, Chevalier."

Coqdor seemed to be thinking, "Tell me, Jean, since geology interests you, will you do me a favor?"

Jean jumped to his feet, excited at the idea of helping his friend to whom he and his sister owed boundless gratitude.

"No not right now. Come to my cabin after coffee."

In his cabin, Coqdor showed some slides that had been transmitted from Paris-sur-Terre by telephoto. They were marked *Top Secret* and the ship's staff had discreetly handed them over to the Chevalier on behalf of Interplan and his old friend, Inspector Robin Muscat.

After the fantastic exploit they had been through together, Chevalier Coqdor thoroughly trusted Jean Farnel, as he did Monique. So, while showing them the photos gleaned from Jean-Marie Spontini's still living brain, he explained to them what had happened and what he wanted from Jean.

"I was on my way to Earth when the message was delivered to me. My friend Muscat is looking for a clue... Jean, you know old stones... Explain to me what that means!"

The young geologist examined the vision-pictures.

"A zodiac, a primitive zodiac, no doubt about it. But it has thirteen signs instead of twelve."

"Do you know of any examples in the galaxy?"

"Very few. But keep in mind that esoteric graffiti is not often clear. On Earth, the portal of Amiens Cathedral is decorated with zodiac signs and other symbols mixed in with them. Imagine that a new zodiac was founded with the twelve traditional signs plus one chosen from multiple symbolic representations among which we find, among others, figures like those of the tarot, well before Oswald Wirth..."

"Other examples?"

"I know that recently, still on Earth, in Tibesti or the Hoggar, where rock signs abound, we found a kind of circle divided into thirteen sections... A zodiac? The symbols were worn off, but I know that there were actually thirteen different houses."

"That's all very interesting. Are there other cases?"

"I think so. I don't remember the ancient lithology course too well but it seems to me that on a planet of Capricorn, we discovered something like this."

"Capricorn? But that's right next door, at least in terms of spatial proximity..."

"A few thousand light years," Monique said, laughing. "Unfortunately, a ship like the *Black Swan* doesn't veer off course like that and doesn't easily dive into subspace, even at the request of our dear Chevalier."

"Very true, beautiful child. Only, I don't have to stay on the *Black Swan*!"

Coqdor, therefore, asked Jean Farnel to study the matter very seriously.

The young man, already excited, assured him that he would get started right away.

"Chevalier, I have documents in my cabin. I need to do a little sorting but I'm sure I'll find some interesting stuff for you."

"Don't brag too much," Monique said. "I know Jean, Chevalier, he gets passionate."

"Indeed," Coqdor laughed. "I remember his love affair with the beautiful priestess Gheldir."

Jean turned pale, then blushed.

"Ah!" he said, annoyed. "I was so young."

"Two years ago. Light years for you!"

"Now I have a degree in geology. And an important one."

"Well, young and brilliant scholar, I will leave you. I'm taking your sister out on the promenade deck to drink some pineapple juice with a drop of gin. You, meanwhile..."

Coqdor and Monique left while Jean returned to his cabin and Râx, tamely, was taken to the animal department for the period of sleep, the established period that replaced the night for cosmonauts.

Jean had taken the slides given to him by Coqdor, who had entrusted them to him like the apple of his penetrating green eyes. These were obviously documents of the utmost importance since Muscat had sent to

Coqdor the fruit of the experiments carried out by Dusaule and Stewe, who had tried to extract the secrets from the brain of a dead man.

Jean examined the documents at length, then took several small collections of personal films from his suitcases. A mini-projector lined up some photos, notes and diagrams from his studies. He compared, examined, noted, scribbled, made maps, erased them and started again.

"A zodiac, there's no mistake," he thought. "A zodiac but with an intermediate sign located between Virgo and Libra, i.e. September 23. A hybrid date for astrologers, since on this day the Earth is sometimes under one sign, sometimes under the other. An unknown constellation, something like a new world? Yes, one more element in the traditional cosmos, from our perspective. Some walk in a street that's not there, which is added to the streets of their city. Others think they're reading an unpublished chapter in a novel they loved, a chapter which has never been written, which never will be. It's the extra statue or painting in the most beautiful museum, the art object that won't be there, the untitled play for which all theater lovers would have liked to write the lines, to bring to life the characters embodying their ideal. It's... Oh! Above all, this is what we're waiting for, what we hope to achieve, the elusive mystery of which we can only grasp a shadow, a counterfeit."

Slowly, without Jean realizing it, the door to his cabin opened a little.

Poring over the documents, he jotted down his observations, finished up the job that would surely facilitate the research of Robin Muscat and Chevalier Coqdor.

"The mystery of what is not..." thought the enthusiastic Jean Farnel again. "And suddenly, from another point of view, this mystery takes form, becomes reality. There are, in the celestial horizon known to Earthlings, twelve constellations which are at the origin of the signs of the Zodiac, plus one, which they do not know about, but which they must be skimming without suspecting it, another world that Inspector Muscat sensed. And maybe it's me who will find the key..."

Someone entered the cabin slowly. Jean did not hear anything, completely absorbed in his work. Following the documents, he drew the mysterious sign.

"The report claims it's a monstrous, winged beast... And those frightening symbols... Yes, that's it, maybe a vampire?"

So, he drew a kind of stylized vampire, trying to transcribe the essence of the thirteenth sign of the Zodiac. But this time, he became aware of a presence.

Caught off guard, he swung around, looking surprised but not at all afraid.

He was no longer alone in his cabin.

But Jean was not afraid. At least, he believed he had no reason to be afraid.

And yet... A few moments later, a loud cry of pain and terror echoed through the corridors of the *Black Swan* spaceship.

CHAPTER V

"It's Jean! It's him, I recognized his voice. My God!" Monique's beautiful eyes had grown wide by the sudden horror she felt.

She was returning from the promenade deck, overlooked by the depolex dome and which practically places spacecraft passengers directly in contact with space, where they experience magnificent visions under the gaze of the stars.

While chatting with Coqdor, Monique was returning to her cabin, next to her brother's, when this frightening howl burst out.

"There's someone in trouble. But, Monique, are you sure?"

"It's him, yes, it's him!"

Like a madwoman, the young woman rushed forward and Coqdor, his domineering forehead suddenly creased with worry, rushed after her. Monique stormed into the cabin and Coqdor, who arrived right behind her, heard the sorrowful moan that escaped her.

There was no mistake, it was Jean who had shouted, a few brief moments before. A single cry. Then silence. The horrific spectacle that awaited Monique and Chevalier Coqdor explained why.

Jean was lying on his back, unconscious, but in a tense attitude expressing both the suffering and the fear that had overcome him. The man's face was pale, his eyelids half-lowered over his rolled-up eyes. Blood had splattered all over the cabin, on the floor, on Jean's clothes, even on the table where he had spread out the documents entrusted to him by Coqdor, documents now stained with red marks.

Coqdor stepped forward. Monique was already kneeling next to her brother. The horror took her breath away. She couldn't say a word.

"God of the Cosmos," Coqdor growled, "what kind of wretch could do this?"

Jean's bloody clothes were a mess, which seemed to suggest that he had fought with his attacker for a moment. But what especially terrified Monique, what particularly struck Coqdor, was that Jean's jacket and shirt had been torn off and his chest was bared, with frightening marks. What could have caused these wounds, which in truth were quite minor, as Bruno Coqdor realized immediately, which reassured the young girl a little.

A dagger? A common knife? Claws?

It seemed as if a kind of rough grid had been deliberately drawn on the skin over an area of about six square inches.

The blood that had spurted stained the flesh and clothes and Coqdor was already taking control of the situation. "Be strong, Monique. He's only passed out and I think he has no other wounds."

Monique, now sobbing, lifted her brother's inert head and placed her lips on his pale forehead as the Chevalier rushed to the sink, took a towel and some cologne, came back, and set about cleaning the slashed chest.

He repeated encouraging words. "It's nothing. Very superficial."

"But he fell... He was knocked out... This fainting?"

"One minute, my young friend. Here, keep washing his wounds. I'm going to wake him up..."

Monique obeyed. She had total confidence in the Chevalier, whose hypnopsychic power she was fully aware of.

Coqdor was already kneeling next to Jean, concentrating and his face was contorted with the inner effort. His powerful, elegant hands, his royal hands hovered over Jean's forehead, covering his skull, while his green eyes sparkled. Jean sighed, blinked his eyelids, and his lips formed a whisper.

"Oh! he lives," cried Monique, suddenly happy.

"I'm going to lay him down on his bunk, it will be more comfortable," said Coqdor.

He lifted Monique's brother with his strong arms and did as he had said. There, with a final mental pressure, he forced Jean to partially regain his senses while Monique finished wiping away the blood, which was beginning to coagulate.

"Jean," Coqdor began, "can you hear me? Do you recognize me?"

"Chevalier... Monique..." the young man stammered.

"What happened to you?"

Jean gasped, tried to speak. He was finally about to say something when Monique, who had cleaned her brother's bruised chest, suddenly cried out, "Chevalier! Look…"

"What is it?"

"The wounds! They're not just random scratches. They form lines, it looks like a drawing as if…"

A striking idea crossed Coqdor's mind.

"If it was...? Oh!"

He leaned down and saw that Monique was right. He recognized the drawing formed by the scratches which had tortured Jean Farnel's skin. A loop and two lines in circumflex accent, crossed by lightning. Below, six small lines arranged three by three.

"By all the devils in the galaxy, this is the symbol, the thirteenth sign of the Zodiac! The crime is signed! Ah! Be damned!"

Jean's cry had been heard by several people and officers were already alerted. Coqdor quickly told them that an attack had just taken place and that they had to investigate. With the *Black Swan* still sailing in subspace, it was hard to believe that the wretch had been able to clandestinely leave the ship.

Certainly, cases had been recorded. But then, you had to use one of the saucer boats on board, or dive into the void with a spacesuit. Again, in this last hypothesis, they would have to admit that the fugitive was at great risk, unless he was awaited in the vicinity by some accomplice spacecraft.

The spaceship was soon in a state of agitation. The rumor of the attack spread quickly, especially since the captain could not conceal the affair, even to avoid panic. In fact, it was necessary that the entire spaceship be searched and that everyone, whether cosmonaut or passenger, was asked to answer questions.

Jean had been taken to the infirmary. He was suddenly seized by a fever and Coqdor had to give up questioning him or even probing his mind.

The Star Knight pondered.

So, the mysterious enemy had appeared again. After the various crimes they were guilty of, after the strange death of Jean-Marie Spontini, the kidnapping of the beautiful Giovanna, the handling of the investigation by Robin Muscat, they did not hesitate to challenge both the Interplan detective and his ally, Chevalier Coqdor, at the very moment when the necessary information was transmitted to him by space television.

Coqdor had left Monique at Jean's bedside with the ship's doctor reassuring the young girl. He wanted to understand and, first of all, see the site of the crime.

The *Black Swan* security officer was there. Coqdor's reputation was such, however, that he was not forbidden from returning to Jean's cabin. The Chevalier did not conceal the fact that he had been in contact with Interplan, that a very secret mission was entrusted to him, and that young

Jean Farnel, in his capacity as an interplanetary geologist, had been asked by him to provide some information of the utmost importance.

"So you entrusted him with the documents that were sent to you by Interplan, Chevalier?"

"Yes, sir."

"They're the documents which are still on the table and which, presumably, Mr Farnel was examining when he was attacked."

"Exactly."

"Do you want to check if there are any missing?"

Coqdor silently sorted the slides and examined Jean's audiovisual dictionary. "No," he said, "it's all here. They didn't steal anything."

"That's weird," the security officer said.

"I think so too," murmured the Chevalier. "Do you still need me?"

"Not right now. Maybe a little later we may have to talk again."

"I think so too, but right now, I'm going back to the infirmary."

Coqdor, in fact, had already thought of this. Jean had been attacked to steal the documents. But at first glance, when he was with Monique, Coqdor, although he had hardly had time to deal with the matter, had sensed that nothing was missing.

"In that case," he thought, "they didn't knock him out to steal documents. These people don't need them. They're informed, much better than us, regarding the Thirteenth sign of the Zodiac. Why, then, had Jean been attacked?"

Coqdor found the answer easily enough. It consisted precisely in the very special wounds made with a knife or a claw at the level of the poor boy's heart.

"The sign, the vampire sign. A signature! And a threat!"

The Chevalier was starting to get angry.

In the infirmary, he found Jean somewhat calmed by the sedatives. He was bandaged after a thorough examination. No other traces. However, the doctor had detected trauma to the Adam's apple.

"He was hit, which caused him to faint. And then the criminal had plenty of time to rip his clothes and play his sadistic little game."

"Thank you Doctor. Tell me, was this attack... this strangulation... caused by a human hand?"

"It's possible. But if so, they had to squeeze very hard."

"You don't see any other theories?"

The doctor, intrigued, returned to his sleeping patient. "See for yourself, Chevalier... Ah! I didn't notice that…"

Taking a closer look, they discovered two small bruises on the side of the neck. Astonished, the doctor looked on the other side and Coqdor, leaning in close to him, felt himself turn pale. Two other small spots, barely visible, but showing a tiny, double hematoma.

"It's almost imperceptible."

"But it's there. Doctor, what do you think?"

"It seems... It seems that the unfortunate man got his throat caught in a jaw... not human, of course, but animal."

Four fangs.

Bruno Coqdor looked at Monique, who had not left the infirmary. She looked distressed. Everything about the attack on her brother was crucifying her.

"Be brave, Monique. The doctor says it's not serious. And I'll tell you the same."

He placed a kiss on Monique's delicate forehead and left.

For a moment, he concentrated his mind, tried to join the troubled thought of sleeping Jean. Something vague had appeared to him. Very vague. An image. But if this image had become clearer, it would have truly frightened the Chevalier.

"I'll know for sure!"

He went to the ship's animal hold where, according to the regulations, the animals had to be locked up during sleeping hours.

Two attendants rushed up. "Chevalier?"

"I want to see my pstôr, right away!"

"At your service!"

Like everyone on board, they tried to please the Chevalier, this man famous throughout the galaxy.

"Tell me," Coqdor said, passing between two rows of boxes where the dogs and cats of Earth were next to the hozz, the vârs, the firebirds of Sagittarius and the terrestrial dolphins of Alcor, so intelligent that they conversed with their masters. "Tell me, both of you, are you sure no one has come to the zoo since sleeptime?"

The two attendants looked at each other. Their hesitation, along with a psychic probe, got him the information.

"Listen to me," he said, "I'm not trying to have you reprimanded by the Captain. Just tell me the truth: have you been playing priks?"

Sheepishly, the two men lowered their heads a little.

"Chevalier," one of them stammered, "you know what it is…"

"I know. I know the game is exciting and that people forget to make the regular rounds. It's all right. Let's go and see my pstor."

Priks, a kind of poker played with small-stepped pyramids, a game imported from the planets of Altaïr, and with which one often gambled so much that it was forbidden on spaceships, had absorbed all the attention of the two attendants. But Coqdor didn't really care right now about having them punished.

They arrived in front of Râx's box. When he recognized his master, he jumped up on his hind legs, spread his imposing wings and began to whistle happily.

"Open the cage. Thanks! Now I don't need you anymore."

The guilty guards didn't have to be told twice. They left Coqdor alone.

The Chevalier petted the pstôr, spoke to it gently. With his strong hand, he opened Râx's mouth and looked at the four formidable fangs. He nodded, then grabbed one of the legs—one of the two hind legs, the front limbs actually being those of a bat—and examined it. His heart sank dismally.

Blood! There was a little blood on one of the sets of claws!

"I wasn't wrong," murmured Coqdor. "He's the culprit... It's Râx. Râx himself! He came into the cabin, squeezed Jean by the throat, hard enough to make him faint, but not hard enough to strangle him. Then... with his claws, it was easy for him to tear his jacket and his shirt, and to carve the cursed sign."

He went back to his cabin with his pstôr who simply looked happy to be with him.

"My beautiful pstôr! They used him as an instrument of crime. They will pay for this... But they are devilishly powerful. They know everything and since they don't have an agent on board, they hypnotized Râx remotely. They dragged him out of the hold and threw him on poor Jean."

But now, a terrible grin crossed the face of the Star Knight, whose eyes shined more than ever.

"They didn't think of one thing. In Râx's mind, in his animal brain, all this left traces. And I will find these traces. They'll put me on the right track that my old friend Muscat is missing."

He arrived at his cabin and locked himself in with the pstôr.

"Here, Râx!"

The monster went over, hissing very softly with happiness and, closing his big golden eyes a little, he laid his formidable face on his master's knees. Coqdor spoke gently to him while scratching the top of his head, an exercise in which the pstôr seemed to take great pleasure. Coqdor's hands now seemed to grasp Râx's head.

Suddenly, without the Chevalier having spoken, Râx raised his muzzle and looked him in the eyes, under the impulse of the psychic call. It lasted for a fraction of a moment, then the beast's whole body shuddered, suddenly stiffened. And Râx slipped to the ground, rigid, as if dead. In truth, it was just a catalepsy.

Coqdor knelt next to him, caressed him again.

"Soon you'll come back to yourself. I won't hurt you. But through you, I will know…"

The Chevalier was concentrating now, his eyes closed. And all his radiating thoughts sank into the neurons of Râx's brain, eagerly seeking the after-effects of the abomination of which the animal had been made guilty, in order to find the instigators.

CHAPTER VI

The investigation by the security officer on board the *Black Swan* had yielded absolutely nothing. The ship had been searched methodically and in detail. No stowaways were hiding on board and, by definition, it was impossible to escape in open space.

Everyone had been questioned, which was quite a job, needing patience and thoroughness along with psychology. Another negative result.

The Captain had to tell Chevalier Coqdor that, unless there was an error, the crew and passengers were innocent of the crime committed by Râx alone, who, moreover, had only been a hypnotic instrument in the affair.

Such results hardly surprised the Star Knight. He expected as much, especially after he had seen the documents sent from Paris-sur-Terre by Robin Muscat were still there. From the start he had sensed long-distance psychic action at work. And what a distance, surely!

Everything had worked in favor of the criminals. The guards on duty, after the last round among the animals, had lost themselves in the passionate delights of priks and, neglecting surveillance, had noticed neither the coming nor the going of Râx.

"They're powerful," repeated Coqdor. "They influenced Râx who is, they realized, an ultrasensitive animal despite his muscular strength. And they even managed to get him to open and close his cage. The demons!"

What was particularly heinous to him, the clairvoyant, the telepath, the familiar with what lies beyond the tangible and the visible, was precisely this mysterious surveillance of which he felt himself the object.

His enemies, these people of the Zodiac, those who used a somewhat old-fashioned method (like out of some old detective novel of the 20th century) of an esoteric symbol to sign their crimes, of a mysterious sign that they tattooed on the heart of their victims, these people—living on what planet, or even in another dimension, who knew?—seemed to be constantly spying on Coqdor's actions.

"They knew right away that Muscat had contacted me to transmit to me the information gleaned from Spontini's brain. They already know that I'm collaborating with him in the search for the Thirteenth Sign and in a short time, they found out about my meeting with the Farnels, the enthusiastic joy of Jean who wanted to help me and it was him, poor boy, whom they attacked."

Anger made his green eyes shine, a hard shine only softened when he whispered, to himself alone:

"Poor Monique! She doesn't need to be involved in this! It's my fault, of course. But by all the storms of the cosmos, I still can't suspect that these people are like living televisions!"

Now, since he was, so to speak, paid to be suspicious, everything seemed suspicious to him. All the same, the Zodiac were going to feel the backlash from their treachery.

They had used Râx. And the Chevalier was already exploring the subconscious of the winged monster, obviously more nebulous than that of a man, to collect some of most interesting images...

The animal thinks, but doesn't really contemplate. His psychic potential is therefore both infinitely less precise and yet much more accessible than that of humans. The little that there is in what we can call his "mind," even if it is only a sketch, has the advantage of not getting bogged down in the endless reasoning that bog down the majority of human brains.

Coqdor, having plunged poor Râx into catalepsy two or three times, had managed to learn a few things concerning those who had enslaved him for a time. Being cautious by experience he kept these things to himself.

Several immediate concerns were bothering him. First of all the safety of Râx himself.

"They're quite capable of doing it again!"

So, several times a day, he sent a cerebral probe towards his familiar. But now Râx was very peaceful. The after-effects of the crime with which he had been heinously accused were fading.

Moreover, by instinct, even though he was a fierce and formidable fighter at the right time, Râx was nonetheless perfectly tamed and remained one of the most peaceful friends possible and he was once again playing with the youngsters.

And then, while spending time soothing Monique and Jean, who was about to leave the infirmary, Coqdor had once again come into contact with Muscat through subspace telecommunications. Thus the Interplan inspector had learned (briefly and to the point) about the drama that had played out on board of the *Black Swan* and of the terrible danger that the Zodiac posed.

Coqdor added:

"I'm on to something, Robin, but I'll be careful not to reveal the slightest clue to you."

"You're right, you old wizard. We're being watched, right?"

"No doubt about it, you old hound. While we talk in subspace duplex, our enemies are listening. From our first communication they knew that I was going to enter the fray."

"Very well," Muscat said. "I'll let you do what you think best. You know something. I also know a little about it from Spontini's post-mortem revelations. This will be enough for me to get back to work, while waiting to see you."

"Hold on, Robin. Where's that?"

"But at…"

A commanding gesture from the Chevalier cut off the name of the planet. On the screen, he saw the policeman biting his lips.

"They're listening, Robin."

"It's annoying, horrifying," the detective growled. "They're following us…"

"All right. Just wait, I'll make an appointment with you. Look at me…"

Light years away, the subspace waves relaying image and sound brought the two old friends face to face in a mind-boggling virtual presence. Coqdor's green eyes cast their imperious shine into the sharp, clear eyes of the space detective. There was a short pause. Then a smile crossed the Chevalier's lips. He had set the trap.

He felt an insidious, mischievous thought creep into his brain. They were going to try to "read" what he was about to reveal telepathically to Robin Muscat, since he wanted to avoid pronouncing the word which risked being captured by the Zodiac.

Coqdor "blocked" his thoughts, put up a barrier with a cerebral process in which he had been trained for a long time. And to reach the only brain to which he was addressing, that is to say that of Muscat, he "channeled" his thought-waves, sending them not in total irradiation, not in an expanding sphere like all the waves so they could be captured in all directions, but only in a very thin beam, a telepathic spear which struck the detective between the eyes, at the level of the pineal gland.

Immediately, Coqdor, who was standing in the *Black Swan*'s communications room, made a sign to the technician. The radio operator cut the communication.

The Chevalier breathed.

"Phew! I felt Muscat catch my message. Him and him alone. The spies, I believe, were wasting their time."

Satisfied on this score, he went to the infirmary.

Râx, now, never left him. During the day, when Coqdor was in the big relaxation room and the children were playing with the pstôr, the human kept the animal with him at all times and under surveillance. Râx, delighted with the boon, slept every night near his master's bunk, only being taken to the animal quarters for daily washing and meals. Again, at the table, he would grab a little meat or fruit that he was fond of. Besides Coqdor, Monique, who now ate lunch near him, the children and many other people willingly stuffed the little monster with treats.

In the infirmary, the Chevalier was pleased to find Jean up and completely recovered from his adventure. Monique's brother's wounds were already closed thanks to the famous intracorol, the plant-based product invented by the famous Venusian doctor, Xol. All that remained on the skin was a very vague, light trace, but which took the form of the Thirteenth sign of the Zodiac.

Coqdor was hardly worried about it. It was not the terrible tattoo that had already killed two men, as far as he knew, and had driven a third mad. He supposed—Muscat, during the first communication, had told him that he was of this opinion—that the special kind of attribute to the chest must be reserved for members of the sect, of the secret society of the Zodiac, which seemed to have as its aim to keep the Thirteenth Sign a secret.

Very probably, this tattoo was at the same time a relay engraved on the flesh of the members—a relay which made it possible to act on the unfortunate people who made the mistake of displeasing, or even betraying the sect. Yum Akatinor, Cladek Halstar, Jean-Marie Spontini, one after the other, had felt its cruel sting.

Giovanna Hi-Ling remained. What had become of her? Kidnapped? Murdered? Locked up like madwoman in some unknown galactic asylum? Or simply "taken out of the picture" for obscure and probably very perilous missions?

At least they knew—the dead man had spoken—that the beautiful Giovanna, too, had the tattoo and therefore belonged to the Zodiac.

What was the goal of these people? Neither Coqdor nor Muscat had yet found out. At least, through the revelations of Giovanna's late lover, they had been able to put together an interesting file, and Coqdor, using Râx as a psychic relay, was not boasting in vain when he said that he was on to something.

He thought Giovanna was the key to the investigation. If Spontini had come to Robin Muscat of his own free will, it was because of the disappearance of his friend. Had she abandoned him on her own? Or at the behest of mysterious sectarians? Had she been their victim, for some unknown reason? In any case, it could be assumed that Spontini, deemed a traitor by those of the Zodiac, had been promptly executed so that he could not speak.

They had not counted, however, on the science of Doctor Frank Dusaule or the speed of action of Interplan and Robin Muscat.

Jean, being back on his feet, petted Râx without resentment. Monique too, overcoming her horror of the first moments, had started playing again with the pstôr who was overly friendly to her. She had listened to the Chevalier who had not had too much difficulty convincing her that the little winged monster was not evil and that under no circumstances should he be incriminated in the attack that her brother had been the victim of.

Coqdor talked with the two young people.

"Jean, do you know that you have brought me a most precious document, which will help us a lot in our research?"

"What's that, Chevalier?"

"Your tender chest that Râx's claws have torn. Indeed, our enemies used his strong claws, well at least one of his claws, a single claw, to mock us and trace their famous sign on your skin. However, until now we only had vague, mutilated, uncertain images of this sign. Robin Muscat got an enlargement of the tattoos of the victims who were struck by lightning, but it seems in both cases that the flash, the deadly spark, had damaged the drawing somewhat. You quoted to me—and showed me a figure—of the Hoggar zodiac. Muscat relayed to me the images gleaned from the brain of the man who was already a corpse. It's all vague, confusing. At least, on you, they were eager to clearly draw the Thirteenth Sign, which has been almost unknown to this day. You see how precious it is..."

Jean said he was glad to help and added that now, more than ever, he was determined to change his plans in order to follow the Chevalier in his search, then battle, against the Zodiac.

Coqdor, mischievously, looked at Monique, "My friend, I see your beautiful forehead darkening."

"Oh," sighed Monique, "Jean is always the brave one as you know all too well. What dangers is he going to face? Isn't it enough that he was half strangled? With a lacerated chest?"

"Exactly," Jean Farnel lashed out. "They have to pay for this!"

"Besides," the Chevalier suggested, "at the next layover, since I'm obliged to leave the *Black Swan* and set off on my own again, my dear Monique will bid us farewell and continue her trip to Earth…"

He laughed at Monique's reaction. A reaction which, of course, he fully expected.

The young girl jumped up.

"Me? Abandon Jean? But you know that mama and papa have entrusting him to me!"

"That's it," Jean was offended, "I'm under guardianship. At my age!"

"You're a young and seemingly healthy geologist," said Coqdor, "admit that your sister is as wise as she is pretty, which is saying something, and that her advice is always valuable to you."

Jean grumbled but Monique held her ground and declared bluntly that if Jean began the fight against the Zodiac, she would be at his side.

Coqdor kissed her and congratulated her. But this did not keep him, at the next layover of the *Black Swan*, from drawing Jean aside and saying a few words to him.

"My boy, here we are in Ulmir. I'm not staying here. I'm leaving tomorrow on a cosmaviso chartered with special authorization from the Martervenux authorities at the request of Interplan. Naturally, Monique and you can come with me. But watch out! At this layover, I have to do some research and, and to do so, go to the red-light district. You'll agree with me that your sister can't come with us to that den of iniquity where the underworld is rampant."

"OK, Chevalier."

"Anyway, my boy, you will come with me. And Râx, too. Monique will wait for us on the cosmaviso, where she will be safe. We'll go down to the dives for only one evening."

Jean was delighted, like all young people from good families who want to have a night of fun. But he wanted to know more.

"Chevalier, I know that you're not talking about it, that you even block your thoughts so that our mysterious enemies can't read what you've learned. But tell me at least…"

"Well, Râx literally served as a transistor. Thanks to the crime of these wretches, I learned various things, including the fact that someone is in trouble in the gutters of this spaceport, and that there are extremely dangerous creatures around this person, with an extraordinary power that I haven't been able to identify exactly. I won't hide it from you, my boy, this expedition will be dangerous. So, not a word to Monique. Do you, still agree?"

"Yes, Chevalier! I'm your man!"

CHAPTER VII

Ulmir was a very ordinary little planet, devoid of any interest for tourists staying or just passing through. Certainly, it was classified among the philohuman worlds, having a highly oxygenated atmosphere which was suitable for humanoids.

But Ulmir was very watery. Its almost perpetually cloudy sky frequently poured, which was all the more unpleasant as the winds gathered loads of spores in the clouds, then dropped them back to the ground in the showers. All this formed a greenish precipitation which polluted everything and seriously damaged the buildings.

As for the boredom that Ulmir exuded, there was no need to talk about it. And the famous green rains, staining people and their clothes, didn't help matters. However, this space-deprived land was the last habitable one on the frontiers of the constellation Aquarius. Also a layover had been established there for spaceships heading towards other worlds in the galaxy, particularly for the relatively close ones of Capricorn.

A real city had been built there but, little by little, the settlers had abandoned it, sickened by such a dismal life.

But the astrodrome remained, a vast area, practical and well located. Naturally, a little life grew around it. Pitiful people, cosmonauts, decommissioned or dropped out, traffickers of all kinds, prostitutes from all parts of the cosmos, and the inevitable civil servants, police, militia, probationary customs officers with their families, for stays of varying length depending on how depressed the climate and the green rains made them.

Everyone lived haphazardly in buildings, most of which were abandoned and neglected, crumbling and sometimes collapsing. Of course, they had luxury apartments, but the views were so bleak...

And in vast, almost deserted streets, the particular wildlife of ports and spaceports crawled around, the mire of the universe.

This was where the *Black Swan* had to make a stop. Here also was where Coqdor left the ship, flanked by Monique, Jean and his faithful Râx.

Naturally, although he had to go down into the underbelly of the spaceport city before re-embarking for a destination yet to be revealed, he was not going to take Monique there. The young girl had to give in.

Besides, on Ulmir decent people almost never got off the ship during the layover.

So, without delay, Jean's sister was taken to the cosmaviso *Comet Hyakutake*, of the Martervenux militia, on which three cabins awaited Coqdor and his companions.

After entrusting the young girl to the officers, the Chevalier, followed by Jean, simply announced that he wanted to research Ulmir and its picturesque suburbs. Monique was sad to see them leave, but Jean was delighted to go with Coqdor.

The lieutenant of the *Comet Hyakutake* figured he was in a position to warn the two men:

"Stay on your guard. The police are on constant patrol, but it's still true that Ulmir is a dangerous city. There are a lot of assaults, even murders, in its bars and in the more than dubious establishments which are everywhere. You can never be too careful."

"We won't dawdle," Coqdor had promised.

Now it was night, the long night of Ulmir which lasts nearly twenty turns around the clock, twenty of the standard Earth hours used as the basis for the cosmic measurement of time, which is not different almost everywhere.

Coqdor and Jean walked down the vast streets, between the tall houses, some of which were falling into ruin while on certain facades, disconcerting cracks could be seen. Some buildings were maintained and the lights were on. There lived the officials and their families, always nervous, on their guard, surrounded by electromagnetic circuits to defend against the multitude of evildoers who haunted the semi-ghost town.

The wide sidewalks and the streets as far as the eye could see, under the street lamps which shed torrents of harsh, magnetized neon light, were pictures of despair.

Especially since over all this, rain was falling. The green rain of Ulmir, its streams seen everywhere, in long repulsive streaks, on the walls, the window sills as well as on the asphalt.

And the long depolex lines of the street lamps did not escape it, coated and dirtied over time by the filthy green mud which was almost constantly falling over this nightmare city.

Pedestrians were few and quickly disappeared either into side streets or under porches.

"Ghosts in a city of death, how cheery," said Jean.

"And we haven't seen everything yet," the Chevalier added.

Râx trudged alongside the two men in the mud that fell from the sky but, being with his master, he never looked unhappy.

A few electrocars passed by, speeding away. Two or three times, one would slow down and the two walkers realized that they were being watched. But nothing happened. The cars left and got lost in the endless, dreary, abandoned avenues.

Here and there, the bright sign of a bar cast a spot of color, contrasting with the rest, unintentionally adding a note of pleasure to the otherwise grim scenery.

Jean knew that it wasn't necessary to question Coqdor since their enemies must be constantly spying on them, although he did not really know how. So, he trusted him, blindly following him through the desperation-filled streets.

Sometimes a female figure would appear, emerging from the shadows where she had been lurking, advancing into some pool of neon light. Venusian or Capricornian, daughter of Cassiopeia or Sagittarius, she murmured some banal and demeaning phrases that were common everywhere, in various languages, or in the spalax tongue that humans strived to teach everywhere since interstellar relations had become commonplace. Seeing the indifference of the two passers-by, the prostitutes went back to their sorry stations.

Finally, Coqdor stopped in front of what had once been a magnificent residence, which the green rain was eating away sinisterly. Naturally, the ever-present neon sign, green and red, traced in the mist the lines of a stylized bird-woman.

"This is it!"

Jean Farnel said nothing and entered the strange place behind Bruno Coqdor.

The interior lacked originality. No doubt, during the short and brilliant period when they wanted to "launch" Ulmir, the establishment had been very luxurious, a sort of *Moulin Rouge* in the outskirts of the cosmos. But now, everything was falling into ruin and the more than filthy clientele were dirtying, wearing out, degrading the veneered tables, the torn sofas, the carpets stained with who knew what stains, around a swimming pool with a lighted fountain, but where half the lights were missing and whose waters, like everywhere in Ulmir, were befouled with greenish mud.

The patrons drank alcohol, like the ztax of Mars, the Old Crow of Kentucky, or the Sagittarian fluz. They all smoked the tobacco. They all stank of drugs. Box-fluggs blared various tunes with their 3-D projections exposing every possible pin-up from the galactic spectrum.

The clientele were just the dregs that Coqdor had been expecting. Degraded people, clients and servers alike.

Among the latter, some were still young, almost beautiful, but already marked by the slackness that had led them to vice.

And drunken cosmonauts fought while robots being remote-controlled by the manager stepped in, slowly, methodically grabbing the fighters and tossing them out to finish the brawl in the green rain.

The boss? The big, red, bald man, most certainly a mixed-race Venusian, but they didn't know with what else. And the one who was obviously his partner, a tall, skinny person with outrageous makeup, dressed in earthly fashion, came and went, smiling at the customers, with that smile that is at once honeyed, complicit, contemptuous and fierce.

Râx sniffed with visible disgust at the fetid atmosphere of the place.

Jean did not feel comfortable, but Bruno Coqdor's emerald gaze reassured him.

They took a seat at a table near the fountain and ordered two Cinzanos of Earth to remember their home planet. Luckily, there must have been one bottle left and a matron came to serve them. She inquired about their health and their desires, probably thinking of sending them companions for the night.

Coqdor was about to question her about the woman he had come to find there when he stopped himself. The manager looked surprised. Jean had understood.

"What's the matter, Chevalier?"

"There's someone here that I know. Just a moment... Ah yes, over there!"

His telepathic gift had served him well once again.

"Excuse me, Madam," said Jean, joining in the game. "Monsieur will tell you what he wants."

After a brief moment of concentration Coqdor asked:

"Are there any rooms over there?"

"Why of course! For the games and also—" she gave a depraved smile "—if these gentlemen would like to accompany our charming hostesses into the salon…"

Jean grimaced.

Coqdor waved the offer away.

"No, hold on. He plays... he's still very young... a hybrid of races. With green skin, eyes heavily streaked with red."

"Oh, yes, I know who it is! A fan of priks and banco. Do you want to see him? I'll take you."

"Thank you. But could you ask him to come here instead?"

A few seconds later, Jean Farnel saw the character described by Coqdor. The guy had obviously had a little to drink and was in a very bad mood, having been snatched from a baccarat table.

"What do you want with me?"

The matron pointed to the table of the two men. The gambler started forward and then shuddered, as if sobering up under the sparkling eye of the Chevalier.

"So it's you, Coqdor?"

"Yes, Holp. You've ended up here?"

Holp the half-breed. One of the four boys that Robin Muscat and Coqdor had tried to rehabilitate, snatching them from reformatories and putting them on the path to safety during a perilous mission during which they had to conquer energy-water.[9]

Holp looked confused, but Coqdor wouldn't let him speak:

"So, you're incurable? We gave you your chance, though!"

"I'm not hurting anyone, Chevalier. I never had a lucky star, that's all."

"Remember Ty, the worst of you all. He died as a hero on the Planet of Fire, to save Gita."

"He's dead, yes. And all the better for him. If he'd lived..."

"Idiot! And Joki, he turned out well! He's now married, a father, and has a good job on Mars in Syrtis Major."

"Joki married Gita. But me, I've got no love..."

"Quiet, idiot! Listen, I need you, since you're here. You're going to make yourself useful for once."

Coqdor took a film out of his pocket. It was a small, color-relief photo. It had been transmitted by space television from Interplan. In it they saw a very pretty girl with slanted eyes, magnificent black hair, a delicate oval face with her skin highlighted in gold.

As soon as Holp had it in his hands, the image came to life and the very soft voice of the subject uttered a few sweet nothings. The film clip had been found in Jean-Marie Spontini's wallet. It was a tender memory of Giovanna Hi-Ling, a precious document collected by Muscat.

---

[9] See *La Planète de Feu*. (*Note from the Author*)

And from the information gleaned from Râx's brain, Coqdor knew that a woman was in trouble in the slums of Ulmir at a placed called "The Bird Woman"; that she was being forced into prostitution and was used as an informer for the Zodiac. He had been unable to find out more, but was convinced that it was Giovanna.

Only, he was disappointed. Holp, who had been hanging around Ulmir for months and knew the entire underworld, nevertheless claimed that he had never seen the woman.

A psychic probe proved to Coqdor that he was not lying. If Giovanna wasn't there, it was unfortunate. But he still had to find the woman in trouble who, moreover, might lead him to the secret of the Thirteenth Sign.

"Chevalier, do you need me anymore?" asked Holp, sighing.

"Have a drink with us. Afterwards, you can go back to your cards and your chips."

"It never changes! You keep reading minds!"

"Sometimes hearts too. Tell me a little about the girls here."

Holp gaped at him.

"Are you interested in them?"

Coqdor asked him to give him a brief overview of each of the hostesses. Then, as soon as Holp had finished, he concentrated and telepathically visited the mind of the targeted woman.

They repeated the experience three times. Disappointing every time. Common stories, pointless destinies.

The fourth creature in the spotlight was, according to Holp, from the Martervenux, but he didn't knew from which planet. Relatively young but plump, with still beautiful eyes in a face that flab was starting to invade. She seemed interested in their conversation and looked over in their direction.

Without appearing to do so, Coqdor was probing her psychically. To his great surprise, he didn't find the usual passivity of this type of person. She seemed to feel the probe. She answered. And their short, mental conversation began.

"Be careful. They're watching you. Don't stay here," she transmitted.

"Thank you, but if I leave, follow me!" replied the Chevalier.

"Impossible," the hostess refused. "If I follow you, they'll find me anywhere I go. They'll kill me."

"Who are they?"

She didn't respond with a mental message this time. There was silence, then Coqdor saw the symbol of the Thirteenth sign of the Zodiac emerge in his mind. She had sent her answer, which spoke for itself.

The Chevalier asked, while finishing his drink:

"Do you bear the sign, too?"

He had the brief image of the naked woman. Too heavy, too damaged, but unscarred and without a trace of the sinister tattoo.

Then she went on:

"They'll attack you. Any excuse! A fight! Get out of here! There's still time!"

Coqdor had already sensed the danger, but he remained firm.

"I know," he said. "I'm waiting for them."

"You don't know. They're... I can't say... You'll see... and then, you'll no longer see... And they'll be here. Always here. They're deadly. Oh, get away, run away with your friend!"

Then the fight broke out in the gaming room. Several men came out arguing. Then blades appeared. The girls started screaming. The robots on duty moved forward with their slow, precise steps, claws out.

Coqdor shuddered. Holp gasped in fear. Jean had gotten up.

The unswerving machines marched on, not toward the fighters but toward them.

Dreadful, merciless.

The trap was closing.

CHAPTER VIII

There were three of them, daunting, terrible.

They moved forward with their heavy, slow, precise, methodical steps, frightening because they imitated humans but did not have their sensitivity; they were nothing but mechanical movements, fixed, planned, with total impassivity in every gesture.

Coqdor saw the danger and, always clear-headed and selfless, he first thought about those around him. About Jean, whom he had dragged there, but also Holp, who was back with him under such strange circumstances, Râx, who was starting to whistle furiously, and even the woman whom he had only known for a few minutes, whose name he didn't even know and who had just warned him so selflessly.

The mechanical bouncers were heading towards them. The Chevalier was looking for a means of defense. It was unthinkable for him to admit that he and his companions were going to be thrown onto the sidewalk of the cabaret by these robot-like common drunkards, or vile cheats. But it was Jean who suddenly exclaimed:

"There are others!"

Then Coqdor saw, on the other side of the lighted pool, the horde of brawlers that three other robots were beginning to grab, two each, to drag them mercilessly out of the establishment. Very quickly, the Star Knight heard in his mind the echo of Jean's exclamations, Holp's strangled cries and the thoughts of the courtesan.

"Three other robots?" he said telepathically to the woman.

"No, there are only three at the *Bird Woman*."

"Where do these come from then?"

He received no clear answer, as if the woman knew, but didn't want to say anything.

"Be more careful than ever. Avoid contact at all costs!"

Even though surprised by this attack, by what he saw, what he heard, and what was suggested to him, Coqdor still had very quick reflexes.

As Jean was about to be grabbed by the pincers of one of the metal attackers, he shoved the machine so hard that he sent Monique's brother diving into the muddy water of the lighted fountain.

Holp trembled as he stared at another mechanical attacker.

The Chevalier shouted:

"Save yourself, Holp! Do something!"

But the young man was frozen with terror, paralyzed by an incomprehensible fear, and barely reacted. Coqdor's cry, backed up by a fierce thought-dart, narrowly saved him and he fled just in time.

The Chevalier again heard the woman's telepathic voice.

"Walk around the fountain. Come to me. I know a way out…"

He wanted to follow her advice, convinced that she was sincere and, with Râx behind him, was about to rush off when the pstôr, standing on its forelimbs, fangs out, faced off with one of the robots.

Coqdor felt himself shudder. He knew Râx's incredible courage. The little winged monster was going to aim for what served as a throat in the metal demon and, while beating his wings, he would try to throttle it with his terrifying hind claws.

But what was dreadful for a man or an animal lost all meaning against an artificial creature. Moreover, Râx had worn down his teeth and claws.

Coqdor whistled to call back the pstôr who faithfully, obeyed and abandoned his attack. The Chevalier then rushed forward, followed by his little monster. The three robots turned to go around the pool where Jean and Holp were splashing. The latter, in his bewilderment, had joined the young geologist.

The Star Knight saw the metallic monsters descend into the green water and, near the fountain, clasp the two young people. A thought crossed his mind, coming from the hostess who stood in the crowd now agitated both by the brawlers battling the cabaret's three robots and by the new fight involving three new robots—but where did they come from, since there were only three in total at the *Bird Woman*?

She telepathically told him while leaning on the bar:

"Short circuit them!"

Coqdor understood, looked around, grabbed a table and threw it at the lighted fountain that literally exploded. A shower of water and sparks erupted.

Two of the robots, hit by the electrified water, flinched and, for a moment, spun around, disoriented by the shock. They made jerky movements, and seemed to no longer know what to do.

The third seemed to hesitate, even though it had remained at the edge of the pool and was obviously not affected by the short circuit. Its attitude stunned Coqdor for about ten seconds. A robot that hesitated? That seemed to be thinking? That, faced with the accident which his comrades had just suffered, seemed confused as to what course of action to follow?

Now was not the time to look for the answer to that riddle. It was necessary to take advantage of the situation, which played in his favor for the moment, since the two other opponents were temporarily out of action.

"Jean, Holp, this way!" shouted the Chevalier.

The hostesses were panicking, too. They were stunned by the appearance of these three new robots, which doubled the number of usual mechanical servants.

The customers were starting to fight back, some siding with the owner of the establishment, others against, accusing him of throwing out those folks whose money supported him and from whom he stole greedily.

The matron, frightened, showed her angular face covered in makeup and the girls ran away screaming. Coqdor still saw his strange ally, who kept her composure remarkably well even though gunshots began to be heard, bottles were flying, and several bodies were already littering the floor.

The three service robots—the real ones—were heading for the door, dragging six furious men who were struggling, foaming at the mouth, but could not escape their iron grip, in the chaos that was spreading everywhere.

"Follow me! With your friends!" said the woman telepathically.

Coqdor whistled at Râx, grabbed Jean by one arm and called Holp. The young man, whose skin was greener than ever, his eyes wide and streaked with red, ran as best he could behind the Chevalier, stalked by the mysterious third robot, the one that had escaped destruction in the pool.

But the matron, who had spotted the culprits, was cursing the Chevalier, yelling that he had to pay for the damage. He pushed her aside with an iron fist. She tried to strike back and her hooked fingers shot up to Coqdor's green eyes. He turned around and used his mesmerizing powers to pin the shrew down on the spot.

The Venusian barkeep came to the rescue of his partner. He had some sort of baton in his hand. He didn't have time to use it. Râx took care of him and when the big man saw the bat wings beating the air, when he came up against the dreadful glare of the pstor, he backed away, frightened.

However, rubbing his eyes, he looked at the strange robot which did not give up pursuit and which was now ready to strike again. As for the other two—and this was something else that was very strange!—they seemed to have recovered from the short circuit. After a moment of mechanical confusion, they followed the third.

A curtain was raised. The hostess left the counter and slipped away after a sign from the Chevalier.

Flanked by Râx, who hissed and stood up, still beating his wings and pushing aside the furious but cautious customers, Coqdor found himself in a narrow, damp back room, pervaded by a musty smell. It was a storeroom. He hadn't let go of Jean and Holp, who clung to him.

"Come!" is all the young woman had said.

She had carefully closed the door behind them and turned the key. Hard blows were struck against the door.

She smiled faintly.

"Robots are strong, but they're only metal. They'll have a hard time breaking down that door!"

She crossed the storeroom, through the piled up bottles, and arrived at another door. She turned around to show them the way, but suddenly she turned pale. Coqdor, Jean and Holp followed her gaze.

The robots were picking the lock! The fugitives saw something poke through, a small object, a sort of tiny metal rod, with which the strange mechanical men were trying to force the mechanism since the door was too strong for them to break it down. Had the robots been equipped with lockpicks? Everyone recognized the little metal thing that jiggled in the lock.

The three men did not understand the fear of the young woman, who repeated:

"Quickly! Oh, quickly, I beg you!"

"But we still have a little time before they open the door," the Chevalier replied.

"No, no!"

Now, she was trembling, sweating with fear.

Suddenly, Râx gave the alarm signal, with a prolonged whistle, the meaning of which Coqdor knew well.

Stunned, like Jean, like Holp, he saw one of the robots suddenly standing in front of the door! It was one of three robots which had attacked them. A robot that was now there, in front of them, on this side of the door, even though it was still closed and the lock had not yet been picked!

Instinctively, Coqdor looked at the door where, a moment before, the lockpick still gleamed. There was nothing there now. But the robot was now in here, with them, and its formidable metal frame threatened the four fugitives. How had he gotten in? Now was probably not the time to wonder about that. Coqdor realized the danger and shouted:

"The bottle rack! Quickly!"

Jean and Holp rushed and joined their efforts with those of the Chevalier. They started to overturn a big, overloaded bottle rack and throw it in the path of the mechanical demon.

The robot seemed to realize what was threatening him, but it was too late. With one united, powerful push, the three men managed to unbalance the mass formed by a light frame weighed down by countless bottles. And it crashed down on the robot in an awful din of dented metal and broken bottles. Varied colored liquids poured all over the cellar floor. Their enemy, trapped under the pile and under the rack, was now struggling like a giant beetle.

Holp looked at the disaster regretfully. Bottles of Dubonnet, flasks of ztax, flagons of Centaurian ambrosia, bulbs of Cutty Sark, broken bottles spilling the delicious yol of Sirius and crystalline barrels of azz from Canopus—all this was emptying sadly while the old Champagne of Earth foamed and bubbled without anyone being able to enjoy it. He heard Coqdor's voice:

"Are you coming with us or not?"

They were already in a narrow corridor. They passed under the building, arrived at the cellars and, from there, reached the underground car park. A small elevator was just big enough for the four of them with the pstôr and, a minute later, they stood outside.

It was raining like it only rains on Ulmir. In torrents. Green torrents, creating a kind of opaque curtain in the night pierced by the luminous spots of street lamps and signs.

"We're behind the building," whispered the young woman. "Go this way, the way is clear. Get away! You'll reach the astrodrome if you keep on this street."

"We're not leaving you," the Chevalier declared.

"Oh, I..." she said with a disheartened gesture.

Coqdor took her by the arm.

"I don't know who you are, nor what your goal is, but I do know that you helped us. and because of that, your life is in danger."

"I don't care. The life of a woman like me…"

"A woman's life, whoever she is, is always precious. And I won't leave you in the hands of the Zodiac. I'm starting to know them…"

"Hurry up! They'll come after you!"

"Yes, yes," Holp grumbled, visibly terrified.

"Well then," said Coqdor, slipping his arm through the woman's, "you're coming with us!"

He meant it. He wanted to save her. But he also thought she could be useful to him. She must know a lot and, in any case, he planned, as soon as the situation was less critical, to probe her remarkably psychic brain.

"In the rain, you have a chance of escaping," she added.

"Why aren't they chasing us?" Jean was surprised

Another mystery. But Coqdor brushed these questions aside. They had to get away. And fast. And take the girl. The one the Chevalier had come looking for at the *Bird Woman*, although initially believing that he would find Giovanna Hi-Ling there.

They walked through the green water that soaked and stained them. In the hot night, there was a kind of fog which blinded them, but, luckily, there were bright lights, and so, they moved in a cottony cloud whose green sometimes turned blackish. It was suffocating and stung their eyes.

They had gone out from the side of the building across the street from the cabaret and no one came out. Screams could be heard in the distance, probably from the drunken or cheating cosmonauts that the service robots had thrown onto the sidewalk. All of a sudden, in the night, in the rain, they heard faint but recognizable whistling sounds.

"They're throwing things at us!"

"Yes, I saw a rock hit the ground."

Coqdor turned around and tried to see. With his human eyes, it was impossible and he didn't try to concentrate because he didn't want to lose himself in a psychic effort. It wasn't the right place, so to speak.

So they sped up, but other rocks were thrown at them, probably from the windows of the building they had just left, and whose occupants, furious at seeing them escape, were showing their anger.

Coqdor shrugged. He walked quickly, helping the young woman. Râx was prancing. Jean and Holp were running alongside them.

Another rock. The sixth. And then, on the deserted street where, they were sure, there had been no one a second earlier, they saw the silhouette of a man. Then another. And another. And yet another...

Six in all. Six big, stout guys with broad shoulders, whose brutal features they could imagine through the rain and the fog. They were blocking their way.

Coqdor shouted out in anger and whistled at Râx. The pstôr flew off and attacked one of the men who collapsed under him. The young woman stood there, petrified.

"Well done, Râx!" the Chevalier shouted. "Come, my friends, let's go!"

Putting his words into action, he pounced on one of the individuals blocking their path. Jean, inspired, followed him, ready to fight. It turned into a brawl in the green rain. Coqdor and his friends fought against the strangers who had suddenly appeared in the fog, without it being possible to tell where they had come from.

Anyone looking for the stones thrown from the building would not have found them either. They had rolled off the street in the green rain, but were no longer there...

Coqdor and his companions were fighting. Alas, they still had five giants facing them. And there were only three of them.

CHAPTER IX

There were only three of them, but the Star Knight alone was worth several men. His physical strength was significant, but his psychic powers were even greater. As for Râx, he had already finished with the enemy whom he had pounced on and who had not been able to put up much of a fight.

The battle began.

In the torrential downpour coating everything in its greenish mists, streaked with luminous pools of neon light that shined everywhere, the young woman could see the bodies colliding, grappling each other, clutching. The fighters puffed and panted in the night, sometimes rolling on the mud after falling with a thud. And there, on the wet ground, the fight went on.

Holp and Jean Farnel were in bad shape.

Who were these strange attackers, who seemed to have appeared out of nowhere?

Coqdor himself, grappling with one of the giants, was amazed at the brute force of his adversary. While fighting, using in turn boxing, judo, karate and even Erdanian ooim, the subtle art of combining mind and muscles in which he had trained for a long time, he was trying to understand the tireless nature of his opponent, but felt alarmed. He was running out of steam; he sensed disaster for his companions, struck down by these brutal, massive thugs who seemed not to feel their blows.

Coqdor's adversary suddenly rushed forward and the Chevalier could feel the danger. Then he saw the enemy face-to-face, up close. It was what he had been waiting for. Despite the night and the rain, the Chevalier's eyes shone in the green darkness. The brilliance coming from his emerald eyes pierced his attacker's skull, and the latter staggered, hit in the brain. He spun around, tried to stand still, staggered and finally collapsed.

Jean was still on the ground, groaning, crushed by the weight of the man on top of him. Coqdor let out a special whistle. Monique's brother almost immediately felt that the formidable weight had just been lightened as Râx jumped on his enemy and quickly took care of him.

Coqdor then rushed to Holp's aid and tried to pull off the giant who was crushing him. But the last two giants, slowly but in unison, methodically moved forward to catch the Chevalier in a vice. Promptly, Coqdor, with a blow to the back of Holp's antagonist's neck, freed the latter.

His mind was working fast.

The demented look of these brutish villains, their behavior, their sudden appearance, and finally what he thought he had read quickly in the brain he had just attacked—all this was spinning inside him and he began to form a hypothesis about the true nature and origin of their enemies.

He was now between two of these monsters. Neither Jean nor Holp, still half stunned, could help him. But Coqdor whistled again and faced off with one of his attackers, leaving the field open for Râx to take on the other one. The result was not long in coming.

Although the Chevalier was worth more than one man, the pstôr alone was worth at least a half-dozen in combat. The man who sought to attack his master quickly discovered what that meant. He fell heavily to the ground, half-strangled, blinded by the large flapping wings, his shoulders torn by the claws of the hind legs which rested on them.

Coqdor, for his part, just stood there and, once again, stared into his enemy's eyes. The giant stumbled and fell. The Chevalier stepped back and watched him hit the ground. This time, it was over. The six giants had been defeated.

Jean and Holp, helped by the young woman from the cabaret, who had watched the fight as she shivered in the rain.

Râx, very fired up by the battle and the smell of blood, fluttered around them, tracing a magic circle that seemed to protect them.

Coqdor called him quietly and he came over for his master to pet him.

Then, they saw three of the giants struggle to their feet but, instead of attacking again, they lumbered away in the downpour, and the thick curtain of green rain soon swallowed them up.

Coqdor told his companions that they had to get away from this hellish neighborhood and reach the astrodrome as quickly as possible.

But Jean, close by, suddenly shouted:

"Chevalier! Look! Look!"

Three of the giants had fled, more or less in bad shape, but three more remained on the ground. The three that Râx had killed. The pstôr had used his teeth and claws, and no man, however skillful, unless he had some kind of special protection, could have survived its attack. Now, these three huge bodies, seeming even bigger in the foul mist, looked like they were shrinking, curling up.

Jean, Holp, Coqdor and their female companion were gawking. It was mind-blowing. The three devastated men—were they really men?—were already taking up only a little space on the asphalt of Ulmir. They were shrinking visibly and at a rate that was accelerating from second to second. As if in a nightmare, they soon disappeared from the sight of those who had fought them.

Not completely, however. In the poor visibility, despite the multi-colored neon tubes, they could see what remained: three big rocks. Nothing but three random stones, which now stood in the place where the giants had fallen.

"It's unimaginable, these stones…" Jean gasped.

"They're the ones that were thrown at us earlier, and that we heard rolling on the asphalt!" said Coqdor.

"But then? What..."

Monique's brother was struggling to understand. Holp, too, was completely stunned by what was happening. Coqdor made a quick decision:

"We have to get rid of them, no matter what. Quickly! Otherwise, God knows what other enemies we will have to fight next time…"

Jean, who still didn't understand, was about to ask for explanations, but Coqdor had already picked up the three rocks. The young woman came forward:

"There! Look! There's a manhole."

Coqdor rushed over and threw in the three rocks, which disappeared into the abyss of darkness.

"And now," the Chevalier said, "let's go! Too bad there are four of us, even five counting Râx. It'll be hard to grab a ride... And there are no tramons in Ulmir…"

They hurried. It was muggy despite the incessant downpour that the warm atmosphere partly vaporized, so that they always kept moving forward through a cloud of steam. The surrounding buildings, riddled with cracks or partly collapsed, stood like specters strangely streaked by the many illuminated signs. And the avenue went on and on, totally deserted at that hour and in that weather.

They no longer saw lights in the windows of occupied homes. The streetlights, resigned to their fate, slowly turned gray with the hideous green leprosy that fell from this hostile sky.

But the young woman knew the way. She guided them and, after a good hour of walking through the bizarre city, they finally saw the lights of the astrodrome. They breathed deeply, feeling out of danger.

Holp followed them without really knowing where he was going, but encouraged because he could not forget how Chevalier Coqdor had once helped him and his fellow delinquents on the planet of fire.

Jean's curiosity finally got the better of him. He cried out:

"Chevalier... Explain all that to me..."

"What happened, my boy? As a geologist, you could have written a fascinating article on the pebbles that I threw into the sewer. But I had to get rid of them, my dear Jean. Indeed, those stones, as you noticed, were what remained of our adversaries, at least those whom Râx had killed. But it was in that form that they attacked us. And they were the robots, at least the fake ones, from the cabaret. And at least one of them was the lockpick that got through the keyhole, then turned into a robot again, and attacked us in the storeroom."

"I see!"

"I believe we're dealing with metamorphs," Coqdor continued. "It's rather strange, and quite troubling..."

They had arrived at their destination. Ten minutes later, they were aboard the cosmaviso.

Monique, who had not been able to get a moment's rest, threw herself into her brother's arms.

"You see I brought him back in good condition, my dear Monique!" said the Chevalier.

"There wasn't much danger, I guess?" she asked.

"Hmm! We'll tell you about it later. In the meantime, thank Râx."

And the young girl, when she found out, placed more than one kiss on the face of the pstôr whose golden eyes glowed with satisfaction at this way of doing things.

However, the *Comet Hyakutake* was scheduled to take off at dawn. From here, Coqdor thought he should go to the constellation of Capricorn, and indeed, the cosmaviso was already leaving on a mission to this region. This was the reason why, in agreement with the authorities of the Martervenux, the Chevalier and those he thought useful to take with him had chosen that ship as a means of transport.

Based on some information gleaned by Robin Muscat, Coqdor figured that at least three planets in this constellation might prove interesting to visit and that there, perhaps, he would find traces of a zodiac with thirteen signs.

Monique, along with some orderlies made available to them by the captain, bustled around them. First of all, they needed to shower, freshen up and change clothes. But the cosmonauts assured them with a laugh that, after the sauna, their outfits would be back in fine condition. The spectacular rain of Ulmir had the reputation of being easy to clean, the spores of plant origin which colored it simply disappearing in a good wash.

Monique took special care of Yloa Flugg—that was the name of their new friend from the cabaret.

Then Coqdor sent Jean and Monique to get some rest. He suggested to Holp to travel with him until the end of his mission, and the misguided youth, feeling that once again fate was offering him salvation, swore that he would die fighting for the Chevalier.

"I'm not asking you that!" said Coqdor. "I hate people who talk so lightly about sacrificing themselves. Living is much harder because it lasts longer. It's also true that it's infinitely more useful..."

Holp, happy now, went to sleep with the cosmonauts.

Coqdor then asked Yloa to follow him to his cabin. Now dressed in a jumpsuit borrowed from the crew—in space, women were dressed like men—she seemed more relaxed, almost beautiful despite the stigma of vice that now seemed to fade away as she was seen in a different light than the sad image she had presented at the *Bird Woman*.

"We'll chat a little, all right?"

Yloa seemed uncomfortable. The Chevalier sat her down and with Râx lying at her feet, purring like a huge cat, he spoke to her of their strange mental encounter in the dive where he had come looking for Giovanna Hi-Ling.

"You called for help, didn't you?" he asked.

She nodded.

"I congratulate you on your mental training. I was looking for someone else..."

When questioned, she admitted not knowing Giovanna Hi-Ling.

"What about the Zodiac?" asked Coqdor.

He watched her bite her lip. Already, he was reading her thoughts.

"You're afraid of them, aren't you?" he continued. "But you don't bear their fatal tattoo, so you won't be struck dead if you speak."

"They have other means to guarantee silence!"

"So you know them?"

This time, he was met with complete silence. And her brain felt like a dam, which meant that this woman had a background that was not in line with the sad profession she practiced in Ulmir.

He told her so, and she began speaking of her past, of her decline.

Born in the constellation of Perseus, in Xow'Tal and not in the Martervenux, as Holp had believed, she had wanted to be a space stewardess. On the Earth-Perseus line, it was not long before she was assigned to the *Spica*.

Coqdor became very interested, remembering the documentation transmitted by Interplan, and urged her to continue.

Yloa Flugg had no problem explaining that she had met Cladek Halstar, the financier who had gone mad aboard the Earth-Perseus spaceship. It was he who, after charming her diligently, had gradually brought her to the idea that serving a very high mission would bring her fortune and honors.

What was that mission? Yloa had only a very vague idea. The zodiac with thirteen signs was involved and unraveling its mystery led either to mastering the universe or putting the cosmos in danger—she didn't know which exactly.

Then, the time came when mysterious "friends" of Cladek Halstar had offered her to work for them, to inform them about the actions of certain passengers on the interstellar line, and even to search their luggage and cabins.

Yloa, very much in love with the financier, had initially accepted but then, little by little, terror had taken hold of her. She had wanted to turn back—but it was impossible! Threatened with being reported to the authorities, she continued her pathetic work until the day she was asked to wear, upon her heart, the sign that would link her to the mysterious order.

This time she refused, even rebelled. Yloa asked Cladek Halstar for protection. The strangers did not insist, but a short time later, the *Spica* took the financier away, and soon after, he went mad.

Coqdor, secretly, promised himself to ask Robin Muscat a little later to verify such statements and to find out if the *Spica* staff, at the time of this tragedy, included Yloa Flugg as a stewardess.

Then, at a layover, Yloa had been kidnapped, brought to Ulmir and thrown into the *Bird Woman*. Under terrible threats, she had to agree to become a hostess for only a few weeks. There, under duress but never seeing the people controlling her, and always threatened to reveal the thefts she had committed on board the spaceship, she had had to act as a spy and try to listen to the conversations of the cosmonauts to find out if they were talking about a zodiac of some kind.

When it was over, Coqdor, with his mental probe, recognized that she would no longer say anything, even though she knew a lot more.

When he said good night to her, she stopped for a moment at the threshold of the cabin.

"I can only say one more thing to you, Chevalier. The name of a planet. Accora…"

"Thank you, Yloa, and good night!"

Coqdor went to the captain and asked him to drop him and his friends off at a layover on the planet Accora, located in the Capricorn constellation. Then he went back to his room, pensive. Râx followed him, with his weird feline-bat walk.

When he got to the door, the pstôr stood up and hissed angrily. There was someone in Coqdor's cabin. A woman...

A woman he had never seen, except on film. Strapped, or rather tightly molded, into a black jumpsuit, she was fascinatingly beautiful with her dark eyes slanted into the oval of a smooth face framed by ebony hair.

Coqdor soothed Râx with a pat, composed himself, smiled and said softly:

"Good evening, Giovanna Hi-Ling!"

CHAPTER X

The film footage hadn't lied. The late Jean-Marie Spontini's girlfriend was truly beautiful, amazingly seductive...

Coqdor could not help but be affected by the fascination that emanated from this Eurasian girl with perfect proportions, and features imbued with an intelligent and sensual personality.

Very much a man of the world, having overcome the irresistible surprise, Coqdor showed her to a seat. She thanked him with a smile that would have damned a monk in the convents of Altaïr, those worshipers whose reputation for virtue is well known—a pointless virtue since they never wanted to believe that the Great Revelation had already taken place on Earth...

Coqdor knew that if the Zodiac sent him such an emissary, it was for a specific purpose in mind—possibly a deadly one.

Giovanna took her seat with feline grace. Her desirable body, fit inside her night-colored jumpsuit, seemed to exude erotic scents. The Chevalier, despite his fortitude, felt uncomfortable. She had thanked him for his invitation with a simple smile and a flutter of her long eyelashes.

"And now," he started, not wishing to be beguiled easily, "I'll listen to you."

Such an introduction, direct and precise, seemed to disconcert her somewhat.

"You'll listen to me, Chevalier?"

"Of course. I imagine that to come here so casually, you have something important to tell me," he replied, quite certain of it.

She was very much alive, and here, in the flesh. He knew that one should be wary of ghosts, of illusions skillfully created by scientists and magicians. More than once, he had encountered semblances of characters created by force-waves, or simply psychic powers.

But Giovanna had managed to appear here while the *Comet Hyakutake* was hurtling through subspace, so she was indeed real. The faint seductive scent she gave off was another guarantee of this. She remained very much a woman and not a mirage.

"It seems you are suspicious of me?" she said, with a half-smile.

"Perhaps, Giovanna, but above all, of those who sent you..."

Her long black eyelashes fluttered slightly and Coqdor noticed that, even when troubled, she still found a way to use her tiniest reactions as elements of seduction.

"I'm fully aware," the Chevalier added, "that you bear here—he pointed with his index finger to her heart—a certain symbol…"

She didn't flinch, just answered:

"Of course! Your friend Inspector Muscat told you."

"So, let's get to the point. To what do I owe the pleasure of your visit, as spontaneous as it may be?"

No doubt she had guessed that Coqdor, as a man, was already the victim of her charms. The irony, the frankness of his words were only intended to mask the trouble that was growing within him.

"Well then," she said. "Let's put our cards on the table. I didn't know you, but I was told by those of the Zodiac—as you call them—that you are a dangerous man. And now, I see why!"

She paused briefly, with another smile which seemed to mean that she was not at all displeased by that fact.

"Chevalier Bruno Coqdor," she continued, becoming serious again, "you're currently seeking to uncover a very ancient secret. But as a matter of fact, you don't even know exactly what you're looking for…"

"I beg your pardon," retorted Coqdor courteously, "but a man has died. Another one became the victim of a fit of madness, sudden but surely provoked. Should I remind you of the fate of Cladek Halstar, now resident, probably for life, in a psychiatric hospital on Earth? The death was that of the cosmomancer Yum Akatinor. Finally, a person close to you, Jean-Marie Spontini, was also murdered through this accursed sign."

"Please, don't bring up such memories," the young woman said, shuddering. "They are so painful for me!"

"No, on the contrary, let's talk about them. They help me clarify my position. It's true that I don't know—not yet—what is at stake in our battle, but it's also true that I'm fighting for a good cause."

"Are you sure?"

"How could I be wrong, Miss Hi-Ling? When one kills, when one destroys a mind? Your friends are criminals. I'm fighting them, that's all."

"Why? You don't even belong to Interplan!"

"They don't call me the Star Knight for nothing. I stand against the forces of evil wherever they appear throughout the galaxy."

He stopped. Bolstered by his noble sentiments, by his passion, Coqdor was getting carried away. And he felt the burning gaze of this seductive creature on him. The beautiful almond-shaped eyes were devouring him. Obviously, she felt passionate about what he had just said; she felt an almost voluptuous pleasure in listening to his words. He realized this and, finding himself ridiculous, changed his tone.

"Let's cut to the chase. You come from those who use as a symbol the Thirteenth sign of the Zodiac, and who protect... I don't know what kind of secret, but surely something formidable, unimaginable. You have threats to pass on to me, so get on with it! I'm expecting them."

Once again, Giovanna looked surprised.

"Threats? Oh my, no, not at all! My, er, my friends know well that nothing could be gained by threatening a man like Chevalier Bruno Coqdor. On the contrary, I was sent to offer you an alliance, and their friendship."

Coqdor put on a gallant but ironic face.

"They couldn't have chosen a more charming messenger!"

A flash of anger, quickly repressed, shot out of her jet-black eyes.

"It was thought, among those who serve the Thirteenth Sign, that it would be useless and stupid to fight you. So I was asked only to ask you not to give up your fight, but to carry it alongside us, for a cause of the highest nobility and well worthy of you, Chevalier Coqdor!"

"Really? So what's it all about?"

"We're inviting you to join our circle. Do you accept?"

Coqdor chuckled and shrugged his shoulders.

"That's all? You disappoint me, Miss Hi-Ling. Do you think I'm stupid enough to say yes, to join a company of murderers when I don't even know what their cause is?"

"If you accept, if you give your word as we just gave ours, you will be made aware of it. That is to say, all aspects of this tremendous mystery—yes, more formidable, more fantastic than anything you could have ever imagined—will be fully revealed to you."

"I can't commit myself like that. I demand to know first!"

"Impossible. You have to trust us."

"I don't buy anything sight unseen, as we say back home."

"Chevalier, it's a matter of the fate of the entire galaxy. Come with us! Join us!"

"I repeat that I don't want to get involved so casually with a gang of criminals!"

Giovanna stood up and her eyes, this time, burned with unrestrained anger.

"The Zodiac are not evildoers! Who cares about the fate of a few miserable scoundrels compared to... that!"

"The life of a man, whoever he may be, is worth more than all the secrets in the universe!" said Coqdor. "And I'm surprised to see you walk so easily over corpses, Miss Hi-Ling—especially when one of them was that of your lover!"

He could read the rage in her eyes.

"Chevalier, please..."

She controlled herself, pulled herself together, anxious to fulfill her mission and not give in to her personal anger. "You must believe me. I am authorized to make you this promise: that nothing will be asked of you that would compromise your honor, nor any of these human lives that you seem to treasure so much, will be endangered by your actions..."

"They're the most indisputable manifestations of the divine, but these are things you probably wouldn't understand."

"Far better than you think..."

She had suddenly changed her attitude. A kind of deep sadness cast its veil over her beautiful face.

"Why the melancholy?" he asked, a little softened because he felt she had been sincerely moved.

"I see I won't convince you," she said with a sigh. "I'll have to report my failure..."

"Come on, Giovanna, it's not so simple. I'm not refusing to hear you out in principle. I'll even gladly accept, if necessary, to meet with whoever sent you."

"Oh!" she said with a slight change in mood. "But will you still think that it's just another trap on our part?"

"Rest assured, I'm used to anticipating traps and overcoming them. No, listen to me! I want to tell you, if not a definitive yes, but at least that I'm willing to talk further. However, I want to know what I'm committing myself to. I want to know the real stakes, the true meaning of the Thirteenth Sign."

"I don't have the right to tell you."

"So you do know..." he insisted.

She showed a slight hesitation, fearing that she had already said too much.

"I'm just a minor player," she said. "I know very few things."

"But even these few would be useful to me and would allow me to make up my mind!" he insisted.

She wanted to speak, but seemed unable to do so. She just shook her head apologetically. Coqdor was smiling, very relaxed.

"Well, I'll just have to solve the mystery myself, which sounds fine to me," he said.

"I don't think," Giovanna murmured, "that it will be possible."

"Difficult, perhaps, but not impossible."

"Chevalier, don't count on your past successes. You have accomplished some extraordinary feats all over the galaxy—but this? No, you won't be able to!"

"Well, my dear Miss Hi-Ling, we shall see."

She sat there now, as if overwhelmed. Her eyes turned towards the depolex porthole beyond which they could see the apparently fixed stars, like priceless gems thrown into this universe, whose most beautiful adornment they formed.

"Come on, don't cry," Coqdor said. "You failed. Surely it's not that important."

"I had no right to fail!"

He edged closer and could not help but feel, so close to her, the aura of her incredibly seductive charm.

"Giovanna, what are you afraid of?"

"They'll punish me. I was supposed to get you to agree."

She was now on the verge of tears.

All of a sudden, she threw her arms around his neck, snuggled against him and he felt her supple body embrace his. There was a sensual, split-second whirlwind! His desire for her passionate caresses grew stronger...

But he was Chevalier Coqdor. He understood intuitively what awaited him if he gave in, and into what abyss of deprivation he would be dragged. Very gently but firmly, he loosened her embrace and pushed the seductress away.

Râx had risen slightly and was looking at them with his large golden eyes.

"No, Giovanna," he said firmly.

This time, he saw hatred in her black eyes—the true feelings that animated her then. She was no longer the friendly ambassador who was disappointed or offended, but a woman spurned. A woman who had offered herself with all her body, all her soul—because she was sincere, Coqdor had read that in her—but who had been rejected.

She wanted to say more and, for a moment, seemed almost ugly beneath the turmoil of her inner thoughts. Abruptly, she stood up, pushed past him and ran towards the door. She opened it and fled into the passageway.

He thought for three seconds, then rushed forward.

"Giovanna!"

But he could no longer see her. He whistled for Râx.

"Look for her!" he commanded.

The pstôr darted forth like an arrow, incredibly fast on its motley limbs. The corridor was empty in the soft light of the magnetized neon.

Coqdor ran, calling out:

"Giovanna! Come back!"

He suddenly felt something under his foot. That something rolled and he fell, furious. He got up quickly, recognized that it was a bolt, a simple bolt, which had caused him to fall, tripping him.

Now angry, he ordered Râx to keep searching, but the pstôr sniffed the air and seemed confused.

Coqdor saw an officer, then a cosmonaut, a little further away. He questioned them but neither had seen a young woman wearing a black jumpsuit pass by.

"And yet," the Chevalier said to himself, "she was here, in the flesh, very much alive!"

On his way back to his cabin, he thought of looking for the bolt, but did not find it. An idea suddenly struck him. But for now, there was something else to worry about.

Back in his room, he lay down on the bed and, while Râx seemed to be watching over him, he concentrated, searching for Giovanna with his mind. But the overwhelming image of this voluptuous girl escaped him and he became certain that he would not see her again on board.

And yet, obscurely, he knew that she was not far away. He tried in vain to find out how she had been able to get onto the *Comet Hyakutake* in the middle of its space flight, and then how she had escaped. Because he suspected that, even if they searched the cosmaviso, they wouldn't find her.

He finally fell asleep, tormented, murmuring before drifting away:

"If only I could have found that damn bolt…"

Four more spins of the dial. Four times twelve Earth-hours. The *Comet Hyakutake* stopped at Accora, the first small planet in the constellation of Capricorn.

Coqdor disembarked with his friends and bid farewell to the captain.

Here, as everywhere, the local authorities welcomed him and made available to him everything he wanted. He had a long talk with Jean Farnel about the geology of the planets of Capricorn in general, and of Accora in particular.

He asked Yloa if she still wished to accompany them and she simply said that she did. Coqdor thanked her. She told him about Accora. On this small planet, lost in space, archeologists had found curious remains of an unknown race, who had undoubtedly disappeared millennia ago.

Coqdor thought that the information was valuable and would save him from searching the constellation from planet to planet, which would have taken months. He sent coded messages to Muscat to inform him of the progress of his expedition.

And then, at the spaceport, he chartered a tankelec to explore the planet's hostile outlands.

CHAPTER XI

Coqdor had been warned: a trip to the outlands of Accora would not be a pleasant excursion.

Accora revolved around a sun to which it was quite close, like Mercury in the Sol system; it was less torrid than its almost uninhabitable counterpart, but was still fairly hot and stifling. Marshes abounded and in the wilderness, some daring pioneers had discovered the remains of an ancient, now-vanished civilization.

Here, as on Ulmir, missions were considered real punishments.

Around the spaceport stood a city that looked just like Ulmir. Only, instead of rotting in the green rain, its buildings were slowly crumbling due to the searing heat—that was the only difference.

Yloa Flugg, however, had pointed to Accora, so Accora it was that they had to search.

The tankelec had taken off. An all-terrain machine equipped with the traditional air cushion device for the best soils, high articulated legs for marshy regions, removable tracks, finally, to be able to move on the chaotic and stony terrain which abounded, it was said, beyond the marshes. Because, above all, it was the marshes of Accora that had to be confronted and conquered.

Since the first landings on this small world, the pioneers had given up exploring such territory. The stagnant waters extending over vast areas emitted a nasty mist under the burning sun. Fevers were rife there and the first expeditions had ended in failure. Epidemics had devoured the brave souls who ventured through these lands. In addition, a formidable, poorly described fauna was reputed to swarm there. Its visual splendors and tangible horrors were lauded. The death moths, in particular, were famous, not to mention certain winged creatures similar, it was said, to the terrestrial gymnotus or the Altaïr pyrornithocus.

But the films and photos were always of poor quality in this swampy universe and the explorers had never been able to bring back any interesting living specimens. Dead, these bizarre animals quickly rotted or crumbled into dust. So much so that legends were rife and led people to believe in fabled regions practically forbidden to cosmonauts.

The spaceport and the neighboring city was built on more solid ground near one of the poles of the planet, a land by definition colder than the rest of the globe.

Coqdor had thanked those who warned him, but he didn't give up so easily. Besides, his mission orders permitted him to try everything.

To drive the tankelec, a volunteer, a Centaurian called Geek, was made available to the Star Knight. And so it was this Geek, a strong, lively fellow, with ever-roaming eyes—which made Jean Farnel say that he saw in different directions like flies on Earth—who was in charge.

Always cautious and thinking about accidents and possible setbacks, Coqdor had advised Jean and Holp, who had come without really knowing how or why, to learn a little about operating and steering such an exceptional machine. He himself also took an interest in the handling of the tankelec, whose atomic engine drove the various means of progression.

Monique, brave and beautiful Monique, was busy classifying both the documents sent by Robin Muscat and those selected by her brother from his archives. They had left most of it in Accora City, keeping only the essentials.

In principle, the expedition was to study the dilapidated monuments which stood on a mountain range, far beyond the marshes, towards what could be called the northern tropic of the planet Accora. A trip of approximately three days of thirty hours given the duration of the planet's rotation. Three days, if all went well...

Certainly, at first, the cosmonauts were interested in the strange landscape.

The farther they moved forward on an air cushion, the more hostile the terrain became. The first ponds appeared, announcing the famous swamps. Rare birds and unrecognized reptiles were fleeing before the tankelec. Already, the atmosphere was becoming heavier, loaded with miasma and steam exhaling from the large swamps.

Yloa Flugg was pensive.

Coqdor had tried to reassure her:

"I won't ask you anymore. I understand your terror. You live in fear of revenge from the Zodiac. But you know that I'll do everything I can to protect you. And my friends will help."

"Thank you, Chevalier. Unfortunately, I know they'll get me eventually."

"Not necessarily, Yloa. Are you sorry that you talked to me?"

"No, I feel like I'm serving justice while avenging Cladek Halstar and avenging myself for what they put me through."

She shuddered and her gaze froze.

Coqdor had taken care of her. He could not forget that this poor woman had been a prostitute against her will.

"Yloa, you told me about Accora. This is crucial. Of course, I knew that in principle, we had to look in the constellation Capricorn, but without you, what a waste of time…"

Since she looked ill at ease, he assured her that she no longer had anything to fear, that he would not bother her and would not try to extract other secrets from her if they were too terrible to be revealed.

He kept his word, of course, continued to be gentle with her and did not even try to read her mind that was psychologically closed with unusual mental strength.

The Zodiac apparently did not accept just anyone among their members!

Despite Coqdor's courage, Monique's confidence and Jean's natural cheerfulness, although Holp on the one hand and Yloa on the other were more passive, although Geek was totally absorbed in his work, still a certain anxiety weighed on them all constantly.

Certain recent facts could not fail to worry them. The very last incident, that of the appearance and incomprehensible escape of Giovanna Hi-Ling in open space, tormented the Star Knight. Only Monique and Jean knew and shared his torment.

Coqdor had come to believe that the bolt on which he had lost his balance in the corridor was none other than the seductive and perverse creature sent to him by the Zodiac.

A transformation, once again.

These damned criminals had found a way to completely modify their molecular structure, the inner arrangement of their atomic elements. And this willful metamorphism allowed them to be humans, robots or who knew what else, until they became simple pebbles, if necessary, a master key slipping through a lock or a sneaky bolt rolling under the feet of a dangerous pursuer.

Therefore, Coqdor and the two young people had learned to be wary of everything around them. So much so that they had deliberately failed to tell their three companions about this. This plastic glass, this simple atomic pencil, this fork, this document, even Monique's wristwatch or bracelet, might they not be one of the members of the Zodiac who had taken this or that form to constantly spy on them, waiting for the right moment to adopt a human morphology or turn into some more dangerous metallic monster?

Nonetheless, Coqdor, Monique and Jean remained on their guard, watching everything, dreading seeing the enemy spring out of the smallest object placed in the cabin of the tankelec or in the sanitary compartments and the sleeping quarters located under the cockpit.

Involuntarily, Coqdor thought of Giovanna Hi-Ling. He came to regret that such a beautiful girl had made herself the accomplice of such bandits, which he continued to refer to them as.

He was lucid. Giovanna's beauty had made a deep impression on him and her memory haunted him, also troubled him. The temptation had been strong and he had been on the verge of giving in.

He tried to forget it, immersed himself in deep reflections concerning the weird zodiac with its thirteen houses.

Or he reflected on the case of Yloa. Sincere? Probably yes. She didn't seem to have any illusions. She had informed Coqdor and now she was following him. Yloa had deliberately agreed to sacrifice herself, probably out of a spirit of revenge rather than justice. But Coqdor, digging deeper, told himself that, after all, given the sad fate to which she had been allotted on Ulmir, she had little better choice.

Moreover, she was making herself useful, helping Monique take care of them aboard the tankelec.

It had been three days, counting by the spins of the dial, since they had left the spaceport. The swamps spread farther and wider over the landscape and the machine now progressed on its large articulated legs, which gave it the appearance of a gigantic insect.

Stops were brief due to the heavy and unpleasant atmosphere, which made internal air conditioning preferable.

Râx yawned, bored. He was allowed a few laps of flight at the stops, then Coqdor whistled at him and the pstôr had to resign himself to being locked in the cockpit. He spent the majority of the time there, his head on the knees of Monique or his master.

No wickedness had been observed from the kitchenware or various utensils. But Coqdor was still not convinced.

Then they stopped for the night. The men took turns on guard duty and Jean had taken the last watch after Holp, Coqdor and Geek the pilot. Monique's brother had slept well and now, with his nose against the depolex wall, he gazed for a long time at the sky where unfamiliar stars were revolving, where huge and colorful meteors were shooting like rockets, where unusual moons were flashing unexpected fires.

Then he looked down at the swamps that surrounded them on all sides.

On two or three occasions, the day before, they had seen what they took for giant birds, very distant. But Geek had explained that they were probably the death moths, the elusive and splendid creatures that no one had yet been able to capture.

In the night, they couldn't see anything. Nothing but the reflection of the starry sky on the rather murky water of the swamps where strips of land sometimes bristling with aquatic plants, varieties of giant reeds, stretched out like the corpses of saurians.

It started and went on and on.

Jean dozed, telling himself that in less than an hour dawn would appear, an Accora dawn whose colors he would be curious to observe. He was not very aware of what was happening, lost in the hazy drift of his thoughts, his eyes now wandering through the clouds which slowly rose from the swamps and rolled, endlessly, around the motionless tankelec on its large metal legs.

Motionless?

Jean suddenly realized that this was no longer the case. Because the machine started wobbling gently, very gently.

Monique's brother jumped up like a spring, wide awake. He looked around. Nothing unusual, it seemed. No animals in sight, and the weather seemed clear. The sky was just beginning to pale over there, very far away, towards what corresponded to the east over Accora.

Jean looked over to the side of the sleeping quarters. Nothing was moving. He heard the regular breathing of the two women and three men. And Râx, curled up near Coqdor, must have been sleeping peacefully too.

"Oh come on! I didn't hit the whiskey last night! But it feels like we're rocking…"

His heart went cold. Another attack from the people of the Zodiac?

Anything was possible and he wanted to be certain.

Without waking his companions—it might be nothing—he took an atomic flashlight, slipped a blaster into his belt and quietly left the cockpit, not before pressing a button to open the folding ladder that led to the ground some twenty feet below the passenger compartment itself.

There, clinging to the ladder, Jean saw that he was not mistaken.

The tankelec was wobbling strangely, though not very much. The large, rigid metal legs were planted in the ground, which had been seen the previous evening to be very muddy. But here and there, now the same terrain of mire and rotten grass was everywhere.

Jean realized that the abnormal phenomenon had its source in the land itself.

He stayed on the ladder, not daring to take the risk of taking a step on the ground, afraid that he might get stuck. Geek had warned them of such danger, ever-present in this region of Accora.

He swept the halo of the atomic light over the ground. And what he saw shocked him.

The ground, the muddy, damp ground, now seemed to have an inner life that was half underwater, half underground. Eerie throbbing created bizarre undulations and noxious bubblings. The tankelec, planted on its feet but resting on such chaos, obviously could not remain very balanced.

Before sounding the alarm, Jean, carried away by the scientific curiosity that was constantly on alert in his nature, descended to the last step of the metal ladder. There, a foot and a half off the ground, he crouched, held on, leaned forward and probed the mystery with the light.

He was astounded to see a huge swarm, as if a million moles—what kind of moles?—had dug into the ground in all directions, as if aquatic monsters—but of what dreadful species?—had been buried there to torture, to ravage, to furrow from below the great lakes of mire and mud.

It was alive. This was obviously not a geological phenomenon, not an earthquake. And it was scary.

More and more, the tankelec teetered.

Jean realized that if this continued, the machine would end up falling over. And that would be a disaster.

He was about to go back up and call his friends when he noticed, with a tremor of horror, that the situation was changing.

Huge larval forms, streaming with mud, swelled to the surface, puncturing it, colliding with the metal feet of the tankelec, already very unstable.

And these hideous fetuses, these unidentifiable lemurs now seemed to be attacking the craft on board which the Chevalier Coqdor and his companions were sleeping.

CHAPTER XII

"Alert! We're under attack!"

Finally, Jean tore himself away from the kind of fascination he was experiencing, leaning over this chasm which seemed alive and which suddenly opened under the metal supports of the tankelec.

In the light of the atomic flashlight, the incomprehensible swarming looked so strange that for a few moments, trying to understand, he could do nothing but stare at the moving ground.

And then he felt the danger as the liquid mud burst under the impetus of the disgusting, shapeless, unheard-of monsters, which seemed to be trying to climb towards the humanoids' machine.

People like Chevalier Coqdor could wake up quickly. And Geek, ever since he had entered the hostile lands of Accora, with their bad reputation, had never been able to sleep peacefully. So, they were the first to leave the quarters, rushing in their underwear to the metal ladder that the man on watch had unfolded and that was at the bottom.

Râx, naturally, was with his master. Holp also showed up, shaking himself out of a heavy torpor. The two women, in turn, got worried.

The vision, in the mixed glow of the flashlight that contrasted with the shadows of the surroundings and the vague, still pale lights which shined down from the sky, was surprising enough for time to stand still for a moment among the passengers of the tankelec.

"Geek, do you know what that is?"

The Centaurian's teeth were chattering, "Devil of the Cosmos! If only I knew! Another trick of these damned countries... Ach, I told you so! Here, you only find things like that. And I have to say…"

Exasperated, the Chevalier cut off his barrage of regret, "No time to whine! You don't know what it is, do you? Neither do we, since we've never set foot on this planet. But we have to do something…"

"Fight it!" Jean shouted. "I'm going to shoot. Get the blasters!"

"Hold on, my boy! Before attacking an enemy, it's good to know what kind it is. Let me see."

And the Chevalier began to descend, joining Jean on the last step of the iron ladder. There, he crouched down, then with his belly on the rung, half in the air, he leaned forward.

"Chevalier! Please!" Monique shouted. "You're risking your life. If these... these things are dangerous... or venomous…"

"You're right to think so, dear child!"

But Coqdor nonetheless remained hanging there, trying to get a closer look at the creatures—because he was convinced that they were indeed living beings.

Râx, still at the cockpit door and obviously not knowing how to descend an iron ladder, whistled sadly at not being able to reach his master, which startled Coqdor.

"Monique, hold onto Râx! If he flies away, he could very well fall into this magma. And God knows what would happen."

The young lady took the pstôr by the collar and spoke to him softly to calm him down.

The viscous, gelatinous masses seemed to be growing incessantly and their moving mass was unbalancing the tankelec more and more as it kept wobbling.

"Curious, I feel like we're being sucked in! That this ground which I think is alive is trying to absorb the metal legs…"

He rose a little.

"The flashlight, Jean, please!"

Jean handed it to him and Coqdor, very closely, examined the increasingly animated throng. From time to time, a shape seemed to rise up, then drop down heavily with a disgusting "plop", and a little mud splashed on the Chevalier.

"We have to shoot into the mass. Jean, do it! Geek, Holp, get guns and give me one!"

He stood there while up above, Holp and Geek disappeared, hurrying to retrieve the inframauve blasters.

Jean didn't have to be told twice. He started shooting blinding bursts at the abominable things. He and Coqdor next to him saw the hit creatures leaping or falling half disintegrated, shaking with jolts that were not easy to watch.

In this mud bath strangely stroked by the reflections of dawn the halo of the flashlight that Coqdor was still holding danced across the bubbling surface.

Monique admitted that the slow movements of the wobbling tankelec were starting to make her feel unwell, a sort of seasickness. Jean shouted to her that now was not the time.

But he himself wasn't feeling very well. Fed up, with a kind of rage, he aimed at the unspeakable monsters who were attacking the support stems, to hit them with the dreadful darts of inframauve.

Geek and Holp came back, armed now, and the two women moved aside, troubled, wondering what the outcome of such a fight would be.

Already, leaning on the ladder, clinging above Jean and the Chevalier, the pilot and the young hoodlum started joining their fire to those of Monique's brother.

Coqdor, less than two feet from the lake of horror, saw the loathsome bodies which, shot to death, shook in horrifying spasms while the mire splashed back on him.

All of a sudden he shouted, "Stop firing! Don't shoot anymore!"

One more jet of inframauve struck.

The Chevalier raised his head, furious, "Stop, you idiots!"

Annoyed but sheepish, the shooters obeyed.

It was getting lighter and lighter. Coqdor turned off the flashlight and they saw that the sky was whitening and they could see much more of the swamp around them.

The tankelec was still teetering a little and they noticed that the point at which they had set down their machine had been rather poorly chosen. A few yards around the place, the swarming stopped and the muddy waters no longer seemed to contain any of the unknown creatures.

Now, suddenly, something seemed to spring out of the frightful ripples. Something unrecognizable but very much alive.

The being that seemed to have been spontaneously created shot up, spreading great big wings, circled for a moment, in perfectly silent flight, around the iron ladder on which the four men were still standing, then rose again and brushed against them all while arousing in them a strange shudder.

The two women, up above, backed away with a frightened yelp.

Râx, whom Monique, fortunately, was still holding, suddenly whistled and tried to fly away in pursuit of the winged thing. But in the glow of the sun, which was rising over the horizon and from which only the first lights were dawning, they saw...

And the horror, the disgust mutated into admiration...

"A butterfly!"

"And what a butterfly! He has a wingspan of at least five feet!"

"A death moth…" Geek said somberly as he didn't seem to share the general admiration.

But Coqdor didn't give them time to lose themselves in such considerations, "Get down, guys! Grab the knives. No need for blasters. You mustn't kill them. Definitely not, we would be committing an unnecessary massacre!"

"Unnecessary?" Geek moaned. "Death moths?"

"Superb insects, Geek. And probably perfectly harmless."

Holp was already putting away the blasters and handing out the knives.

Astonished, everyone watched Coqdor who bravely, because this time he knew the true nature of the creatures, jumped into the mud, weapon in hand. And he started doing what he had just decided to do.

Wading in the mud, buried up to his thighs without worrying about the surrounding foulness, he grabbed the long, quivering masses with his bare hands and attacked the first with a curious treatment: With the tip of his dagger, he delicately split what looked like the outer shell. Something appeared, something bright, colorful although still unrecognizable. But this something, freed from its prison, struggled, literally seemed to stretch out and, finally, spread wide wings that had until then been folded up, still clumsy, virgin wings, fledgling wings that had never been used.

Monique, still holding Râx, suddenly understood and exclaimed, "Ah… They're chrysalises! Giant chrysalises!"

"Yes, Monique. A veritable nest of what they call in Accora, this sad country we're visiting, the death moth."

Now, Jean and Holp also understood and no longer hesitated to follow Coqdor's example. They jumped down alongside him, got bogged down enthusiastically and started freeing the chrysalises, opening the doors of life to the large insects, as Bruno Coqdor called it a moment later.

Geek looked on, growling:

"Aren't you disgusted?"

He himself was disgusted and went back to the cockpit. He wasn't ready to deny the legends of Accora and took a very dim view of it.

Monique and Yloa, watching over Râx who wanted to give chase to the newly born moths that the three men down below were helping to hatch, looked at the superb insects which were beginning their first flight.

Still a little awkward, stiff, clumsy, they seemed to be struggling to get started, but then, driven by the marvelous instinct which governs the living, they asserted themselves in less than a minute, gained altitude and, in the dawn of the little planet under one of the suns of Capricorn, they rose up and soared above the desolate swamps, above the hostile lands that they decorated like living flowers.

Coqdor, Jean and Holp worked tirelessly.

The shell of the chrysalises was thick, in proportion to the large dimensions of the strange butterflies, which would have been the joy of entomologists throughout the cosmos. None of them even thought of capturing one, of keeping it, because it would have been necessary to kill it to do so.

They split the pulsing gangue and released again and again a new moth.

Each time, the process started again. Slow unfurling of carefully folded wings, initial palpitations, tearing of the envelope, first beatings around the iron ladder, a little above the swamp itself. And then, in absolute silence, displaying their magnificence, all with their large gold-bottomed wings spotted with big, alien eyes, azure blue, crimson red, turquoise green, they soared off, glorious, dazzling Monique and Yloa who watched as they lost themselves in the infinity of the dreary horizons.

As the operation went on, the tankelec finally stopped pitching. Soon, the last chrysalises had been split open and the moths had taken to the air in a carousel of fire, in the burst of the new sun, thus the danger was completely averted for the astronauts.

But there was no point in lingering. Coqdor and his friends were eager, after such an incident, to set out again to unveil the secret of the thirteenth sign.

Coqdor, Jean Farnel and Holp hastened to clean up. It was not for nothing. They laughed about it. They were covered in mud, up to their faces. What did it matter! As the Chevalier said, they had saved the tankelec that the slow work of the chrysalises would perhaps have ended up completely overturning. Moreover, aiding nature, they had accomplished a good deed, launching into the sky of this deprived world a magnificent horde of gigantic and splendid insects.

Geek, who didn't need to wash, took the controls. Yloa made coffee for everyone. And the tankelec left.

The journey lasted another day and night. They discovered, towards the horizon, some rather high peaks. No doubt this was the mountain range reported by the unfortunate explorers of Accora, at least those who had been able to escape the fevers and the poorly described dangers which were rife.

But there, too, stood the very famous ruins where Coqdor thought he would find vestiges of the mysterious zodiac with thirteen signs.

He was keeping in touch with Muscat, who was still on Earth, occupied with various investigations and who was still thinking of joining him. A small space TV facilitated their talks but they continued to communicate discreetly, always fearing espionage practiced by the formidable sect.

And then, on the fourth morning after their departure, they approached the mountains, weary from having crossed the hopeless swamps, taking care to avoid fevers. They didn't see the death moths anymore, no more birds, no more anything. They moved forward, a little anxiously.

"A storm is brewing," Monique remarked.

"I only see a very faint cloud… Yes, there, over the mountains…"

"But I heard thunder."

"Me too," Yloa said.

"And me," Jean added. "Hey, a lightning flash! And another!"

"But the sky's clear, except for that cloud. So what does that mean?"

On its big legs, like a strange animal, the tankelec advanced towards the first foothills. There, depending on the terrain, they would use the air cushion or more often the tracks for the ascent.

Except that they looked towards the sky, fascinated, towards the funny little cloud. Shapes appeared in it and, at times, lightning flashed. Then they had the impression that the cloud with the strange silhouette was coming toward them.

The streaks of lightning started falling like infernal rain.

CHAPTER XIII

Geek was afraid and his eyes, his fly eyes, as Jean said laughing, expressed all the emotion he felt.

"The lightning birds! The sacred birds! We have to go back, leave at once. They can destroy us all…" He gasped.

He had never seen them, these strange birds of prey, since in principle they only haunted the distant hostile lands of Accora. But their reputation was enough to plunge him into terror.

"Geek, what are you doing?"

Without asking the mission leader's opinion, the Centaurian was already executing a strange maneuver. Coqdor, Jean, Monique, Holp and Yloa realized without understanding anything that the tankelec was behaving strangely even if this time, as Jean said out loud, they were no longer wading through a nest of titanic butterflies.

But the big machine was swinging around to the strange rhythm of its support legs.

The Chevalier suddenly leapt on the Centaurian:

"Geek, are you crazy? Who gave you permission? Who ordered you to turn around?"

Because that was exactly what he was doing! Panicked by the appearance of the cursed birds known for sowing death and destruction, the poor pilot, without asking anyone, was going back to the Accora spaceport.

The Chevalier grabbed him, but the Centaurian struggled. Jean and then Holp came to the rescue and Râx, understanding that something amiss was happening and it displeased his master, started whistling in a menacing manner. Coqdor had to trust the pstôr with Monique so that he would not harm the panicking pilot.

With the help of Jean, he snatched Geek from his command seat, "Holp, take his place!"

The ex-con, devoted body and soul to the Chevalier, hastened to obey.

"Do you know enough to take over? Can you take control of it?"

"I think so. I'll try, Chevalier."

Geek was trembling, no longer trying to resist, "You'll see! Misfortune will befall us. Sacred birds are evil. They're set on striking down anyone who comes near the ruins…"

But suddenly Coqdor's green gaze met his and he fell silent, subdued simply because the Chevalier had hypnotically soothed his fearful mind.

Well, it was true that the strange birds, until then gathered in the mass of the light cloud which formed a kind of screen for them, were rushing towards the tankelec.

"All exits must be blocked. Jean... Monique... Yloa... Check carefully. I think the attack will be a hard one."

Râx, overly irritated, feeling the electricity which seemed to ionize the atmosphere all around the machine, hissed angrily and could no longer hold still. There was no doubt that if they had petted him the wrong way, they would have kicked up a whole nest of sparks.

Lightning streaked the air around the cosmonauts. Now the cockpit was carefully closed but the jets of lightning dazzled the passengers and, almost everywhere, flames appeared, little globes of fire, fortunately only fleetingly after they were born spontaneously from the strange charge.

Interested in this living mystery, Coqdor watched.

"No doubt, it's birds that cast the fire. Magnificent birds, by the way!"

"But," Monique shouted, "they're eagles... Or they look just like them!"

"You're right. Morphologically, they look exactly like the eagles from our home planet."

Big and majestic with their powerful claws, their curved beaks, their beautiful golden-brown plumage, these extraordinary eagles, in close flight, were circling and sometimes they half-opened their beaks and a long spark could be seen emerging.

Coqdor observed.

Now he was silent. But on board, the situation became untenable. Subdued, Geek was no longer moving. Yloa was trembling. The others felt the effects of the electrification.

Even though the cockpit was hermetically sealed, the craft, whose entire structure was non-metallic, suffered the effects of the multiple discharges which, fortunately, only rarely hit it.

"If this continues…" Jean murmured.

"We should protect ourselves," Monique added. "A lightning rod? Did we bring anything like that?"

Coqdor seemed to come out of his reverie.

"Monique's right. Let's make a lightning rod with the radio antenna! It's lucky that lightning hasn't struck us yet!"

More and more lightning flashed while the fire eagles continued to circle above the tankelec.

"A lightning rod... Conductor... Catalyst... It can be made! Get to work, kids!"

They improvised, in fact, using the antenna carefully disconnected from the radio and video sets. A metal wire was connected from the base and a crude Franklin device was made with some drinking water from the tank, which was suitably insulated with plastic elements.

Just in time.

Barely had the little job been completed when a tremendous explosion shook the entire cockpit of the tankelec. They were thrown against one another. The two women screamed, Râx hissed, Jean cursed, Holp swore. Only Geek, completely despondent, remained silent.

They barely had time to get up. Twice, in quick succession, the formidable sparks fell on the antenna which quite naturally attracted the animal lightning, and the discharges dissipated in the makeshift installation.

The fantastic eagles, as if emboldened, now descended very low. They were flying all around the cockpit and they appeared to spit their lightning at the adventurers with great accuracy.

"I can assure you that we're not in any danger," the Chevalier said.

Yloa covered her face. The poor girl's nerves were shot, she couldn't take it anymore.

Monique, despite her usual courage, was trembling. "I can't look at them. It's beautiful, but it's terrifying!"

Jean growled, "It feels like I have ants all over my body! It's unbearable!"

"My boy, we're all feeling the same thing."

"But when are they going to leave? We really didn't need this."

"I imagine, as soon as they have..."

Coqdor cut himself off. He jumped up.

"Jean, your documents! Quickly! Quickly!"

A little surprised, Monique's brother stared at him, but the Chevalier nudged him.

"The slides! Don't you get it?"

Jean, stomped off to get what was asked of him without understanding why.

In front of Monique, Coqdor picked out a document. "Look at this one."

"But... it's the photo taken of Jean's chest after the attack on the Black Swan!"

"The scar, yes."

"My scar!" Jean grumbled, clearly in a bad mood.

"Look! The thirteenth sign! We thought it was a stylized vampire like all the other signs of the Zodiac. Look closer now and compare it with what we've just seen."

"Oh!" Monique cried out. "I get it! It's a thunderbird from Accora!"

"Right you are, dear Monique! A double loop, a circumflex accent. With the two Z bars symbolizing lightning. And these are actually talons, not claws, which are represented below."

Jean snapped out of his bad mood, "But then, what I still have on my skin…?"

"The thirteenth sign of the Zodiac isn't a myth but the representation of a reality. It's these extraordinary lightning eagles that are probably only found here, in this one place in the entire galaxy."

"But then that means…"

Coqdor turned serious.

"It means that we're very likely reaching our goal. Multiple forces have attempted to keep us from coming this far. But we came. And we encounter these lightning eagles, these torpedo-like birds of prey that have spawned all kinds of interpretations among the different races, religions, myths…"

"It's Zeus," Jean said. "The lightning-bearing eagle! Who would have thought that he'd been born here, in a world of Capricorn, before heading down to the Olympus of our Greco-Earthlings."

"Yes, Jean. And it's also the symbol of the evangelist whose name you bear."

"It's true," Monique continued. "The eagle is the apostle John!"

"Nothing is due to chance," the Chevalier said. "I'm beginning to glimpse the truth… The Great Initiates who led the world undoubtedly took paths that only they knew, followed the paths traced by Fate, marking them with symbols capable of being understood only by evolved spirits."

He fell silent. Around them, the flashes of lightning continued their strange sarabande and in the cockpit, which was bathed in electricity despite the insulation, sparks were still appearing.

They could see Râx's back quivering. The animal seemed to feel the unusual storm even more than the humans.

But Holp, taking advantage of the hours of study that Coqdor had pressed him to spend on handling the tankelec, was proud because he had succeeded in rectifying the situation. With some clumsiness, the machine set off again and stubbornly headed towards the foothills of the mountains where they were to find the ruins reported by the first explorers of Accora.

All of a sudden, as if obeying an invisible signal, the lightning eagles took off in perfect unison.

The makeshift storm stopped. They all breathed a sigh of relief, feeling the atmosphere clear, freed from this weight of anxiety which was crushing them all.

Geek was relaxing, coming out of his torpor.

They were heading towards the mountains again. Up above, the birds of prey merged into a kind of cloud that blended with new clouds. And they saw nothing more, except the sky of Accora and the mountains towards which they tirelessly plodded.

Coqdor examined the landscape.

"We'll have to change how we're moving. Holp, do you know how to change the legs?"

"Yes. I know how it should be done."

"Well, stop! Fold up the legs and get out the tracks!"

It was a more flexible gear system, more manageable and hugging closely to the rough terrain, which they needed to begin the ascent. On the bumpy land, the air cushion also became impractical. As for the large support rods serving as articulated legs, they were obviously to be avoided because the imbalance would have threatened to overturn the machine with every step.

Now, although nothing out of the ordinary seemed to be happening, Chevalier Coqdor and his companions were in a state of permanent alert and the slightest thing panicked them.

Yloa, aware of having directed them there, was closed up in total silence and only carried out her duties with a face expressing the anxieties that were gnawing away her.

Geek also kept silent. He must have regretted having agreed to pilot the tankelec into hostile lands. But there was no going back. Even if he said nothing, the fleeting glances of his bug-eyes spoke volumes and one could easily read his disapproval of these imprudent astronauts who, landing on a planet as formidable as Accora, recklessly set out in search of the accursed ruins. It meant they had to face the death moths, the lightning-breathing eagles, not to mention a thousand other perils still to come, which the survivors of previous expeditions had not said much about since they were so terrified by them.

Coqdor was worried. Râx sniffed the air, constantly disturbed.

Holp "seconded" Geek, who had taken control again. The mixed-blood was fortunately quite passive.

As for Monique and her brother, they were whispering together in a corner.

They had faith despite everything and since Coqdor had figured out the true meaning of the thirteenth sign, they went back to the documentation and tirelessly searched for new clues.

This is how, without any incident, while the machine was climbing the moderately high mountains, they ended up discovering the ruins.

Little remained of what had undoubtedly been a city countless years or centuries ago on Accora. Dilapidated buildings, nine-tenths of them collapsed. This type of simplistic architecture was mostly built as cubes. Monique saw it as a kind of huge game for the children of titans, and the comparison seemed full of meaning.

The tankelec got on even ground—archaic causeways had been established and were now invaded by the bizarre plants of the Accora mountains—then they went back to moving on a cushion of air, a great deal faster, and the astronauts cruised for a moment through the dead city.

"If only we had time..."

Jean was taking photos and Monique was pointing a small camera. At least they would bring back documentation because these statues eaten away by time, these bas-reliefs still vaguely discernible remained the eroded but faithful witnesses of a civilization of which nothing was known.

A pile of cubes, which had also collapsed, dominated or rather had dominated everything. In all the towns of their mother country, like in all those that Coqdor had visited during his interstellar travels, such a construction meant a temple, palace or both at the same time with a strong political, religious or similar meaning. So, they headed for it.

Coqdor jumped to the ground, of course followed by Râx. Monique and Jean also started to imitate the pstôr but, seeing the faces of the three others, Coqdor ordered them to stay on board for a moment longer or at least not to go anywhere not within sight.

He only half trusted Geek. And Yloa, despite everything, was still a riddle to him. He felt that she must have regretted telling him so much, clearly fearing the vindictiveness of the Zodiac.

He said a few words to Holp, whom he felt was much more devoted, recommending that he notify him by personal radio in the event of an incident.

In the end Coqdor, Monique and Jean put on the jumpsuits, flexible and light but equipped with a miniature arsenal and similar to, although less resistant than, the spacesuits. Thus they ventured through the ruins.

Bruno Coqdor had to keep whistling at Râx, who had a tendency to move ahead.

"He smells something."

"Yes... smells, or hears!"

"Weird! It's absolutely silent. No wind, and no animal life around here. It really is a city of death."

"Let's be careful. There are, in the various worlds that I have visited, these cities which are only apparently sleepy... until an imprudent person wakes them up."

They were still advancing in the open. There had been ceilings to these galleries, to these rooms, but they had collapsed centuries ago. They sought to understand the meaning of the artistic works of which vague vestiges remained.

"Hominid figures, undoubtedly. Animals. Ah, here we can see the butterflies."

"Yes... and other unknown beasts."

"Look here! The lightning eagles!"

"Yes... Here, as among the Greeks... and the Christians!"

Now they headed into places that were still covered and suddenly, around a bend, they entered a very dark place. The atomic flashlights revealed one then two vast rooms almost intact. In the corners, exits led to crumbling stairs that sank into the ground.

With short breath, silent, the light pointing in front of them at all times, they descended, Coqdor keeping Râx close to him by psychic force.

Darkness, old stones, more stairs... Three floors...

"We're deep underground in the very heart of the mountain."

"I hear something," Monique said. "It's far away, but…"

"And I smell something," Jean said. "I'm an idiot. It's like... a plant scent, very pungent, very sensual…"

They kept moving, not understanding. The lights only partially revealed the rooms, staircases, rotundas, pillars.

"Look," Coqdor said suddenly.

A section of the wall still stood and they could see an engraved figure there, almost erased by the centuries.

"It looks like... a horned beast... a ruminant. No it's…"

"It's a Capricorn, kids!"

"And when you say Capricorn," Jean said glibly, "you say the Zodiac!"

And this earned him a sarcastic compliment from his sister, assuring him that when they returned to Earth, she would now allow him to cross the street alone. This witty remark relaxed them a little but, five minutes later, following the Capricorn gallery, which they had automatically entered, they slowed down.

Coqdor had a feeling that they were finally arriving at their destination.

"This glow, still dim..."

"But pretty. A little green... bluish…"

"Like a beautiful summer evening."

They came out into a new room and there, speechless, they turned off the now useless flashlights.

The three travelers with the pstôr pressed against his master's legs, gawked. The room was a huge rotunda and, unlike other parts of the temple-palace, it remained perfectly intact. It was at least a hundred feet in diameter with beveled corners and had openings almost fifteen feet high, all alike. Above each opening, carved into the stone, there was a sign.

Trembling with emotion, turning around, they discovered these signs, absolutely not surprised to find them there but overwhelmed with joy.

For there were thirteen doorways around the rotunda! And thirteen signs! The twelve signs of the traditional Zodiac plus the famous thirteenth sign symbolizing the sacred eagle, the lightning eagle, located between the symbols of Virgo and Libra.

But the openings attracted them because out of all of them came, inexplicably, various lights, strange scents, assorted noises, very soft but clear.

Coqdor didn't want the discovery to remain obscure so he decided to call his friend Robin Muscat. He removed from his belt the small space-radio video set with a miniature screen and called the future commissioner of Interplan via subspace waves. Almost immediately, the Earthling responded and his image appeared on the screen.

"This is it, Muscat! We found one of the zodiacs with thirteen signs!"

Quickly, Coqdor explained. The face on the screen looked pleased.

"That's wonderful! I'll try to join you as soon as possible. But first I have to go back to Paris."

"Where are you then?"

"Currently, you caught me in the Hoggar, in the middle of the Sahara. I came here to study very special mountains here in North Africa. You know that for centuries, these caves are famous for the rock drawing that's still unexplained but which probably represents a humanoid from space, who came to Earth millennia before the Christian era."

"I know it!"

"Thanks to you, Jean Farnel had told us of the existence of engravings resembling the Zodiac with thirteen signs in this region. Well, what if I told you, Coqdor, that I too am under a mountain in a kind of rotunda? A rotunda with thirteen doors!"

"What?"

"But it all collapsed. A very old earthquake, most likely. It's hard to get our bearings. However, in the rubble we can vaguely see what remains of the zodiac signs, if we try really hard.

"And the doorways? The thirteen portals?"

"Almost all filled in except two or three."

"Too bad."

Monique and Jean were listening, deeply disturbed. Thus, there was on Earth a neglected, abandoned replica of this sanctuary that they had come so far to find!

Coqdor was about to ask Muscat something else when Râx, whom he had no longer been watching since he had turned on the screen, suddenly took off, ran, flapping his wings, towards the opening surmounted by the sign of the lightning eagle, the thirteenth sign, and he rushed into it.

"Rax! Come back here! Râx! Come here!"

Monique cried out, "Oh, on the screen!"

Coqdor held the screen at arm's length. He was dumbfounded, amazed.

At the cry of his sister, Jean had come closer. All three contemplated the incredible.

And Muscat, as stunned as they were, exclaimed into the microphone:

"But... Râx is next to me! Râx is here! Is that Râx? Yes... It's not another pstôr, there are so few in the galaxy! Coqdor, didn't you take him with you? I don't understand anything."

The Chevalier, with a lump in his throat, had nothing to say. Like Monique, like Jean, he watched the incomprehensible spectacle.

In less than ten seconds, passing through a doorway, Râx had just traveled a truly crazy number of light years.

CHAPTER XIV

A dizziness worse than being in mortal danger.

This was what all three of them felt.

Coqdor clenched his teeth, held on, knew that he had to react, to take control of the situation before letting himself be overwhelmed by it.

On the small screen he saw an astonished Muscat who was obviously wondering what it all meant and a Râx who seemed very happy to have found his old friend who always spoiled him when Coqdor was visiting.

"Muscat, we're going to try…"

"Try what, by all the devils in the galaxy?"

"Muscat, I'm going to call Râx."

"Râx? But you left him on Earth? Well, that's what I figure… unless this one is just pstôr ectoplasm?"

"Pet him. Talk to him… and you'll see that he is indeed the good, the true, the one and only Râx."

And on the screen they saw that the Interplan officer and the bulldog-bat scampering and jumping around him were getting along normally.

"I repeat, Muscat, I'm going to call Râx… and you follow him!"

"Follow him? Look, Coqdor, what is this nonsense? I'm on Earth… with Râx. And you're in the constellation Capricorn, which is not exactly in the suburbs."

"Muscat, we could talk like this for… let's not waste any more time."

Jean and Monique, silent and contemplative, were observing the scene.

"Rax! Rax! Come, my beautiful monster, come!" Coqdor raised his voice and whistled. He whistled between words, as he usually did to call the pstôr.

On the small screen, the brother and sister saw Muscat visibly stunned and Râx turned his head, seemed to be searching, sniffing the air. He heard the call and suddenly the image shook.

They didn't see much anymore. No more Muscat, no more Râx.

Coqdor's green eyes sparkled, "Monique, Jean, look! Look at the door of the thirteenth sign!"

Together, the young girl and the geologist turned in that direction.

Râx appeared, whistling with joy as he rushed towards the Chevalier. Behind him, they found Robin Muscat who was, just a few brief seconds ago, on planet Earth in the Hoggar Mountains...

He understood less and less but, to prove that he was not the victim of some mirage or some devilry the Chevalier opened his arms to him and the officer hugged his old comrade.

"Muscat, let me introduce Monique Farnel and Jean, her brother, whose research has helped us so much."

There was no doubt possible for the future commissioner. This was all reality. Râx, clearly pleased to be the innocent cause of this impromptu reunion, licked his lips eagerly.

"Come. Everyone follow me," Coqdor said. "Don't forget where we are. We're on Accora, a small planet of Capricorn. In a thousand-year-old temple. In a deep crypt. In the very heart of a mountain."

"Why specify all this, Chevalier?" Jean asked.

"So that we all keep in mind the truth of the present. And for what follows not to confuse you, so that you'll all understand."

He took a step, stopped. "Muscat, you've passed through behind Râx one of the only doorway that is still more or less passable, right? Did you notice under what sign it was?"

"Of course and it seemed logical to me, in fact. Although the bas-reliefs were crumbling, it was surely the sign of Capricorn."

"... which comes out here, in the world of Capricorn, under the sign of the lightning eagle."

"So there's intercommunication from one world to another?"

"Not just from one world to another but from one world to all others. At least to the twelve worlds constituting the celestial horizon of Earthlings, to which is added the thirteenth, which is that of Earth! The Earth whose constellation, seen from the cosmos, is that of the Eagle!"

"But," Monique exclaimed, sensing the truth, "that would that make thirteen similar rotundas?"

"Nobody will deny that, beautiful child? Thirteen signs corresponding to thirteen rotundas located in a kind of inter-world in which we find ourselves. But we need a demonstration. Monique, you have the honor: choose your birth sign."

"Leo!"

"So let's go through the Lion's Gate!"

The four of them with Râx rushed through the doorway marked with the sign of Leo.

In the soft glow that shined everywhere, in the fantastic domain, they first came out into another rotunda, quite similar but quite damaged.

All they had to do was continue towards the door marked with Leo. Taking this, they immediately found themselves in a rural, marvelous setting, in front of a monumental natural waterfall beside which Niagara was no more remarkable than Park Montsouris.

They were in a world where everything was on this scale, where the thousand-foot leafy trees rose up to a bare sky the color of emerald. They saw gigantic birds, glimpsed enormous monsters. It was all very beautiful, impressive, and the air was scented.

"We're somewhere," Muscat said, "on a planet in the constellation Leo!"

"Exactly. But in a jungle that hides the entrance to the Zodiac crypt. Let's go back!"

As in a dream, they returned and then passed through the doorway marked with Cancer, the sign of Jean's birth.

Another rotunda, another doorway opening onto a shore where a golden ocean rolled under a fiery pink sky. Strange beings, half-men, half-birds, were moving in the sky where metal islands were floating, visibly placed in orbit at a very low altitude and which must have been the habitat of these creatures. It was one of the worlds of Cancer.

They didn't linger there and repeated the experience with Sagittarius, then with Virgo.

They first saw an ultra-technical universe where flying ships, in staggering numbers, attacked planets covered and caparisoned with metal fortifications in an interstellar battle that defied all imagination.

Then, it was an idyllic, big sky which led them to an elevated platform overlooking a chain of titanic mountains. They contemplated white and golden cities under a triple sun.

Then they returned to the initial crypt. That of Capricorn. They were all stunned by the incredible journey they had just taken in a few steps. At least Coqdor, Jean and Muscat were. Because Râx, for his part, licked himself with gusto, little interested in such instantaneous transgalactic wanderings. The Universe was always his for the taking as long as he was there in the company of his master.

"And here we are again in Capricorn," Coqdor said. "If you feel like it, we can still visit the constellation of Libra, for example, or Pisces."

"Yes," Jean said, "but... where did Monique go?"

"I saw her a minute ago," Muscat replied. "As she was going through the last door, she was fixing her mitten."

"Monique? Where are you?" Jean was going back to Virgo's doorway and calling out to her.

Monique didn't answer.

Coqdor frowned and Muscat grumbled something. They ran, went back to the rotunda with thirteen doors that opened onto the world with the raised platform. No Monique.

Jean suddenly panicked, "Disappeared! She got lost!"

"Impossible, we were all together."

"But the rotundas all look the same! She got lost!"

"I don't believe it,. Jean. Stay here!"

But the young man ran and came out again into the world of Virgo. He had to realize that the platform, obviously a natural formation reworked by humanoid hands at the top of a formidable mountain forming a plateau, was totally isolated. The rotunda there was the only thing protruding from the ground flattened everywhere else, except where the construction had been cut into the rock mass. All around, there was no trace of the young girl and elsewhere, the completely sheer cliffs which surrounded the building forbid any idea of escape or even kidnapping.

This was what Muscat and Coqdor were thinking, but Jean did not give up so easily.

"They could've snatched her, taken her on some flying machine."

"Râx will help us. Let's go back!"

They went back to the starting point of these mind-boggling explorations which defied all means of spatial and subspace transportation.

Coqdor looked at Râx and whistled softly. There was silence. Muscat was used to this kind of practice and knew that the Chevalier was giving his orders to the pstôr. Coqdor's green eyes sparkled and Râx's golden eyes expressed all the intelligence of the strange animal.

In the end he stood up, stretched his wings and began to sniff around the crypt. He scrupulously retraced the route that they had all followed since the arrival of Muscat, who had emerged with Râx from the doorway marked with the thirteenth sign representing the Earth. They saw again the fantastic forest of Leo, the extraordinary inhabitants of

Cancer, the battles of Sagittarius and the enchantment of Virgo. Finally, they found themselves again in the Capricorn rotunda.

But Râx did not stay there. He took the doorway aptly marked Capricorn, which took them back to the planet Accora. Coqdor, Jean and Muscat followed him and the first two retraced the path that had brought them there, from the point where they had left the tankelec.

The Chevalier, always driven by intuitions which rarely misled him, felt anxious as they approached the entrance to the Zodiac temple. He was almost not surprised when Râx, who was picking up his pace, emerged in front of them and let out a long, forlorn whistle. The machine had not moved and was still in its place, appearing perfectly intact.

However, in the cockpit, they found the two men, Geek the Centaurian and Holp the mixed-blood. Both motionless, they were visibly unconscious and didn't appear to bear any trace of harm. Dazed, the two men looked at their rescuers without seeming to understand.

Where was Yloa? To this question they could only stammer an answer.

As they came to their senses, terror appeared on their faces. Finally, they managed to fully revive them with some good, strong Earth alcohol and, it must be said, a few well-timed slaps—following the Muscat system.

Then they knew there had been an attack, which they had already suspected a little. But by whom? They were unable to say.

Geek was terrified, his bug-eyes were rolling in all directions and, naturally, he started blaming "this damned country" again, declaring bluntly that he wanted to return to the spaceport.

Coqdor stopped listening to him and went at Holp. The green-skinned mixed-blood said that he thought it was the scrawny plants growing around the entrance to the ruined palace that had lunged at them.

"Probably the usual phenomenon," murmured the Chevalier. "A spontaneous mutation of these evil shapeshifters. Okay, and after?"

But Holp had been knocked unconscious and couldn't remember.

There was nothing to learn from Geek. They asked him to keep quiet after assuring him that they would leave soon.

And Yloa? The Star Knight was very worried about her. The poor young woman had in some way betrayed the Zodiac by informing Coqdor as best she could. The Zodiac who had persecuted her so shamefully and had driven her friend Cladek Halstar insane. They had to fear the worst for her and it was very probable that the attack, vegetable or not, was carried out to seize poor Yloa and make her pay for her alliance with the forces of good.

Coqdor, Jean and Muscat discussed the situation. Jean was mad with grief. He thought of Monique, who had undoubtedly fallen into the hands of the fantastic creatures who had such formidable power.

"And, what's more, they possess the secret of the thirteen-sign Zodiac which allows them to move instantly from one constellation to another."

"And thereby easily dominate a good part of the galaxy!"

They were baffled by the revelation of the frightening secret. But now was not the time for speculations. Shouldn't they be thinking above all about saving the two young women, possible victims of the vengeance of their terrible adversaries?

Coqdor, once again, tried to use Râx. The pstôr had found a trail, but a trail that was somehow cut off. They watched him as he couldn't sit still and was searching, still searching...

The Chevalier got him back in the gaze of his green eyes, whistled for a long time and pronounced Monique's name clearly several times. The winged monster seemed to listen and once again took off.

He did not go towards the temple and the entrance to the underworld this time but into the maze of the dead city, among the avenues deserted for centuries and centuries. Coqdor ran behind him. Jean, naturally, was hot on their heels. Muscat was with them and Holp, now without asking permission, tried as hard as possible to stay in the Chevalier's shadow.

At a certain point, Râx soared away.

Jean cried out in despair, "We won't be able to follow him anymore!"

"Calm down, my boy! I'm with him mentally. He saw something and I hope..." Coqdor broke off.

They could see the pstôr whirling, beating the air with his bat-like wings, and descending in increasingly narrow circles. The astronauts ran that way and Jean started dancing for joy.

"Monique!" He saw his sister, his sister who was walking a bit like a drunk woman but visibly unharmed.

Yloa, near her, stumbled forward in the same way.

When Monique saw Jean, she threw herself into his arms and started crying. Jean hugged her, comforted her.

Coqdor said a few words to quiet her down, but Yloa was livid and turned away without saying a word. Monique, sobbing, admitted she knew nothing. What had happened? Neither of them knew.

The flowers had attacked. Yloa confirmed this. Afterward...

They had lost consciousness and found themselves in the ruins of the dead city. Monique had not noticed the separation since her companions had left her behind in the crypt. Anyway, the two of them had woken up, as if under a telepathic impulse of unknown origin, and realized what they both immediately verified, but not without a sudden horror that almost crushed them.

Now they both bore, over their hearts, the infernal sign, the sign of the lightning eagle, the thirteenth sign of the Zodiac, symbol of the great galactic secret.

Yloa had escaped it until then; Monique had just succumbed to it.

John was horrified. He knew what it meant. His sister, like Yloa, was now under the control of the Zodiac. From a distance, whenever they wanted, they could either strike with lightning or drive the two young women insane or subject them to this or that type of abuse of their choice. The small group stood in shock at this catastrophic revelation.

"We'll do something. And fast! Back to the tankelec!"

So they went. But an unpleasant surprise awaited them. There was no longer any tankelec.

The truth was easy to figure out. Geek, in a panic, had abandoned them and returned alone to the Accora spaceport. In fact, they saw it from afar, in the marshes of the death moths, the metallic silhouette of the machine marching on its large articulated legs.

Coqdor shrugged his shoulders:

"Poor guy! He's foolishly betraying us! But it doesn't matter since now it will be easy for us to return to Earth without having to cross the spaces of the great void."

Jean, who was afraid for his sister, murmured, But... the others? What else will they try against us?"

He hugged his sister, terrified at not being able to protect her enough against the cursed mark which marred her breast and could kill her at any moment.

Coqdor looked at Monique, then at Yloa, "There's a way. And we're going to do it. Right away! I ask you both for a little courage, and you will be free."

CHAPTER XV

"Are you ready, Monique?"

Jean was looking at his sister with unrestrained anxiety.

But the courageous young girl, although very pale, had the strength to smile. "I'm ready, Chevalier!" And with a simplicity more touching than a long speech, she added, "I trust you."

He looked at her, moved.

"Prepare yourself. Jean, I hope it's not you who's going to cave in?"

The young geologist tensed up, but he wanted to show strength. He approached his sister and with a hand that did not tremble, unclasped the magnetic closure at the top of her jumpsuit.

Yloa looked at them. She didn't move, she didn't say anything. It seemed as if all the terror in the world had fallen upon her.

Muscat, at a wink from Coqdor, knowing what was going to happen, had moved away, pulling Holp with him.

Râx, always in the shadow of his master, had lain down, his muzzle resting on his folded wings. He purred under the Capricorn sun that lit Accora.

Geek's defection had deprived them of many things since most of their equipment was on board the tankelec. However, even though Muscat, surprised by the events, found himself launched from one constellation to another in simple safari attire, Coqdor, Jean and Monique, in their special clothing, still had the mini-arsenal of planetary explorers.

"Monique, I won't be able to give you total anesthesia, but at least with this concentrate of ethyl chloride, I can numb relatively well the affected region."

Monique nodded, thinking that the few essential pharmaceutical elements provided with the food tablets, the inframauve pistols and the bladed weapons, the multi-tool knives, not to mention the radio and television communicators, came as safety measures from experienced people who had the task of equipping astronauts in need of adventurous planetary expeditions.

So, she was readying herself.

There was no need to waste time. The Zodiac, as a challenge to their enemies, had taken pleasure in marking the two young women with their fatal sign. If they wanted to avoid unfortunate consequences, it was through immediate action.

Monique had opened the jumpsuit and, calmly, slipped off her bra. They were out in the open, among the walls of the dead city that were invaded by wild plants.

Coqdor, with a blaster in hand, adjusted the terrible flame to a half-millimeter. Like this, skillful surgeons had used it as a scalpel for certain field operations. And this is precisely what the Chevalier wanted to try on Monique, then on Yloa.

A tiny pill crushed on Monique's breast created a zone of insensitivity which would last a few minutes.

"Lean on your brother. And you, Jean, hold her! Hold her tight! The slightest wrong move could have serious consequences."

He leaned over the delicate breast, examining the sign.

More stuck to the epidermis, by an unknown process, than truly tattooed in the dermis. So, in principle, what he was going to try could have a chance of success.

Monique, when questioned, said that she was ready to risk anything to escape the influence of the lethal thirteenth sign.

The blaster moved closer.

Monique closed her eyes. Jean clenched his teeth, also affected, if not more than his sister. But he held her fast.

Coqdor, with a hand that didn't fail, aimed the ultra-short beam straight at the mysterious mark, and went at it.

One minute...

The smell of burnt flesh, faint but unpleasant, hit all three of them and Monique, turning pale although not feeling much, held back a scream.

Yloa looked at them, stupefied. Râx, intrigued and worried, stood up and engulfed them in his golden eyes.

The Chevalier took a step back and turned off the blaster.

"The intracorol! Quickly, Jean!"

He let go of his sister who fell rather than sat against a section of collapsed wall and he handed the healing ointment to Coqdor who, tossing aside the blaster, cauterized the small wound.

He stared for a moment, then stood up, "I think I did it. No more trace. When the intracorol has taken effect, in half an hour, the cells will reproduce and I think the scar will be hardly more visible than the one you have yourself, my young friend!"

Jean covered his sister's forehead with kisses, the beautiful forehead stained with drops of sweat.

"Thank you, Chevalier!"

Coqdor smiled at him, then turned to Yloa,

"It's your turn. You see that Monique is free. It's important that you get the same treatment."

"No! No!"

To their great surprise, Cladek Halstar's friend seemed to be in the grip of utmost terror.

Coqdor tried to reassure her.

"As you can see, the patient barely flinched. Anesthesia, however imperfect, makes the pain very bearable, doesn't it, Monique?"

"Absolutely," Monique agreed as she was readjusting her suit. "Be strong, Yloa!"

But the young woman, whose teeth were chattering, still shook her head no.

"Come on, it's a matter of your salvation. You know only too well what happens to those whom the Zodiac hold under their control by this dreadful means. It won't hurt, maybe just a little."

"I'm not afraid of the pain, but…"

Coqdor said to her gently, "Will your modesty be offended? But believe me, I'm like a doctor, like a surgeon…"

Yloa made an evasive gesture and suddenly seemed very sad. Talking to her about modesty, after what she had experienced…

The Chevalier wanted to insist but suddenly she ran off like a madwoman through the ruins.

"God of the Cosmos! What's that all about? We can't let her get away!"

They set off in pursuit of Yloa, who was fleeing desperately. They were shouting at her to stop, to come back, but she didn't listen. She was about to turn at a crossroads in the ghost town when she screamed and stopped.

It was Robin Muscat who appeared and grabbed her mid-run. He brought her back by force. She was crying and screaming.

Coqdor coldly declared:

"We have to save this woman against her will, right?"

Monique, Jean and Muscat nodded.

It was hard to hold her steady and it was Monique who undid the suit and took off the bra. Jean took care of the anesthesia and Coqdor adjusted the blaster a second time.

Yloa moaned softly, held by Muscat and by Holp who had been called to the rescue. They held her down on the ground and Coqdor, on his knees, leaned over the fatal sign that had to be eradicated, torn off the victim's flesh. When he cut into her skin, she let out an inhuman scream. The Chevalier, however, held his ground and kept on working.

Monique and Jean, peeking from behind him, suddenly opened their eyes in terror. And Muscat and Holp felt that under their iron grip, something extraordinary was happening in Yloa's very organism.

As Coqdor, with his burning scalpel, destroyed the mark of the thirteenth sign, Yloa seemed to transform in front of their eyes. They only realized it a minute later.

Her somewhat heavy body, her dull face, marked by suffering and vice, which the young Persian woman had been forced to endure, all of this no longer looked the same. Her whole body seemed prey to a terrible tension and violent spasms shook it while she constantly cried out.

Was she in pain? This was indisputable, but it probably had nothing to do with the little operation that Coqdor was performing.

They saw the color of her skin change, the features of her face shift and her hair suddenly darkened, becoming a beautiful lustrous black. Her waist became slimmer and her very pronounced chest, instead of remaining busty and less than graceful, became more refined and shrank until it it was quite modest.

Coqdor got up, sweat on his forehead, and let go of the blaster.

"She's not the same woman anymore!" Jean shouted. "And she still has the sign!"

It was Muscat, recognizing her, who declared the real name of the transformed creature:

"Giovanna! Giovanna Hi-Ling!"

"The main accomplice of the Zodiac," droned the man with green eyes.

"My compliments, Chevalier Coqdor."

The voice that made this last comment did not belong to any member of the group.

The adventurers, except for Coqdor in whom the light was gradually dawning, just stood there overwhelmed, stunned under the harsh sun of Capricorn which had once again illuminated such a wonder.

Unable to move, Muscat, always on the defensive like the good policeman that he was, turned around with the zeal of a bloodhound who is never caught off guard and faced forward, aiming his blaster.

The slightly ironic voice, the one that had just spoken, then added, "Please, inspector, besides, see, I'm alone. And you realize, I'm the most harmless of men."

Monique, Jean and Holp, between the two galactic heroes, saw a strange character appear among the wild plants growing in the ruins. A small, middle-aged individual, rather sickly with a thin, ordinary face and myopic eyes behind thick contact lenses. He was wearing a planetary outfit, one of those jacketed jumpsuits that had been in fashion half a century ago. In short, the portrait of the small, insignificant civil servant, like millions of others who existed across all the planets of the civilized galaxy.

Giovanna stood up, still weak, fragile, shaken by the mutation she had just undergone under the burning scalpel, which had restored her natural form.

They all looked at the newcomer and noted that, indeed, he did not seem at all frightening.

"Who are you?" Muscat asked.

"A poor man among the poor men of the cosmos," the man replied. "A planetary citizen without originality or problems. And yet, I must make it clear—I am, though not the leader, at least the Guide chosen by what you call the Zodiac."

A shiver ran through Coqdor and his companions.

"Miss Hi-Ling can confirm that," the stranger said.

Giovanna, on whom all eyes were converging, nodded in agreement.

"How about following me?" the thin little man said. "Let's go to the crypt of the temple, where twelve doors give access to twelve different worlds, which means to twelve planets in the twelve constellations of the Galaxy!"

He sensed their hesitation, because he hastened to add:

"Oh, you're in no danger! Not at all! I admire you... Certainly and mine with me. Nothing stopped you. You fought to the end despite the pitfalls that we laid, that our duty obliged us to lay in your way. And yet, you ended up discovering the truth. Without ever giving up. Which proves that you deserved to learn the great secret of the Zodiac. But I'm rambling... Will you follow me?"

This time, he set the example and plunged into the ruins.

Everyone hesitated but Coqdor, with a nod of his head, indicated that he agreed. So, he followed the little man, flanked by Râx.

Monique, whose side Jean no longer wanted to leave, set off after them. Holp was even more passive than the pstôr. Giovanna kept her eyes cast down, ashamed of having been so absurdly found out. Muscat brought up the rear.

The walk underground came with no surprises until they reached the rotunda still illuminated by the soft light coming from no one knew where.

The little man spoke a few words in an unknown language.

They saw big insects and reptiles scurrying along the ground. Instinctively, Monique jumped back in disgust and Râx hissed in anger.

"Don't be afraid, Mademoiselle!"

Suddenly there were no more insects or reptiles. But seats. Huge armchairs that seemed to be made of stone, massive but in fact very comfortable.

The little man smiled and pointed to them.

"If you'd like to take a seat."

Here again, they hesitated and he had to insist.

"Yes, you're suspicious because you've just witnessed a spontaneous mutation again. Insects... and then armchairs. Excuse me, we have no choice. And since I have to speak to you, I can't decently leave you standing, especially Mademoiselle and Giovanna Hi-Ling."

And he added, inviting them with a wave of his hand:

"Do not fear any treachery. You know that my companions are experts at changing their appearance and even their nature. But before the God of the Cosmos, I swear that you are now our guests, our friends. When you forced Giovanna's transformation I judged that the adventure had ended. But you're entitled to explanations. After... afterwards, you will choose, because we no longer feel we have the right to forbid you from using the secret of the thirteen signs as you wish since you have earned the right to know."

Coqdor and Muscat took their places and the young people imitated them.

Giovanna sat down as well, still distant and uncomfortable.

The simplest way is sometimes the best. "Do you know the Marquis de Mesmay well?" I asked, bluntly.

"I've never met him," she replied, equally bluntly, but added: "I don't really have much opportunity to enjoy the company of men; this is a rare privilege for me— but to answer the question more fully, I do know a good deal more about Antoine than most men, because he's married to my niece."

I must have looked more surprised than the revelation warranted, because she continued: "Even Sisters of Shalimar have actual sisters. Mine was Aethne's mother. Aethne and I aren't close nowadays, but we are still in touch. She used to seek my counsel quite often; it's less frequent now, but communication hasn't entirely ceased."

"Giving the Sisters of Shalimar a line of communication to the heart of the Orphean cult," I said.

"Not its heart, Master Rathenius, or even its wing… but a part of it, yes."

"Do you have other nieces married to Dionysians?"

"Alas, no… which might, I admit, give me slightly distorted view of that rival cult, most of whose members are probably meek clubmen. Still, just as there seem to be some Orpheans who regard the Dionysians as the direct descendants of the murderer of their founder, so there are rumored to be some Dionysians who regard the Orpheans as the treacherous slanderers of theirs. It probably seems as absurd to you as it does to me that a vendetta occasioned by an imaginary crime could extend over more than three thousand years, still drawing blood, but there have been political complications and schisms, as I suppose you're vaguely aware, which have served to keep hatred alive and occasionally to stoke it up. Even if that document is utterly meaningless, as it might well be,

119

the mere fact of its existence and its history has been enough to cause murders in the past, and might continue to do so in future."

"Would you care to tell me why? Given that I'm currently holding the object of desire in question, albeit reluctantly, I'd like to know why someone might be prepared to kill me to take it from me—if, in fact, your judgment in that matter is correct."

"You're probably correct to doubt it—I'm uncomfortably aware myself that my knowledge of the world is limited to what I can obtain from books and the fragile lines of communication opened to me by a few confidantes. I might be completely mistaken—but I'll tell you what I know… except that some of it, I fear, is mere conjecture. No one really knows the truth, because no one really knows how to decode the myth of Orpheus' excursion to the Underworld.

"The legend pertaining to the manuscript of which your parchment is a partial copy claims that that when Orpheus succeeded in charming the shades with his music—including Hades and Persephone themselves—he was able to do it because he was inspired with the ability to play or sing the language of sighs: the language of the dead, which only Hades and the infernal judges were supposed to know how to write. Having learned to sing it, though, when Orpheus came out of the Underworld again, he contrived to write down the song he had sung: the song that has the gift not merely of charming shades, but of charming Hades, the god of death, himself. Whether he supposedly wrote it in Hades' own script, or whether he invented his own notation, is unclear, as is the precise content of what he wrote, which is probably more akin to a sequence of musical notes than words.

to preserve this secret. The origin of our society is lost in the mists of time seeing that no one knows exactly when the Zodiac was discovered. We are therefore the Zodiac, initiates who have no personal interest and whose mission is only to prevent, by all means, lay people with evil intentions from becoming aware of such a secret."

He paused and made a slightly weary gesture.

"You know humans! They monetize, they exploit everything. Even what is sacred."

"Of course," Coqdor agreed. "Some tyrant, some ambitious scientist or some unscrupulous trafficker, knowing the secret of the Zodiac, could eliminate Time and the distance between the thirteen constellations for his own benefit and use it either to set up a dangerous dictatorship or to perform risky experiments or even more sordidly to launch a crudely commercial enterprise even if it means massacring, enslaving and ruining the honest people of the world."

The little man looked satisfied.

"I knew you would understand! I confess to you, I had to—we had to—fight against you, anticipating your wisdom and your subtlety. We assumed your intentions were pure, but we were wary. Certain potential initiates—those we call our 'Black Lodge'—intoxicated by the prodigious secret, have already tried to betray us."

"Yum Akatinor," Muscat said. "And Cladek Halstar, among others."

"Yes!"

Giovanna choked back a sob. Monique came to her and kissed her gently.

"Giovanna under the influence of Halstar almost betrayed us too."

"And Jean-Marie Spontini?"

"We had to remove him because he was going to betray us in turn. Out of love. Out of spite, too." The little man looked at Giovanna with pity. "She had abandoned him for Halstar. And her punishment was that she be our agent on Ulmir... to befriend you in the guise of the prostitute Yloa Flugg. Thanks to our metamorphic power, you know how she was able to try to seduce you, Chevalier, by temporarily becoming Giovanna again. But it failed, like everything else. You are strong!"

"I'm just an honest man."

There was silence. Everyone was thinking. Except Holp, probably.

Then the Zodiac Guide stood up and made a little salute, which seemed comical. But his guests did not laugh.

"You went all the way. You have defeated us. You know now. I must therefore comply with the rules of our sect."

He indicated the thirteen doors with a sweeping gesture.

"Mademoiselle... Chevalier... Commissioner... Messieurs... No one will try anything against you ever again. This is the moment of choice. Decide what you're going to do. Reveal the secret of the Zodiac or exploit it for your own benefit. Our old master once decided. And we respect his law. If you use or cause to be used the rotundas of the thirteen gates, we will enter darkness. I only ask you to consider the consequences of your actions, if you choose so."

Chevalier Coqdor stood up.

"My friends are free to choose. As for me, my decision is made."

He looked at the Zodiac Guide. He said nothing but his powerful thought pierced the brow of the little man, who smiled at him.

"Thank you, Chevalier!"

"By the God of the Cosmos," Muscat growled, "such a secret is dangerous! I'm not a telepath like my friend Coqdor but I know what he decided!"

Monique and Jean stood up holding hands.

The young woman said, "Let there be silence about all of this! I hope that your brotherhood continues to jealously ensure that vulgar humans never ever become aware of the meaning of the thirteenth sign of the Zodiac!"

They walked towards the Eagle Gate, followed by Holp.

Beyond, just a few feet away, was the Hoggar cave, the place where Muscat's men were waiting, those who had brought him there to work. In half an hour they would be back in Paris-sur-Terre, with the helijets.

Coqdor waved goodbye to the little man and Giovanna Hi-Ling. Then the Star Knight, Monique and Jean Farnel, Holp and Râx, one by one went through the passage that spanned light years.

Which, moreover, thanks to the fantastic doorways, practically did not exist...

EPILOGUE

A few days later Robin Muscat celebrated his appointment as commissioner.

On this occasion, he told his friends that an earthquake had shaken the mountains of Hoggar and destroyed or filled in certain caves in which bas-reliefs had been found, mostly worn down of course but very curious.

No doubt there had also been, in recent times, a certain number of similar earthquakes on a dozen planets across the Galaxy...

L'ÉTOILE DE SATAN

MAURICE LIMAT ★

★★ANTICIPATION★★

Editions
"Fleuve Noir"

Cover art by René Brantonne

THE FOURTEENTH SIGN OF THE ZODIAC

CHAPTER I

Paris-sur-Terre could rightly pride itself on having one of the most advanced psychiatric centers in the Martervenux, or even in the entire galaxy.

With its elegant buildings and air-conditioned gardens, the complex that the former Sainte-Anne hospital had become, after the reconstruction of the City of Light following the world conflict which marked the end of the Great Decadence, held more than one luxury residential estate as a place where the most rebellious cases defying the mysteries of the mental sciences were treated.

In principle successfully, but sometimes also without any tangible results.

In the vast office from which Professor Fougerin, director of the hospital, reigned as absolute master, it was precisely a question of one of these incurables who was affecting Rémi Lucas, a trainee recently graduated from the Centaurus University of Medicine, literally driving him to despair since he had first gone through his file.

"You shouldn't be so affected by this Cladek Halstar, my young friend!" Fougerin insisted in a dry tone. "He's a madman from whom we were never able to learn anything during the years of his internment. As if his body were an empty shell that all spirituality deserted ages ago! You just have to see it to understand!"

"I disagree with you, Professor, if I may," Lucas replied. "The spirit does not leave like that, it does not go out like a candle that is blown out. I'm sure that this man still has a spark of consciousness and I intend to bring it out! Besides, I've already told you, I intend to focus my thesis on this case which challenges your wisdom because..."

"A waste of time, this project of yours!" Fougerin broke in. "There are much better subjects to study than this. We got nothing out of him, you won't get anything out of him and what's more, it's going to cost us a fortune for cherry stems! The Health Administration will oppose it, I'll bet you!"

Certainly, the professor was a great scientist, curious and passionate, but his very Cartesian personality and years of inevitable routine for civil servants ended up disillusioning him somewhat. To him, Halstar was an oyster that had been closed for years and surely dried up inside. No need to bother trying to open it, there would be nothing inside. Not the tiniest pearl, in any case.

Lucas was not of this opinion. Halstar, the elegant Martian, had been a highly esteemed financier, director of Solexport , a powerful multiplanetary company based on one of the planets of Perseus, and his fame reaching far beyond the limits of the Martervenux had been more than enviable. He had known no enemies, no romantic escapades or troubled passions that could have led him down a fatal path. His ex-wife, an Earthling who ended up filing for divorce after the tragedy, had only been able to mention secret, very confidential trips, probably linked to business needing to be handled with the greatest discretion.

Apart from that, she had also alluded to contacts that Halstar would have had with several members of a very mysterious occult organization, adept at cosmomancy. If there was one odd item in the file, it was this one. Otherwise, not the slightest gray area. But from there to explaining why and how the financier had suddenly fallen into dementia aboard a ship on the Sol-Perseus line, that was another story!

"What if Halstar's madness was linked to cosmomancy? I'm not very familiar with black magic rituals nor their derivatives as developed by the adepts of chaos and non-being, but I think they can have harmful effects on predisposed minds."

"Nonsense, young man! Fairy tales to frighten children!"

"Or to induce hallucinations, seconded by attacks of space sickness, Professor. Our Martian maybe thought he saw terrifying things during the subspace dive, like others see them in the clouds and sometimes read catastrophic omens there."

"I'm not someone who deludes himself, you know that. For me, the irrational has no place in our well-ordered Universe and neither does superstition. You know, I once witnessed a phenomenon of communication with souls wandering at the limits of the afterlife, in an indefinable domain called interlife, and the 'voices' that patients heard in their spirit became very physical when a brilliant scientist I know, Doctor Stewe, operated a curious robot-medium.[10] So... this cosmomancy story, for me, is a fool's errand and if Cladek Halstar lost his mind, it's because of the money that this gang of charlatans extorted from him. The vertigo that swept him away was the vertigo of the bottomless abyss into which he let his fortune sink! Let's go see our patient, it will be much better than to keep talking about nonsense."

Lucas was careful not to answer. Finally, the old doctor was handing him a rare opportunity on a silver platter, without being asked to do so. The meeting of this enlightened intern with the madman would save him a lot of time and energy because Lucas had no plans to abandon his thesis subject, especially after he had seen the pitiful Martian. The meeting had to take place as quickly as possible!

But Fougerin, who did not know the young graduate very well, did not know, for example, that the more the case was off the beaten track, the tighter he would cling to it.

At the other end of the grounds, in a pavilion slightly away from the rest of the center, patients classified as lost causes spent more or less peaceful days depending on the disorders from which they suffered and the crises induced by their individual ailments.

Cladek Halstar was not one of the restless ones, quite the contrary. Like all Martians, of whom he was one of the last representatives, he was a humanoid of tall stature, formerly thin and slender but now debilitated, haggard and gaunt since his crisis which had irreparably cut him off from the rest of the world. His delusions were of the contemplative type, focused on images that he believed he saw appearing before his eyes and which, after having beguiled him, ended up terrifying him beyond measure. He then shut himself up in total silence, huddled like a fetus in a corner of his padded cell. Quite frequently, between his ravings, he sang in a loop an earthly melody dating from the early days of the Great Decadence,[11] which he had furnished with lyrics of his own adapted to his home planet. And he accompanied himself on the kem, the octagonal guitar, also from Mars.

When Fougerin and Lucas entered the pavilion, they were greeted by the harmonious sounds of plucked strings and of the infinitely sad tones of a voice that was certainly thin but nevertheless very moving.

It's snowing on Syrtis Major

---

[10] See *Les Portes de l'Aurore*.

[11] Mort Shuman, "Le Lac Majeur."

And the last Martian is no more
By an Earthling's inframauve blasted.
Of the old world nothing has lasted...

"Listen, Lucas, it's our singing madman!"

"Halstar? Him?"

"Well yes."

"So he can still express himself!"

"If you call the fact of repeating this refrain and nothing else, you can say so."

The canals stretch lifeless,
Across the plains in extremis
And the forests of crystal
Fall to domes of metal.
Mars or Earth, same future.
It's snowing on Syrtis Major...
Mars or Earth, same future.
It's snowing on Syrtis Major...

Lucas stood still. There was no way he was going to show it to the icy Fougerin, but the song was upsetting him.

Here, elsewhere, the conquerors
Will always massacre.
To the ends of the Universe,
Humans will carry their wars...

"Shake it off, young man! Do you think I'm going to spend all day here?"

The intern put an index finger to his lips.

"One moment, Professor! What if there's some clue to be gleaned here?"

Fougerin grumbled, but kept quiet. Deep down he was impressed by Lucas' stubborn curiosity.

It's snowing on Syrtis Major
And the last Martian is no more.
I hear the roar of the thrusters,
It's the five-hour Mars-Earth transporter...
Deep down in my body it's cold and somber.
It's snowing on Syrtis Major...
Deep down in my body it's cold and somber.
It's snowing on Syrtis Major...

A final series of chords played out, then the music stopped. Lucas turned away and secretly wiped his eyes.

"Let's go, Lucas!"

The two men walked to the door of the ex-financier's cell. Just as the professor was about to punch in the code on the keypad lock, a shout rang out and abruptly stopped his hand.

"Venus in house seven! Trine in Neptune! Aquarius, you who spread the fluid of life... Cancer... Glimmer coming from darkness, non-being gnawing away at the cosmos like an incurable evil... Aries, you who ward off all perils in your eternal course... Virgo, eternal feminine of light and truth... Sagittarius with the fiery features... Rampart of the castaways..."

"Here we go again, Lucas! This is one of his famous delusions..."

Suddenly, a cry of terror, a blood-curdling howl, strangely accompanied by a low discord from the kem as it fell on the plasticized concrete floor.

"Horror! It's coming... Your arrows, Sagittarius! Protect me, shoot... Shoot, I beg you! Ah, the bird... The great bird of the galaxies... Woe... Its plumage of stars... It fastens its claws on me... It takes me with it into the sky... I run... My feet... Oh, my feet burning with fire... This height... These abysses... And my eyes which bleed, my eyes which are flayed by the glare of the distant suns..."

As Fougerin reached for the keypad again, Lucas tried to find a common thread in the flow of Halstar's ramblings. There was the Zodiac, obviously, behind the flood of words. And other things too.

"This man may be insane, Professor, but there's some lucidity in his madness! A lucidity born of fear, of total panic. The great bird..."

"Come now, Lucas! Halstar was driven mad by astrology, that much is obvious. God only knows what charlatans caught him in their nets to imprison him in such a state!"

"The great bird of the galaxies is not part of the Zodiac, Professor. It's a legend known to all cosmonauts who travel the abyss of the cosmos, a haunting linked to the prophetic appearance of a fantastic and gigantic bird to announce that a tragedy will strike a ship.[12] The archetype of the emissary from beyond, from a nothingness about to open up in order to swallow..."

Lucas stopped abruptly. The poor Martian began screaming again.

---

[12] See *Le Grand Oiseau des Galaxies*.

"No! Pity! Ah... It's not the great bird of the galaxies... It's worse... The lightning eagle... God of the Cosmos... No, not the lightning eagle! They want to kill me, they are sending me the storm bird... Oh, my heart... My chest... I hurt... This bite of fire... No! I didn't do anything! Not me! Not the lightning eagle... Not this death... Noooooooooo..."

The professor, hardened by all the experiences among the most varied forms of insanity was no longer impressed by such displays and finished pressing the keys in the appropriate order. With a faint metallic click, the lock turned and the door opened.

Cladek Halstar lay on his back, unconscious, staring into some horrifying vision with his bulging eyes. Seeing this and becoming concerned, Fougerin rushed towards him, knelt down and unfastened the top of his long white shirt. Then he examined him summarily.

"He's not dead, Lucas," the doctor reassured the intern who was standing still beside the patient. "But... What is that?"

As if scientific curiosity had suddenly awakened in him, the hardened old man was examining the patient whom he had never looked at closely.

"Look there, young man! He has a curious tattoo on his left breast... It looks like... Not possible! Are you somehow right, in the end?"

The design was simple, almost childish.

A circle, a few lines, all blackish in color.

Like a burn mark.

Unquestionably possible, the image of a stylized eagle...

After their visit to the Martian, he was taken care of by a specialized nurse and subjected to a neuroleptic injection then placed under remote monitoring. The rest of the day passed without another crisis. At midnight, Halstar was sleeping like a baby and had been for several hours.

A deep calm had settled over the psychiatric complex. With all measures taken and checked every evening to ensure safe nights, no one had to worry.

And yet...

On the flat roof of the incurables' pavilion, a pitch-black silhouette had just materialized, as if emerging out of nowhere. Its bodysuit, flexible and tight-fitting, covered it almost entirely and a mask hid its face. Like a modern variant of those cat burglars who, at the beginning of the Great Decadence, had been the favorites of so many cheap adventure serials, the stranger had an extraordinary means of transportation attached to his belt, full of colorful little buttons with mysterious purposes: a transport disc.

This marvel, the result of a technology unknown to ordinary mortals, allowed its wearer to teleport over short distances from or to a much larger base device on the express condition that the linking hyperanionic beam was not interrupted during the trip. What was most similar to it was the photonic disk developed by the Cygnus scientists for bioluminic transfer. But this secret was lost with the victory of Earth, helped by the Sirians, over the dangerous pirates of light.[13]

In the present case, there was no risk of interference. The transmitter was located on board a spacecraft currently hovering at mid-altitude above Paris-sur-Terre, more precisely above the Sainte-Anne hospital, where air traffic was regulated. All that the associate of the man in black, who remained at the controls of the ship, had to do was not to disturb the air traffic, which was fortunately very rare at this time, and not alert the agents monitoring the proper functioning of the three-dimensional luminous grid surveillance which marked out the night sky of the capital of the Martervenux. In this, the fairly cloudy sky of this October night was a welcome ally.

The burglar-spy did not waste any time. Thanks to another device in his possession, he jumped from the roof terrace and landed on the ground, fifty feet below, with the lightness and silence of a feather.

It was child's play for him to unscramble the coding of the entrance whose sliding doors vanished with a hiss, then to neutralize the two guards whom the noise brought into the hall of the pavilion. Their nervous centers inhibited by a paralyzing shock, the peaceful guard dogs would sleep until the following morning and would remember nothing when they woke up.

Then the man in black went directly to Cladek Halstar's cell as if the place was perfectly familiar to him and he unlocked the door using his pulse transmitter again.

Like a silent shadow, he approached the bed on which the Martian was resting, motionless and with relaxed features. He took a small, faintly shiny object from a pocket of his suit and unfolded it, exposing a very fine metal mesh which he delicately placed on the madman's skull.

This done, the stranger took a few steps back, pressed one of the many buttons on his belt and began to mentally count the seconds. He was reaching ninety when the expected phenomenon occurred.

---

[13] See *Ici l'Infini*.

With extreme slowness, like a puppet that its handler makes rise little by little, creating the illusion that he is giving life to it, Cladek Halstar began to rise on his bed. The head, the neck, the upper chest, one arm, the other...

As if animated by invisible strings, the Martian moved and, most importantly, his eyelids opened to reveal eyes that were certainly still filled with fog but whose brilliance betrayed something other than the haggard flame of madness.

"Where... where am I?" Halstar panted in an unsure voice. "And you, who are you? Why..."

"You can call me Monsieur D.," the strange visitor in black said. "I'm a friend."

"A friend... It's been a long time since I had one."

"I will explain, but not here and not now. We have to leave right away. Come..."

Saying this, Monsieur. D. approached the bed and helped the patient to stand up. The poor man staggered, almost fell and was caught by his savior.

"Where?"

"Am I taking you? To a safe place, first. Then to find your past, your immense fortune, those of your kind."

"It was so long ago... They..."

"They made you a wreck, a barely human wreck with a mind drowned in darkness. You will soon be able to take revenge on those monsters!"

"Revenge... I still forget a lot, but horrible images haunt my memories... They must pay!"

"And they will pay!" Monsieur D. affirmed. "You'll be able to delight in their sufferings as they delighted in yours."

The Martian's red eyes now glowed with a wild, cruel flame. And his lips curled into a grin as fierce as a shark's smile. No one would have been able to see in him the harmless lunatic he had been just a few hours before.

"Fortune and power, weapons of my destructive anger... Ah, what a future to look forward to."

Meanwhile, the man in black and his ward had climbed back onto the flat roof of the pavilion. Given the mild temperature maintained in the immediate environment of the center, there was no need to give the Martian any extra clothes.

Monsieur D. took a second transport disk from his belt, an exact copy of his own, and hooked it to Halstar's shirt.

A moment later their two silhouettes vanished.

In the escaped patient's cell, the only remaining trace of his stay was the traditional kem from his home planet.

CHAPTER II

The huge planet Arpam, satellite of star A in Sagittarius, rolled across the multi-colored background of the peripheral nebulousness of the near center of the Milky Way. Around this celestial giant orbited a black mass with a ragged, bristling surface like the quills of a sea urchin, turrets housing the most powerful radiant batteries, platforms posted with flashing lights used to guide the war cruisers coming back to their base.

This space fortress was the heart and central brain of Arpam's military fleet.

In the largest of the conference rooms of this mecca of interstellar warfare, Generalissimo Y Zeon, supreme master of the armies of Arpam, received from his squadron leaders the status reports needed to develop the strategy for the next battle.

The outcome of an immemorial conflict, or at least its reorientation, was indeed going to be played out very soon in the vicinity of the fifth moon of the planet Xanta.

"The Raophi'i have regrouped their forces in the Xanta sector and are making the twelve satellites of this world the main assets of their supposed superiority," the leader of the first squadron summarized. "There are at least 300,000 heavy units deployed there."

"They built a veritable network of space beacons both to guide their potential reinforcements to the theater of combat, avoiding hyperresonant minefields, and to give the alert in the event of an intrusion by enemy ships coming as scouts or for isolated offensive actions," number four said.

The officer in charge of the fifteenth squadron reported in a somber voice "They stationed 850 octagonal platforms, each equipped with 32 missile-launcher batteries and capable of firing 1,000 complete salvos. We've also spotted asteroids armored with molecularly densified steeloplastex and stuffed with thermonuclear charges."

"So those arrogant hozz did it!" Y Zeon exclaimed. "They've got the famous projectile meteors whose existence our spies had reported at the prototype stage."

"And finally," number eight completed, "the Raophi'i have equipped each of the twelve moons with energy envelope fields, which will prevent any enemy in distress from taking refuge on one of those small worlds."

Somehow, the Lord General was not completely surprised. War had raged for millennia between Arpam and Raophi, the other ultra-technological giant planet in the constellation. The race populating the largest natural satellite of the star B of Sagittarius was certainly human-oid and thus very close to the Arpamas. Nevertheless, the two civiliza-tions had become rivals from their first contact and had not taken long to declare war on each other, an increasingly harsh, increasingly sophisti-cated war, mobilizing ever more sophisticated weapons, and which would only end with the total annihilation of one of the adversaries.

Fortunately, the enemy brothers had never spread their antagonism to the rest of the Galaxy—which would then hardly have had comparable means to oppose them!—and only had very rare exchanges with it, al-most exclusively focused on the export of fluz, the very famous local liqueur served in most of the famous bars in the known Universe.

Lord General Y Zeon thanked all of his squadron leaders and an-nounced to them that the next meeting would take place the next morn-ing. Until then, the rather taciturn and withdrawn strategist would have devoted his time to constructing a battle plan which would give him the best chance, if not of triumph, at least of not suffering a defeat with too heavy losses. Because the means he had to throw into the balance were in no way inferior to those of the Raophi'i, quite the contrary. The key was to mobilize them wisely by building tactics capable of striking the enemy with blow after blow by his own forces.

Drawn up and revised many times by its designer, the plan would be presented to the specialists responsible for its execution and probably amended, modified in a few details, until everyone accepted it. But until then, hours of intense reflection awaited Y Zeon. Hours during which he needed to be alone, because he only knew how to think when completely withdrawn into himself.

The Lord General had turned off almost all of the magnetized neon lights that lit the vast amphitheater, leaving only a few railings illuminat-ed directly above his platform and his desk. Immersed in contemplation of the terminal's flat monitor connecting it to the central military com-puter, he feverishly lined up the complex sketches on the sheets laid flat in front of him.

Toward the back of the room, a fluorescent ink pen remained on a tray. One of the squadron leaders had forgotten it and Y Zeon had not noticed it. Had he done so, he would hardly have been concerned because what could be more innocuous than an object of this kind that its owner would pick up the next morning?

But for that to happen, the pen would still have to be one... And here, appearances could be deceiving.

Because suddenly, the little cylinder of colored plastofiber seemed to lose its materiality and pass into a fleeting, hazy, unknown state. A loose nebulosity rose from it, without giving off light, gradually densifying, growing—up to the approximate size of a human.

A shadow among shadows, the silhouette was there. Very material now.

And it moved forward with silent steps, leaving the area of relative darkness.

It was the mental sensation of a presence that made the Lord General raise his eyes. More precisely, the impression that something had just appeared out of nowhere and stealthily entered his personal space. He held back an exclamation of feigned surprise and tried to scrutinize with a cold eye the visitor whose entrance he had not witnessed.

And for good reason! Y Zeon, however, knew of the powerful process used for such materialization.

A face with fairly fine features, a greenish complexion, framed by a very smooth and carefully trimmed cord of black beard. Had the Arpaman been an expert in the ancient history of the Earth, the comparison with an Assyrian would have immediately come to mind.

In his face, two eyes with a dark glow, as if shining with a cold light.

For clothing, the visitor wore a loose brown hooded robe, a sort of cape tightened at the waist by a black belt. Underneath, a light beige shirt. One important detail: no visible weapons.

"You possess the power of the Masters and yet you are not one of them," the Lord General ventured in a slightly unsteady voice. "Or... are you replacing one of them? I don't understand... Brown would have warned me if one of the Masters had died! Which one is dead, if that is really the case? And why this visit?"

The intruder spoke with an almost contemptuous tone, "Well, great supreme leader of the armies of Arpam the Great, have you lost your memory? Have you forgotten one of your former victims... a Persean whom you killed yourself... and who was my own brother?

"Yum Akatinor!" the Sagittarian gasped.

"You got it, Y Zeon! Yum Akatinor."

"Was he your brother?"

"Indeed. I am Noa Akatinor. Cosmomancer—and follower of the Non-Being."

The Lord General froze.

"The Masters of the Zodiac are the only ones to have the gift of metamorphism! Would you have become one of them? Impossible! You're nothing but a traitor, just like Yum was—for which he paid with his miserable life!"

"Who really betrayed who, Y Zeon?" the Persean replied. "Even as a Master, I believe that you do not have all the keys to know..."

The Sagittarian felt a flood of blind anger rising within him. Not only did someone dare to come and interrupt him in the midst of strategic preparations of the highest importance but, what's more, an impostor and perjurer to boot was bragging about possessing the exclusive power of the Masters!

Focusing all his energy, Y Zeon transformed. The morphology he adopted was the most appropriate for him, that of a monstrous vâr, a triple-bodied serpent that had the ability to spit lightning bolts.

Instantly, Noa Akatinor became an immaterial creature, a thinking globe of the planets of Aldebaran, impervious to any electrical discharge or physical embrace.

The Lord General could do nothing against him, so he returned to his original form.

Soon imitated by the Persean who, with a gesture of defiance, stood right in front of him and half opened his ample cape then the ecru shirt he wore underneath.

Stunned, Y Zeon saw the incredible tattoos engraved on his enemy's chest.

And the six medallions hung on a chain around his neck.

Six symbols... Six figures...

Virgo, Libra, Leo...

Aries, Cancer, Gemini...

A frightening vision for its implications...

"You bear six of the signs... Cursed assassin! You have killed six Masters!"

The Lord General almost collapsed. If this enemy was here, if he had revealed himself like this... then the Sagittarian would be his seventh victim!

Y Zeon was going to die a most hideous death...

If he did not resist with all his being, if he did not fight with all his energy and all the resources drawn from the depths of despair...

Listening only to his anger, mobilizing the potentially enormous forces contained in his psyche of a Master, the Lord General threw himself headlong into a battle whose outcome nevertheless eluded him.

Both adversaries went through a frenzied succession of states and forms which gave their confrontation the appearance of a carousel of living hallucinations, of a cosmozoological kaleidoscope such as might have arisen in the twisted imagination of a demiurge struck by creative hysteria.

It was all a complete waste...

The protagonists of this prodigious duel were of equal strength. At any metamorphosis of one, at any monstrous morphology supposed to be able to defeat the enemy, the other answered by adopting an even more terrible form or, if necessary, one utterly invulnerable to the weapons deployed by the other.

In a very prosaic way, the clash of the titans ended with the exhaustion of their resources and their imagination.

The two Masters suddenly faced each other again in their original appearance.

And now, the Persean had a decisive advantage. Unbeatable, unpredictable. While the Sagittarian, psychically defeated, relaxed his concentration for a moment, Noa Akatinor made a weird gesture like in a magic trick and, by making sure to divert his victim's gaze, extended his strangely counterfeit right hand from which shot a deadly discharge of what might have been a condensed dart of psychic energy.

Shortly after, he leaned over the corpse of his opponent and gave his right hand the appearance of the claw of an algomaus from Wolf 424. With his talons, he tore the bronze breastplate off the Lord General, baring his chest on which was tattooed over the heart, under the right breast and not the left, the sign of the Sagittarius.

Cutting into the epidermis with surgical precision, the Persean uncovered a metallic medal and removed it, still bloody, from the flesh in which it had been implanted. Then he unclipped his necklace and added the small engraved disk to the six others that he had already appropriated through criminal means.

That done, a shadow among the shadows, Noa Akatinor returned to the back of the conference room and dissolved into an immaterial mist.

A few moments later, the small cylinder of colored plastofiber was again on the tray where one of the squadron leaders had conveniently forgotten it.

The next morning, the discovery of the mutilated corpse of Generalissimo Y Zeon aroused not just worry, but the ominous conviction of defeat among the armies of Arpam the Great—and spurred an investigation that led nowhere.

A perfect example of a closed-room murder, the death of the Sagittarian warlord was quickly classified among the insoluble cases.

CHAPTER III

It was in Paris-sur-Terre, at the Interplan headquarters. In his simple office on the 15th floor of the ultra-modern building built on the hill of Montmartre, Commissioner Robin Muscat waited for the most recent recruit of the interplanetary—and interstellar—police to arrive to touch base on the mission which had been entrusted to him.

Muscat was in charge during the absence of Lepinson, director of the terrestrial headquarters, who had gone to enjoy two weeks of vacation in a space center somewhere near Gemini.

Arriving early, as usual, he stole a few minutes to smoke a pipe of faoz from the plains of Mars. And he railed once again against the drizzle that fell on the Dazzling City, a minor but discreet spring rain.

At the appointed time, Marc Verano entered his superior's office. The young inspector was of medium height, with dark, curly hair, energetic features and a gaze sparkling with intelligence barely filtered by small round glasses.

"Hello, Verano," Muscat said with a smile.

"Top of the morning, chief," the young inspector replied. "So, any progress on the great mystery?"

"Yes and no. The Black Circle is still full of mystery and I still have no information as to its origins or its history, meaning that it isn't helping much in our investigation."

"All we know, then, is that the organization is like the Mafia of the old twentieth century and that this octopus extends its tentacles to the Centaur, Perseus and even Altaïr. But from where, that's another matter."

Vérano seemed sorry to admit that he had got no further.

Muscat let out a long sigh,

"Even though I've beefed up checkpoints and surveillance, nothing works. These people avoid all traps, slip through all nets, as elusive as if they were immaterial... or as if they had means infinitely superior to ours. The powers behind it are colossal, starting with the finances. Because in the end they've got to have technology that defies the imagination to foil all our tricks, unless we're dealing with ghosts."

"No, Commissioner, you don't have to worry about that. You probably don't know that among my direct ancestors there's a rather exceptional man, Teddy Vérano, who was rightly called the ghost detective. He was active in the 1960s and left memoirs in the form of stories that recounted his battles with the occult. Very rare are the cases in these testimonies that seem to relate exclusively to the purely supernatural. Men who are particularly twisted and prone to evil have always been able to control and manipulate more fragile, sensitive souls. Perhaps here we're also dealing with people who are flirting with the world of shadows—but there's something else at stake, something tangible and material!"

"I hope you're right, my young friend! At the risk of surprising you, however, I have the start of a trail to show you. Here you go: The Interplan, or rather its Venusian representation, has picked up some clues pointing to the underbelly of Ishtar Terra as the site of a rise in activities that are more suspicious than usual."

Vérano stared at him with a penetrating gaze.

"Ishtar Terra... Oh, if we have to go and dive into that modern-day Court of Miracles..."

"And yet... There could be a woman there, a mixed-race Terro-Venusian named Luse Borek, who might play a leading role in this famous Black Circle. We will therefore have to think soon about poking around there. And you, young man?"

"I wanted to see you this morning, boss, because by remaining very down to earth, I managed to locate a cell of the Black Circle not very far from here... Right under our noses, you might say."

"Where?"

"In Melun-3!"

Muscat rolled his eyes up.

"Melun-3... That's all we needed!"

Among the peripheral towns which had once grown to form the suburbs in a very broad sense of the former capital of France and where, in reality, Paris concentrated, in a way, everything that it refused to put up with inside it, many cities that came out of nothing before the Great Decadence had experienced the very unenviable fate of becoming refuges for undesirables and outcasts of all origins. Sordid tragedies caused by intolerance, violence, racism and other scourges ingrained in human stupidity remained attached to notorious names like Evry, Corbeil, Rosny or Cergy-Pontoise.

As for Melun...

There, it was not a matter of horrors spawned by the basest instincts of the one who believed himself to be the king of Creation. Was that reassuring though? If the number 3 was added to the name of this town today, it was because the small town, originally cheerful and friendly, over time had become a living hell of the worst kind and had been razed twice. The first, following a catastrophic accident in the neighboring thermonuclear power plant and the second, a century later after decontamination and reconstruction, was due to a viral epidemic accidentally imported from the planets of Cetus by a ship in distress that had crashed on the edge of populated areas.

Marked by fate, Melun today made up the lower end of the Dazzling City. Some would have said the cesspool or the manure essential for the flowering of the most beautiful species, but they had never dared to step down there in their pretty shoes made for right-thinking salons!

And when the forces of order ventured there, it was for expeditions more perilous than the exploration of the most cursed worlds in the Galaxy. Each operation resulted in the capture of so many delinquents of all kinds that the special section of the Interplan called JVM, "Jeunes Voyous du Martervenux" (Young Punks of the Martervenux), saw its three-year workload plan in terms of re-education, rehabilitation and reintegration— for the least hopeless cases—increase nearly 150 percent.

"Melun-3, indeed!" Vérano exclaimed, tearing Muscat away from his bleak musings. "I've drawn up the outline of the intervention we need to launch... But watch out, it first needs special authorization and then the call to one or two paramilitary contingents of the Imperial Militia of the Martervenux.

The commissioner acted as if he had not understood. In reality, the declaration astounded him to such an extent that he had to hear it twice to acknowledge its absolute necessity.

"No problem for special authorization. And for the other point, did you say..."

"One or two paramilitary contingents, boss!"

"You're insane, young man! This is not about going to war against the human octopuses of Fomalhaut! The forces of Interplan will be more than enough to..."

"I'm afraid not, Commissioner! The spotters who have been on the lookout for about six months have observed, more and more, the excessive means that you spoke of. The members of the Black Circle are amassing weapons whose design and purpose remain undecipherable to the most experienced experts. An unprecedented arsenal is being built up there, in a complex of abandoned but now ultra-secure hangars. And when we see these thugs training in the surrounding wastelands, they're no longer men we are looking at..."

"What then, by a thousand comets?"

"These individuals demonstrate hyper-augmented physical strength, are capable of moving so fast they're almost invisible, display extraordinary endurance...

"Conditioning?"

"No, not really... I'd rather say an anabolic substance, a doping product of unknown origin... Or even a drug with metabolic catalysis—but that absolutely does not come from us."

The further Vérano went in his explanations, the more Muscat became interested. And the more he regretted having reached the rank he had recently reached, because it kept him further and further away from the front lines of the operation by pinning him behind a desk for tasks that were always frustrating.

"If I understand correctly," he summed up, "you're asking me to seek the support of the Military."

"Exactly, boss."

"All right, I'll call Admiral Delta."

The commissioner tapped the keys of the communicator integrated into his desk and it did not take long to connect with the HQ of the Martervenux armed forces. Shortly after, the square, energetic face of Admiral Delta appeared on the screen.

Muscat summarized the context and the situation, explained the ins and outs of the planned operation then requested authorization for intervention as well as the support of a paramilitary contingent.

The background of the affair was sufficiently disturbing that the senior officer, knowing his colleague, who was not a man to judge lightly, immediately granted his request.

"It's done, young man," Muscat announced when he had cut off the communication. "But on one condition..."

Vérano turned pale, "I'm being removed from leading the assault because I'm too green?"

"No not at all. Delta likes you even if you haven't been with us for a long time, and he trusts you. No... The condition is that I supervise the operation with you. Faced with enemies of the caliber of the Black Circle, the presence of a seasoned veteran like me will come in handy in the event of a reaction beyond your expectations."

"We'll be in touch remotely, that's good enough! There's no question of you exposing yourself on the front lines, boss! You're indispensable and irreplaceable..."

Muscat brushed aside the objection with a brisk gesture. "Like many others whose successors took the job with much more success! Besides, if I stay at a distance, I won't see anything live or in real time. Especially not the kinds of details which might slip by you but won't fail to alert me to the enemy's potential and the immediate reactions needed to oppose them."

Vérano let out a sigh of resignation, "No need for me to insist, right?"

"Right. Thank you for your concern, my friend, but don't worry, I know how to protect myself."

The cloud cover had thickened with the evening. Fortunately, the rain had stopped. Shortly before midnight, the ultra-silent Interplan electrautos had parked around the edge of a circle half a mile in diameter with the hangar complex occupying the center, then the police forces had begun to cordon off the perimeter. Fifteen armored gliders, totally discreet thanks to their anti-detection coatings but armed to the teeth, had quickly reached the theater of operations and the men of the paramilitary contingent sent by Admiral Delta had joined those they were soon to support.

Camouflage outfits, night vision masks, shields and strong-wave blasters, individual paralyzers and inframauve guns—these only to be used if the situation turned dire for the assault commandos... No normal, ordinary adversary was likely to oppose such a deployment of means.

But for that they were pretty sure that the Black Circle didn't fall into this category.

The eight warehouses had initially belonged to an import-export company selling luxury furniture whose managers, young and inexperienced, had been misled by the site contract, which was far too cheap to be honest. Given the environment, it was almost immediately necessary to put in place very sophisticated protection and security systems, which were also very expensive. Their effectiveness only lasted for a short time.

Just enough time to put to rest the distrust of the owners and let the local underworld infiltrate the security teams, who were easy to corrupt. A year after setting up, one night of looting and pillaging completely emptied the premises, then burned them down, and the company went bankrupt. Since then, no one has reinvested in this risky area.

Except the Black Circle... Whose dissuasive means, not to mention their ways of keeping the status quo with the gangs of delinquents of Melun-3, must have been convincing enough to remove from anyone's mind the idea of entering the place.

And yet, from the outside, they saw nothing. Not an electrified fence, not a strong-wave network, not an electronic surveillance eye, not a sentry... Nothing. The two groups of four square buildings were much more innocent in appearance than many buildings occupied by official administrations.

"If I didn't have confidence in you, young man," Muscat said, "I'd scold you for making hasty conclusions and we'd go back immediately!"

"That's the whole problem, boss. A week or two can go by without anything moving here, and suddenly there's excitement. Worse than a crazy hive! Between these periods of hyperactivity, it's as if there's no one here."

"What do you want to do, then?"

"We take advantage of the dead calm to attack. Let's see what we can find inside these hangars."

"OK, Vérano, go ahead!"

In less than a minute after the signal to go, the place had transformed into a pandemonium of fury, violence, flashing lights and screams.

As if the attackers had awakened them from a lethargic trance, the thugs of the Black Circle had descended on the forces of order at the very moment when they had broken down the big main doors of each of the warehouses. It was as if the police and soldiers had crossed invisible anti-intrusion beams and simultaneously triggered all the alarms of Creation!

Individuals in full night-colored suits, armed with disintegrators and inframauve guns, burst out from every nook and cranny inside the buildings. Some running, some diving from on high, some springing from the ground... Faced with the magnitude of the defense, the intruders were forced to use the most violent tactics, to strike mercilessly to avoid being shot, and given the aggressiveness of their opponent, they did not hold back.

At the same time, explosive charges had detonated everywhere, completely destroying the stocks amassed by the Black Circle.

After half an hour the operation was over. The men of Interplan counted five losses, there were two deaths among the ranks of the paramilitary contingent. On the enemy side, apart from around fifteen prisoners now immobilized by strong-wave containment grids, there was not a single survivor.

Marc Vérano was satisfied. And Robin Muscat did not fail to congratulate him.

"As far as a success, that's not bad!" he declared. "I don't think the Black Circle will come back to set up again here any time soon."

"The prisoners will be valuable to us," the young inspector added.

"As long as they allow themselves to be interrogated... Which is not yet a done deal," Muscat warned.

A minute later, a call from an electrauto confirmed his fears.

"This is Captain Xérix. All the prisoners have just committed suicide!"

"Hell and damnation!" Muscat exploded. "I knew it... What happened?"

"They went up in flames, Commissioner. They caught fire like torches just as we were getting them loaded into the vans."

"And what did you do?" Verano asked.

"We sprayed them with dry ice, to no avail..."

"Don't move, I'm coming!" Muscat announced.

Before running to the vehicles, he turned to his young colleague.

"Search what remains of all this mess, Vérano! You never know, there may be hard drives or computer disks in good enough shape to still be readable and provide important information about the Black Circle."

"I'll take care of it, boss. Look, over there, Dupuis has already found something."

"Good, keep it up!"

Muscat rushed to join Captain Xérix. The old officer, looking perplexed and a little lost, stood near several bodies very seriously damaged by the strange process of spontaneous combustion.

"I've read things saying that it was possible, Commissioner, but to see it with my own eyes..." The man shuddered. "It's incredible! No, worse—it's spooky!

"Pyrotechnics work wonders when it comes to fireworks, Verix!" Muscat reassured him while leaning over a corpse less charred than the others. "You know, science and technology…"

He left his sentence hanging.

The victim's outfit, which was wide open at the level of the torso, revealed the entire left part of the chest. And there, just over the breast, near the location of the heart...

"By Altaïr's spells!" Muscat muttered. "It's starting again..."

Tattooed on the pale skin, impossible to miss, a distinct design.

That of a lightning eagle.

"It's the Thirteenth sign of the Zodiac again."

Suddenly, an old classified file had just resurfaced.

CHAPTER IV

"Gently, my beautiful monster! Yes... You felt it, I finally got good news for you! But stop acting crazy as if your wedding were tonight!"

Somewhat tempered by the deep harmonics of his master's voice as well as the soothing waves emitted simultaneously with the words, the magnificent pstôr came and sat down next to Bruno Coqdor's armchair and placed his bulldog-like muzzle on the edge of the work table.

"Here's where the letter comes from, Râx. Sender: Chevalier Riccardo Ohaniero, Palazzio Vendramin, Venice. Ah, Italy, the City of the Doges, its palaces with their age-old mysteries and their dark legends, its sometimes spectral bells...[14] You'll soon see this pure marvel of the past that human technical genius was able to save from the eternal waters... And this Ohaniero also has a pstôr! Apart from me, he must be the only Earthling who does. And the miracle, little demon of Dzo, is that this Venetian pstôr is a female!"

Coqdor patted the head of his favorite animal.

"The noble Signor Ohaniero is simply sending us a marriage proposal! Shô is younger than you, smaller, she hasn't experienced a fraction of your adventures but look... Isn't she wonderful?"

So saying, the Earth Knight placed a 3D photo in front of the bulldog-bat nose on which Mademoiselle Shô was smiling with all her teeth while rolling her eyes—enough to make any healthy male of her race melt.

"I'll answer 'Yes', don't you think?"

Râx gave a very deep purr which soon broke into a sequence of tiny yelps of almost ecstatic joy. He stood up, unfolded his bat-like wings that served as his forelimbs and for a moment his master thought he was going to fly away... and put in danger all the objects on display in the vast office.

"Calm down, terrible beast!"

The pstôr understood. When Coqdor spoke like that, it was better to take it easy.

Above all, don't forget to respect the master's sacred things.

---

[14] See *La Maleficio*.

And, truth be told, there were a lot of them between these four walls!

The huge room was located on the third floor of an antique building, meaning it was built a good century before the Great Decadence, in this little microcosmic jewel in the heart of Paris by the Ile Saint-Louis. From the two impressive windows of the office, he had a breathtaking view of the immemorial spiritual heart of the former French capital: Notre-Dame Cathedral.

Coqdor's choice had not been for nothing. Whenever he came back from one of his many interstellar epics, after having pitted himself against beings and powers sometimes verging on the unimaginable and the demonic, being able to contemplate for hours this monument so rich in spirituality, wholly in the glory of the God of the Cosmos—and not only of the divinity which, in a rather reductive way, had given birth to the Catholic religion—gave him the possibility of recharging himself on the plane of moral elevation and the invincible force of the spirit.

It sometimes happened that Râx, taking flight from the roof of the building, flew across the sky to perch there alongside a gargoyle and adopt the latter's frozen pose. Anyone of the many human and extraterrestrial visitors or pedestrians who crowded around the cathedral in all weather and, by chance, saw him coming, rubbed their eyes in disbelief.

But the most beautiful moment was when the pstôr, always playful and teasing, left his perch and his immobile companion a few minutes later to dive at the stunned, frightened onlookers... suddenly convinced that a macabre spell had just given life to one of the hideous stone figures that lined the pinnacles, flying buttresses and corbels of Notre-Dame!

The absolute and never-to-be-broken prohibition, on the other hand, was to unfold his wings in the office in the hope of being able to slip through one of its open windows. Just to tempt it spelled sure punishment. Because here, nothing should be broken. And the master was not joking around about this rule...

On invisible shelves of strong-waves were in fact lined up here all the "souvenirs" brought back by the Star Knight from his adventures in the four corners of the Galaxy... and elsewhere. Or the works of art that he had got made in the rare cases where it had not been possible for him to bring back a physical piece. To all this were also added the gifts regularly offered to him by his "dear star cop," Robin Muscat, to commemorate his own solo journey when by chance a mission or an investigation sent him without Coqdor into a world where danger lurked.

Thus, this delicately ornate chitin structure was the lower part of the abdomen of a Venus zlan, in other words the light source of the over-sized firefly. Muscat had brought it back from the swamps of the Tmex'x mountains where he had been tracking an individual accidentally dema-terialized by lightning and become a half-mad demigod.[15]

The small iridescent gem next to it came from the Living Stone Temple of Evkeer-bis, in the constellation Eridanus. It was a gamahé, a kind of talisman capable of recording images and sounds then restoring them with the right mechanical or photonic stimultation. The policeman had followed the trail of a rather disturbing trafficking story there and had witnessed the petrifying of a young castaway from Earth with his companion from the indigenous Lowoxi race, those strange firefly-men.[16]

The piece next to this was a translucent block recovered by Muscat in the Trembling City on the planetoid Arethusa, one of the largest stray rocks that revolved between Mars and Jupiter. It was one of the rare ves-tiges of the hypnotron, the formidable machine for materializing dreams that the intangible and invisible Owods, from their incredibly distant universe, had had human scientists build with a view to conquering the Solar System.[17]

Even stranger was the small vial of emeraldine glass connected to a very disconcerting incident experienced by Robin Muscat himself. On the trail of a secret organization called the Space Dragon, the policeman had discovered the unthinkable traffic set up by Doctor Aknôr between human worlds and his home planet Weïdimir. A traffic based on reduc-ing living beings to a liquid state by the action of the ZZ frequency—an experience which Muscat himself had suffered and which had made him stay for a time in this very ordinary-looking flask.[18]

The next object in the "Muscat collection" was a metal ring pierced with radial holes and fitted with a handle in the middle supported by two perpendicular diametric rods. In fact, a photonic shield designed and manufactured by the Cygnian scientist Vaô. From his ultra-modern la-boratory set up in an old castle in the Balkans, the Earth scientist Wolf

---

[15] See *Les Foudroyants*.

[16] See *Lumière qui tremble*.

[17] See *Les Créatures d'Hypnos*.

[18] See *Fréquence ZZ*

Stagg, a specialist in light, had developed a process for the bioluminic transportation of living beings, the essential details of which had been provided to him remotely by the people of Cygnus using the duplex communication established with them. Stagg had facilitated the escape of a man sentenced to death for a crime of passion through jealousy, Rod Armauri, in order to pick him up for the sole purpose of having a subject to be sent by photonic means to the Cygnus. But the contemptible pirates of light had intercepted him and planned to use for their own purposes the gift of total knowledge of the inter-time course of events acquired by Rod during his transport. Because he had then literally embraced the Universe and reached the past, present and future limits of infinity. Muscat himself had to make the photonic journey to kill poor Armauri who had become a threat through the scope of his premonitory visions while the Sirian interstellar militia put an end to the wicked abuses of the light pirates.[19]

On the next invisible shelf was firstly the hyper-realistic representation of a spaceship with a sinister appearance, the Red Eye, the cosmic beacon concealing a phantom spacecraft that the inhabitants of the planet Dzo regularly sent to the edges of the constellation Hercules in order to lure possible travelers and then lead them to their home world. The Dzos had certainly achieved immortality thanks to a successful experiment of one of their scholars, but the acquired eternity had proven to be a ruthless curse because it had condemned them to sterility and boredom. So, they hoped, each time, that their forced visitors would agree to kill them... The Star Knight's first mission had brought him to Dzo where, apart from the unexpected resolution of the problem of induced immortality and, consequently, saving an entire people, he had won the unflagging friendship and faithful company of Râx, his pet monster.[20]

Very simple in appearance, the small galena crystal of Mars was one of those vibrating stones which, set up in a certain way, could transmit radio waves. Coqdor had lived on the Red Planet, then in the process of terraforming by the creation of a breathable atmosphere from the melting of its polar ice caps, and had an unusual confrontation with the last Martians opposed to the colonization of their world. Many natives had already emigrated to Venus, much more hospitable than dying Mars, and some had later returned to their homeland alongside the Earthlings. Oth-

---

[19] See *Ici l'Infini.*
[20] See *L'Etoile de Satan.*

ers, however, had retreated to the interior of Phobos, the entirely hollow "potato moon," from where they had tried everything to stop the occupation of their planet. And it was paradoxically the cataclysmic impact of Phobos, dashed against Mars, which had completed the terraforming process by speeding up the melting of the ice and causing rain to fall on the red deserts for the first time in tens of millennia.[21]

The tenfold metal box from Sirius, decorated with inscriptions in ftoopahg, the sacred language of the planet Pyr, had ephemerally housed a chronon, a parcel of time—the only zero particle ever successfully isolated, capable of disrupting the very existence of the Universe if it had not been destroyed before it was too late.[22]

Between this shelf and the next hung on the wall a painting made using the holographic painting technique and signed by the brilliant Montmartre artist Tami Euclimar. Based on the descriptions provided by Coqdor, who had made an exception to inspire them with some hypno-suggestive impulses, the painter had produced a striking representation of a vast sector of intergalactic space visible from the dead planet Syrrax, located at the extreme edge of the Milky Way, somewhere at the antipodes of the Solar System. An area which seemed empty of all matter and light, even at these immeasurable distances where, in all other cosmic azimuths, the reassuring spots of very distant island universes usually sparkled. Nothing had been neglected, down to the characteristic details of what was considered locally and relatively erroneously as the "supreme planet" of the entire known Universe: the whitish reptiles and the big pale birds, the beautiful Syrrax in golden breastplate and emeraldine coat, so strikingly realistic that one would have thought they were ready to shout their friendly "Zaiao!" to the observer fascinated by the painting, their fantastic factory for recreating images of the past, sunk in the waters and reconstituting scenes of the exterminating war waged against Syrrax by the conquering Hobbals endowed with a third eye. There were also the ghost stars and those ghost ships which assumed an ephemeral materiality when the Great Livid Ray, that beam of indescribable light emanating from who knew where, sometimes flashed through the absolute nothingness of that which, for lack of a better word, had been dubbed the after-world.[23]

---

[21] See *Et la Pluie tomba sur Mars*.

[22] See *Particule Zéro*.

[23] See *Ici finit le monde*.

To this day, the mystery of this area, which aroused the fear and anxiety of the great unknown, had not been elucidated. Some assumed that it was not a total vacuum but rather a concentration of dark antimatter following the bizarre laws governing the balance between the positive and the negative of Creation, but this was still an unproven hypothesis.

Near Deneb, the Star Knight had one day accidentally landed on a planet made entirely of crystal, more precisely of extra-pure carbon with undetectable traces of an unknown substance which made it capable of emitting in the ultraviolet. The small ultradiamantine gem on the next shelf was a tiny fragment. Thanks to these formidable stones, Coqdor was able to restore normality to Agoââ, a bleak world located in the heart of the Livid Nebula whose negative stars and vampires, in addition to the radiographic effect on living organisms, kept the planet in a bleak atmosphere, "in black and white," and had gradually dragged an entire people into the most unfathomable of depressions.[24]

Crystal, always crystal... Very close by, well secured in a transparent display case with a coded lock, was a tiny cage carved from the same kind of mineral, a spidery architecture obeying very subtle mathematical laws because it had to shelter, without the possibility of escape, a tiny flame oscillating between blue and green. A minuscule piece of the Torch of the World that the Wemyx of a sun planet lost on the outskirts of Sagittarius jealously watched over, a living fire that, obeying a song, could heal the wounded and resurrect the dead, but also mercilessly destroy when ordered to. The telepathic powers of its guardians forced him to create circles of flame capable of striking at great distances in the cosmic void.[25]

Right next to these extraordinary and yet natural things, the next small object looked common, innocuous, almost out of place. And yet... On close examination, this very simple 3-D photo revealed a series of very strange flat figures, close to human in appearance. It was one of the only visible proofs of the attempted invasion of the normal universe by two-dimensional beings from a cosmos plane "perpendicular" to ours, through whose fault certain events, at first incomprehensible, had spawned a storm of panic on the worlds of the Martervenux and elsewhere... Thanks to the studies and experiments hastily carried out by the brilliant Doctor Stewe, Coqdor himself had agreed to dive into the two-

---

[24] See *Les Soleils Noirs*.
[25] See *Le Flambeau du Monde*.

dimensional continuum to establish contact with its weird inhabitants and then, alongside one of them, to guide an Earth expedition to the confines of the Monoceros constellation. It was there, in fact, that the 2-D human-oids had struck for the first time, depriving a space freighter and all its passengers of the third dimension. They had discovered there, literally on the fringe of the two universes, a normal solitary planet but curiously endowed with flat moons, whose colossal deposits of prism gems had finally allowed the two-dimensional creatures to acquire the much de-sired thickness, thanks to a process derived from anaglyphs. Unfortunate-ly, as soon as their dream came true, a great number of these beings were instantly petrified because of the panicky fear that had seized them fol-lowing the surprise attack of native snake-plants. And all the others had then fled, no one knew where...[26]

The Star Knight kept another very special memory from this incred-ible adventure, whose existence only he and Doctor Stewe knew about. And for good reason... In secret, the subtle physicist continued to work on two-dimensional diving and applied the principle, tested urgently, to the development of a transportation-re-emergence process over pre-programed distances. He had thus designed and developed a small dis-coidal device of around six inches in diameter and less than an inch thick. Adjusted beforehand and attached to its user's belt, it temporarily made the user lose his third dimension to allow him to instantly travel the desired route, in a completely undetectable manner, by borrowing an "external" singularity from the usual 3-D universe. Coqdor had around ten copies, carefully stored in a safe with a coded lock. And no one, not even Robin Muscat, knew about them.

It was common knowledge that ice and snow melted above zero de-grees. Nevertheless, these two particular states of water had manifested themselves in totally inconceivable conditions on countless planets when they were affected by a strange snow in the collective psyche following the appearance of a star with inverted and refrigerating light, the ice sun. The object kept by Coqdor as a souvenir of the crazy adventure he under-took with Muscat was a complicated assemblage of regular hypergeo-metric figures, a fractal sculpture executed with an inframauve micro-laser in a mass of previously ionized depolex. It represented none other than the crystals of intelligent snow from the ice sun, such as the two men had encountered during their dive into the infinitely small, their minds transported by flagellate-vectors with which they had won a first

---

[26] See *La Terre n'est pas ronde.*

victory over an enemy of an unprecedented kind. The final battle had taken place on Mars, on the plains of Phison, and it had been terrible.[27]

More prosaic but of striking purity and beauty, the golden dagger which came next was the admiration of all the visitors of the Star Knight. More precisely, its sculpted guard magnetized the visitors who could not stop staring at the perfect female form represented. It was that of Gheldir, high priestess of the night-colored god, who had committed suicide out of jealousy when the entity had preferred a young Earthling. This had happened on the planet Uzaow where superabundant gold had supplanted all other metals in everyday life. Uzaow where, in time immemorial, a shipwrecked extragalactic astronaut had been mutated into an enormously enlarged brain by means of a lake of raw phosphorus and had risen to the rank of deity, enslaving an entire population to his perverted will out of loneliness and despair.[28]

Placed on a small easel of Centauri veined wood, the delicate embroidery displayed next was made of oxiiz silk produced by the spiders of the planet Mîo of Aquarius. It bore the symbolic motif of the Arcana of the Science of the Magistral City of Maakeldar, thanks to which the scholar Frank Dusaule was able to risk a voluntary foray into the borderlands of death. The Chevalier Coqdor, for his part, had to accept the inconceivable experience of disincarnation in order to save the other Necronauts threatened by the demiurge desires of Doctor Kowi, who had attempted nothing less than recreating life by luring wandering souls into masses of synthetic protoplasm.[29]

Farther away, a small, ordinary-looking bottle contained a liquid just as ordinary in appearance. Water, yes... but crossed here and there by slight flashes reminiscent of storm lightning. This energy fluid came from a world of Bouvier, a satellite of the giant Arcturus, where Coqdor and Muscat had led a group of four young delinquents with the aim of conquering the energy of the formidable waters and, at the same time, offering the four ruffians a chance of rehabilitation. When they found out that the human body was to serve as a living catalyst in the experiment, Ty, one of the teenagers, had sacrificed his life on this remarkable quest.[30]

---

[27] See *Le Soleil de glace*.
[28] See *Le Dieu couleur de nuit*
[29] See *Les Portes de l'Aurore*.
[30] See *Planète de Feu*.

Another object from the "Coqdor collection" was a piece of bas-relief brought from Accora, a grim swamp planet in the constellation Capricorn where the Star Knight had learned of the thirteenth sign of the Zodiac after a tumultuous journey. The sculpture adorning the gray stone was none other than the symbol of the lightning eagle, the famous thirteenth sign representing not the inter-world rotunda connecting the twelve other transdimensional doors but indeed the Earth, from where the prodigious network had been developed, no one knew when or by whom.[31]

From a more recent mission which led him to the vicinity of the giant Saturn, jewel of the Solar System, where entities beyond comprehension had decided to start a Creation on the scale of the Titan satellite, the Star Knight had brought back a curious object stolen aboard the misanthropic Marsupial's cobbled together spaceship.[32] From afar, the strange box looked like the Sirian nesting box which had once housed the chronon. For this reason alone, motivated by an almost superstitious fear and apprehension that was backed up by his sometimes vague and inexplicable premonitions, Coqdor had never dared to open the box. Having somewhat understood the complicated personality of the space pariah, of whom certain allegations suggested that he had been able to establish contacts with beings bordering on the inconceivable, he had become intimately convinced that the box harbored an immeasurably dangerous secret. The thing fascinated him and scared him at the same time. Maybe one day he would give in to temptation and in the worst case scenario he would pay for it with his life...

The melodious five notes of the bell at the front door yanked the green-eyed man out of his brief meditation. Râx made a soft whistle, suggesting that he was expecting a visit from a friend.

Coqdor got up, left his office and crossed the vestibule. One look at the intercom screen, and his face lit up. The visitor was none other than Robin Muscat.

"Glad to see you again at last, old Milky Way cop!" the Chevalier said cheerfully, stepping aside to let his friend enter, whom the pstôr immediately welcomed.

---

[31] See *Le Treizième Signe du Zodiaque*.
[32] See *Flammes sur Titan*.

"And me too, my dear wizard!" the policeman replied, whose face instantly turned dark, even though Râx's behavior cheered him up a bit and he responded with many affectionate caresses.

"Did you swallow radioactive stones?" Coqdor asked. "Or drink some tainted ztax? You look very upset, my friend..."

"Can I sit down?" Muscat asked. "And if you have one of those Cutty Sarks up your sleeve... just as a pick-me-up..."

"With pleasure, old star cop! So what's got you so upset?"

"The Zodiac is back," the commissioner stated in a blank voice. "I'll tell you everything."

Half an hour and two glasses of excellent aged whiskey later, the Star Knight was informed in detail of all the events that had occurred over the past few months. The disturbing activities of the Black Circle, the clues of the vague trail leading to Ishtar Terra, the assault on the Melun-3 warehouses the night before. And finally, the tattoo of the lightning eagle discovered on the chest of one of the "suicide" victims of the operation mounted by the young and brilliant Marc Vérano...

"Are you sure it was the Thirteenth sign?" the green-eyed Chevalier pressed. "Sometimes a simple birthmark... or a tattoo for fun..."

"Come on, Coqdor, don't take me for a blockhead! I wasn't the only one to see it, there are photos, and I checked when I got back to the office... It's definitely the fire eagle we know. The gang of criminals is starting to strike again!"

"Criminals... A bit exaggerated, in my opinion. People who wanted at all costs to keep a secret likely to cause all galactic civilizations to shake on their foundations..."

"And they killed for that! Remember Jean-Marie Spontini, executed before my eyes. And Yum Akatinor, also murdered. Cladek Halstar, driven to madness..."

"It's true they didn't go in for subtleties. Their Guide whom we met on Accora in Capricorn, however, didn't give me the impression of being an unscrupulous murderer."

Muscat sat quietly for a few seconds.

"Time's passed since then... Quite a lot, even. And I've just got proof that the Zodiac are now working hand-in-hand with the Black Circle. From there to assuming they're the instigators and pulling the strings isn't a great leap. What I can say is this: the armed intervention in Melun-3 caused the death of all the local thugs of this newfangled mafia...

But keep in mind that during the last six months, no one had managed to corner them. To the extent that we thought they were invulnerable!"

"Because they had serious resources provided by the Zodiac, right?"

"Exactly!"

"And Melun-3, then?"

"A gambit, as they say in chess. Deliberate sacrifice of a pawn to smoke out the opponent."

The Star Knight pondered for a few moments.

"It all makes sense, I admit. It sounds like an opinion entirely in line with the logic of an experienced police officer and criminologist. But... it's not mine."

"Why?" Muscat objected. "What's your take on it, then?"

"Well, it's quite simple after all. It all starts with the end, that is to say with the Guide. This innocuous little man, this Mr. Everyman, as short-sighted as a mole and dressed as normal as could be, really had nothing of a potential culprit capable of acts as monstrous as the 'exterminations' that set you on the case. Nor the beautiful Giovanna Hi-Ling, manipulated as she was to cover her tracks and above all prevent us from knowing the secret."

"Innocents who hid their thoughts behind a mental screen that I couldn't get through? Well done, green-eyed monster, your insight was kind of in a slump... You didn't sense the psi powers they had? It's because they put you to sleep and exploited you!"

"Of course, I haven't been able to read them either. But Râx... Remember, he didn't show any aggression towards them. And he's not fooled, as good and simple an animal as he is. Instinct-wise, I trust him. I, too, will grant these people the good graces they proclaim. The Zodiac is not a criminal organization!"

Muscat waited two seconds before taking his parting shot.

"One day, you will explain to me how the death of Spontini fits into your painting of the Holy Innocents, my friend..."

Seeing the Star Knight's reaction, he said to himself: Score one for me!

Coqdor closed his eyes and seemed to concentrate. Clearly he was puzzled.

"I won't explain anything to you, you overly Cartesian rationalist... I'm far from having the answers to all the questions, but I will answer this one with two simple words: gut feeling. It wasn't a malicious act on their part. And that's all."

The commissioner took one final stab.

"There's something else, to wrap up... Remember that we're sworn to protect the secret of the inter-world rotundas and as such, we haven't revealed anything about the matter to anyone. We have passively 'covered' the members of the Zodiac. Well, it's over. With the Black Circle and everything involved with it, today I have to first refer it to Interplan. Later, perhaps, it will also be necessary to involve the Imperial Militia of the Martervenux."

Coqdor jumped in his chair. He was scandalized.

"No! Under no circumstances should you do that. We promised..."

"At a time when everything the Zodiac did was still legal or almost! Well, they've changed their tune. From now on, we're dealing with premeditated murders, armed attacks, trafficking..."

"Against which the police and the space army will be powerless! All the more reason to observe the law of silence... and act on our own, as lone wolves if necessary."

"For anyone who didn't live through Melun-3, it's easy to say! If you'd seen those fighters and their determination... all the way to suicide by spontaneous combustion! No, my friend, here we really have to do something. This time I'll give my full report and talk about the Zodiac!"

Without saying a word, Coqdor nodded slowly.

"Well, in that case," he added, "grant me one request. It's Friday, give me until next Monday to try to unravel the mystery. Meaning, either get on the trail of our quiet little clerk or trace it back to Giovanna Hi-Ling. If I don't have anything in three days, I'll let you know and it'll be up to you. Whatever you want to do."

"Okay, okay," Muscat conceded, though unconvinced. "I'll prepare the file in the meantime because I'm sure that you won't succeed."

"We'll see about that! He who doesn't try, gets nothing, right?"

The star cop stood up. With Râx on his heels, a little less cheerful than before, the Star Knight showed him to the door.

For the first time in their whole career together, Bruno Coqdor and Robin Muscat took leave of each other without the feeling of being their usual duo.

They had set themselves on opposite sides of an invisible barrier.

The limit marked by two different concepts of duty.

And respect for giving one's word.

Alone again, Coqdor returned to his office and looked at the towers of Notre-Dame for a few minutes. Lying on the richly patterned wool carpet, the pstôr respected the meditative silence of his master.

When the Star Knight finally moved, it was to type on the keyboard of his personal computer.

It didn't take long for the Zodiac folder to appear.

Coqdor skimmed through it once again, quickly arriving at the synthesis and conclusion.

Apart from the mysterious little man with the thick glasses, there remained only two people in close connection with the organization centered around the thirteen signs.

One was the Earthling Giovanna Hi-Ling, the statuesque Sino-Italian with no known family, raised on Mars in Syrtis Major, disappeared under mysterious conditions then resurfaced in a no less enigmatic way on Ulmir, in the guise of Yloa Flugg, and as herself on Accora of Capricorn.

But where had she gone since then?

This question did not arise for the other person: the Martian financier Cladek Halstar who had fallen into inexplicable insanity and spent his surely peaceful days in Sainte-Anne hospital, knocked out by the chemical straightjacket of tranquilizing pharmacopoeias. Although the man was always within reach, his condition unfortunately made him completely useless.

Out of curiosity more than hope, Coqdor dialed the number of the psychiatric center. The charming face of a pretty switchboard operator was framed on the telecom screen. Kindly, she immediately transferred him to the management of the establishment.

"I'm the intern, Dr. Lucas," a young man with a serious and thoughtful expression announced. "Hello, Chevalier Coqdor, what can I do for you?"

"I've called to inquire about the health of one of your patients, the man named Cladek Halstar. How is he?"

Lucas's expression changed in a flash. He looked like the evening Earth-Moon shuttle had just crashed on the toes of his shoes. "Cladek Halstar? Sorry, Chevalier... I would be hard-pressed to answer you."

"Is he dead?"

"No... Although... We don't know... He disappeared!"

"Disappeared? When?"

"A little over six months ago... The same day I saw him for the first time."

"You alerted Interplan, I assume?"

"Obviously. The next morning, when we discovered that he was no longer in his cell."

"No news since then?"

"No... Nothing from the police about him. The investigation wrapped up quickly. There were no traces or useful clues."

"Thank you, Doctor," Coqdor said, surprised, before cutting off the communication.

About six months... The coincidence was too perfect to put it down to pure chance. Hadn't Muscat said that the Black Circle discreetly surfaced six months ago or thereabouts?

If the commissioner didn't know about this, which was likely since he hadn't mentioned it during his visit, he would soon find out.

And by Coqdor himself.

So only Giovanna was left. Before being a hostess on the Spica, which ran the regular Earth-Perseus route, the attractive young woman had lived on the Moon, more precisely in Tycho City where her fiancé, Jean-Marie Spontini, had been a technician of the wind tunnels supplying breathable air to the domed city. She had later been unfaithful to him by becoming the mistress of Cladek Halstar on whose behalf she had "spied on" the Sol-Perseus line.

During the trip from Ulmir to Accora, aboard the Comet Hyakutake, she had paid Coqdor a visit as baffling as it was disturbing, after which she had vanished again.

When she reappeared on Accora, she announced that she had become a member of the Zodiac.

This provided, at the same time, many and few clues about her.

Where to start?

Where to look for her?

And how to find her?

Suddenly, five melodious notes... The front door again.

Râx stretched and stood up, his whole being exuding an almost tangible worry.

It's not Muscat this time... thought Coqdor.

As a precaution, he grabbed a small paralyzer before walking through the vestibule.

The intercom screen showed no image.

The pstôr uttered a heartbreaking groan.

Silently, the Star Knight unlocked and cracked open the padded door, which swung completely open behind the weight pushing against it. The weight of a body that Bruno Coqdor barely had time to catch in his arms before it collapsed on the floor.

A bloodied, panting body, shaking and trembling, which only the worst fears can cause.

The body of a woman of statuesque beauty, even though she was blushed from all the vital fluid she had lost.

"Please, Chevalier Coqdor, help me, I beg you!" Giovanna Hi-Ling cried before fainting in the saving arms of the green-eyed man.

CHAPTER V

No sooner had Coqdor laid the inert young woman on the ground and closed the door three quarters than all hell broke loose on the wide landing.

Three dark figures came up the steps of the stone staircase, one step at a time. While releasing short bursts of inframauve, they performed an agile forward somersault then landed in front of the door.

There they stood still for a moment.

Which, on the one hand, allowed the Star Knight to identify them. Greenish skin, a dark collar of beard... Perseans! Night-colored suits... Minions of the Black Circle? In any case, killers tracking Giovanna Hi-Ling with the goal of eliminating her. Once and for all.

The very brief pause also gave him time to prepare his defense.

A very special, modulated whistle and the pstôr was crouching at his feet. Ready to take off as soon as the master fully reopened the door. Which was done a split second later. The winged beast soared off with astonishing speed while Coqdor emerged from his residence like an almost spectral apparition.

It had only taken a few seconds for him to concentrate and gather all his mental energy, which, in the form of zigzagging sparks, then seemed to spring from the pupils of his green eyes, literally glowing, to strike each of the three adversaries for the first time right on the forehead.

Destabilized, the Persean killers fumbled.

Râx dove at them and threw them to the ground, starting to attack them with strong blows of his membranous wings.

Then Coqdor sent out a second wave of psychic energy, combining it with ooim, the very special technique developed by the natives of the planets of Eridanus. A mix of athletics and philosophical meditation, it executed a kind of transcendental judo with dazzling holds to which no uninitiated person could block or escape.

The assassins barely had time to stand up. They bit the dust again even harder than the first time.

An ominous, ephemeral flash arose out of the chest of each of them.

They stopped moving.

The pstôr uttered a mournful howl as if he had foreseen the worst and understood that only a funeral oration was in order.

The Knight leaned over the three inanimate bodies. Pushing aside the collar of the suit of one of them, at heart level, he saw a zodiac tattoo.

Same thing for the other two.

On the other hand, it was not one of the signs already seen in this strange affair.

"This time, it's Scorpio," whispered the man with green eyes. "Stranger and stranger..."

A voice whose faintness could not mask its warmth answered him softly, "They're Cladek Halstar's minions!"

Coqdor turned around. Giovanna Hi-Ling had just woken up.

"Thank you, Chevalier... You saved my life... Their mission was to kill me—and they were going to take the opportunity to get rid of you too."

Slowly, the young woman stood up and Coqdor helped her to her feet.

"Forgive me for being a little too practical, but what should we do with the bodies, since they haven't auto-destructed?"

Briefly, he told her what Muscat had witnessed at Melun-3.

"It depends on how they're being remote-controlled," Giovanna replied. "Given my standing, I can make them disappear. Give me a minute..."

Still supported by her rescuer, she turned towards the three corpses, seemed to concentrate for a few seconds... and the three corpses vanished in an eerie greenish flame.

Coqdor stared at her with an inquisitive look but held off questioning her. Obviously, explanations would come shortly.

"If you want to use my bathroom..." he suggested. "You can clean yourself up to befit your natural beauty."

Offering her a supportive arm, he led Giovanna to the room decorated with iridescent marble imported from the jaspered planets of Gemini.

"Take your time, relax in the water. You'll find an oxiiz silk bathrobe in the wardrobe along with the towels. In the medicine cabinet, there's everything you need to treat your wounds. Intracorol, bandages..."

The Sino-Italian waved off the offer.

"No need, Chevalier... You know about my metamorphic faculties. Well, self-healing and even tissue regeneration—to a limited degree—are possible for me."

She entered the bathroom and, without any shame, without even turning her back to her savior, unfastened her tattered, blood-stained clothes.

Coqdor couldn't help but keep his eyes glued to her. Deep down, Giovanna troubled him. At that moment, the memory of the visit she had paid him aboard the *Comet Hyakutake* came back to mind. He had been on the verge of giving in to her intense femininity...

It was then that he noticed the tattoo on her left breast. The traditional symbol of Capricorn had replaced the lightning eagle.

"I have a lot to explain to you, Bruno Coqdor. You'll soon know all of my secrets... and more."

With his curiosity as aroused as his sensations, the Star Knight nodded in agreement.

"Meet me in the living room when you're done. I'll prepare a pick-me-up snack and drinks."

Before leaving, he whispered a few words, very quietly, to Râx,

"Stay here, my beautiful monster... Watch over our little friend. And take action if anything suspicious happens to her."

His large topaz eyes fixed on the grained wooden panel behind which Giovanna was washing, the pstôr sat down in front of the bathroom door. A Cerberus both comforting and disturbing at the same time, the front of his body enveloped in his bat-like wings, forming an infernal robe...

Half an hour later, draped in the Aquarius silk bathrobe whose monochrome patterns further enhanced her hybrid beauty and her very discreet but oh so harmonious shape, Giovanna had settled into one of the comfortable armchairs in the living room. Nothing was visible of the injuries she had received.

On the other side of the coffee table, near which Râx had inevitably come to lie down so as not to take his eyes off the woman he was to guard, the green-eyed man had also taken his place in a comfortable chair. Between him and his guest, on the inlaid tray, an appetizing snack was sitting with a whole range of non-alcohol drinks, cold and hot.

By chance, Coqdor had prepared a pitcher of blue tea from Canopus, with slightly euphoric properties, and a pot of wazuk from Sirius, the main competitor of earth coffee but endowed with more stimulating power. As the evening promised to be long, they would have to resist the inevitable onslaught of sleep.

Through the large windows decorated with geometric stained glass, the late afternoon sky displayed shades of colors presaging a shimmering twilight.

After eating some toast, nibbling two white Venus nectarines and drinking a large glass of Centaurian ambrosia, the young woman lit a faoz cigarette and began her story.

"You see that I bear the sign of Capricorn, Chevalier. Well yes, I reached the rank of Master of the Zodiac shortly after our final meeting on Accora. The one who introduced himself to you as our Guide, that ordinary, innocent-looking little man called Edward Brown—a name that will be useful for you to remember—inducted me into the higher circle of the brotherhood as a reward for the services rendered during your... intervention in our affairs. Even in spite of my first failure aboard the *Comet Hyakutake*."

Giovanna flashed a mysterious smile, the hidden meaning of which did not escape her host. He preferred to change the subject.

"In your organization, there are Masters, supreme initiates... and un-derlings, minions responsible for all kinds of activities. The three killers, for example..."

"Servants of the lowest rank, exactly!"

"However, their signs look pretty much the same as yours, to the laymen that I am..."

"Simple magnetodynamic microfiligree tattoos, thanks to which the Masters can control these individuals and even, if necessary, probe their psyche and remotely influence their behavior."

Coqdor was starting to understand. "People like Cladek Halstar, to drive him crazy, or Jean-Marie Spontini, to kill him?"

"Yes, dear soothsayer of the distant stars," the seductive mixed-race woman whispered. "Both were still on the lower rungs of the ladder—but they hid their double-dealing from us damn well. Take Halstar... The Martian banker managed to become very close friends with Brown and Rumia Dolon, the previous Master of Capricorn. In fact, he had suspect-ed that the Zodiac concealed a great secret of galactic if not universal magnitude and his only goal was to find it after having infiltrated our ranks."

"The dark story of cosmomancy, how does it fit in?"

"I'm getting there… Yum Akatinor, the Persean, is the one who somehow introduced this particular movement. Among his followers, Cladek Halstar, Jean-Marie Spontini and Luse Borek, who is also the founder of the Black Circle of which Jean-Marie was also a member, all belonged to another very secret group, the Cabal. Except for Luse, everyone operated so cleverly with Brown that he unhesitatingly marked them with the sign of the lightning eagle, the symbol of the constellation in which the Earth revolves if viewed from the twelve other worlds. When Rumia Dolon died, apparently of natural causes, Brown became suspicious. As if he suspected something, even though ignorant of the existence of the Cabal. Because Cladek had made it clear on several occasions that he desired to be inducted to replace Rumia Dolon. Which obviously didn't happen."

"And you, how did you fit into the affair?"

"Brown knew me as Spontini's fiancée and Cladek Halstar's mistress. He asked me to infiltrate the group. I operated with enough subtlety and discretion to quickly uncover the existence of the Cabal, without however managing to track down the whole network or identify the person or people who run it behind the scenes. After I told Brown about it, he summoned the other Masters of the Zodiac…"

"Did you meet them then?"

"No… I didn't participate in that strategic meeting. But I know who they are. Anyway, let's get back to the subject. Lord General Y Zeon, Master of Sagittarius, and thus the high commander of the space armies of the giant planet Arpam, came right out and declared that an occult movement like the Cabal with unclear motivations had to be nipped in the bud. The warlord had such charisma that he easily convinced a majority of the other Masters to vote in support of him. Yum Akatinor was sentenced to death and murdered. I was able to intercede on Cladek's behalf and save him from being eradicated because he wasn't an inherently bad person. This is why he was struck with dementia. Like this he was neutralized but without paying with his life."

"And your so-called fiancé?"

"Y Zeon, as a very discerning strategist, quickly understood that Jean-Marie was trying to manipulate Interplan in order to find me."

"It's true that you too had disappeared somewhere on the Sol-Perseus line…"

"I had to! I was risking a lot after the role I had just played. The few financial associates of Halstar involved in the Cabal, too trite to need to be eliminated and Noa Akatinor, Yum's brother, also a cosmomancer, were surely going to hunt me down to avenge the dead... So, Spontini was judged as a proven threat by Y Zeon. Brown saw things his way and decided to put him down. Which your friend Robin Muscat witnessed."

Bruno Coqdor nodded without responding. This silent assent allowed him to launch a discreet psychic probe into the mind of his fascinating visitor and to verify her sincerity.

Giovanna had perceived the mental intrusion and had not resisted it, quite the contrary. She gave him an unequivocal smile and wet her lips with the tip of her tongue so sensually that it would have damned an Altaïr monk.

The Star Knight only responded with a deadpan stare of his green eyes—a look that spoke volumes.

The beautiful Sino-Italian woman poured herself a cup of wazuk, took a sip and resumed her tale.

"As you can imagine, it was thanks to Brown that I was able to disappear at the right time. Shortly after, he proposed me to succeed Rumia Dolon. I then received the Capricorn sign, both subcutaneously and on my left breast, thus attaining the rank of Master. I could now use the Accora rotunda to make inter-world journeys and I also benefited from the incredible powers which initially allowed me to throw you into total confusion on board the *Comet Hyakutake*."

"The inexplicable appearance and disappearance, a common bolt that almost made me trip in the corridor then turned out to be impossible to find... And Yloa Flugg who 'stepped aside' for you as if by magic, on Accora..."

"Yes, metamorphic talent is the prerogative of the Masters. My entry on the scene under the identity of the Persean girl from Xow'Tal, thrown into the decadence of the Bird Woman in the sinister underworld of Ulmir, was a test of loyalty imposed on me by the other Masters. My mission was more to guide you—remember, I was the one who gave you the name Accora of Capricorn—and at the same time to judge you, to evaluate you. In this, I wholly satisfied them. You too, by the way. Because without Brown's agreement, you would never have reached the Capricorn rotunda."

"And that's when it all ended for us. As you know, neither Muscat nor I have ever betrayed the secret of the inter-world gates. We respected our given word..."

"An important factor as far as I'm concerned! Some time after your return to Earth, the other Masters ratified my induction and our brotherhood once again withdrew into the shadows."

"Until its recent reappearance, indirect if I may... So what happened recently for the Zodiac to resurface?"

"Good question, Chevalier! There are, everywhere in the Universe, people who are stubbornly resentful and whose desire for revenge never wanes once it takes hold in their minds. Noa Akatinor is one of them. A formidable being for his stubbornness, his tenacity, and also his attachment to his brother... Noa never gave up, even if no one noticed anything. Through extensive underground work, he ended up learning the great secret of the Zodiac. How and by whom exactly, we have no idea... But from the moment he became aware of the identity of the Masters, in particular those who had voted for the elimination of Yum, he has been set on hunting them down and eliminating them one by one."

"How many deaths are there on his blacklist?" Coqdor asked casually.

"Seven... I can tell you who they were, given what is planned for you," Giovanna declared mysteriously. "Geo Martus of Virgo was the first to fall victim. Noa took his medallion and stole all his powers. Then, he was able to kill the wise Met-Pa Na'Tou, Master of Cancer, the fiery Dolxa Roren of Leo, the ardent Serah Li'ing of Aries, the whimsical Boarg Dar of Gemini and the generous Armaa Annabi of Libra. Very recently, after a more difficult encounter, he defeated the charismatic Y Zeon from Sagittarius, as if he had saved the best and most symbolic for last, the one who was the first to call for the death of Yum Akatinor."

"Did he attack you too?"

"No... I was inducted after the famous vote. Those guys chasing me, as I told you, were cohorts of Cladek Halstar. He escaped from Sainte-Anne a little over six months ago, in a way that no one has yet to understand. You might think he had regained his senses because since then he has apparently acted with full knowledge of the facts. It was he who eliminated the enigmatic Annepie Wagre, Master of Scorpio, whose medallion he took. The henchmen of the late Annepie thus came under his control and he set them after me, also in revenge since I once betrayed him."

"Do you think they helped him escape? And that those who did this also rescued him from his madness?"

"There's really no other logical explanation... It's unheard-of, even among initiates of the Zodiac. But we don't have the slightest idea about who 'they' are or the slightest clue that could lead us to these people..."

Bruno Coqdor thought for a moment while contemplating the sky which was turning purple over Paris. The first air traffic beacons were turning on, the magnificent network of lighted lanes began to take shape. And at the tip of the towers of Notre-Dame, the two star-shaped lights shined more and more brightly.

"I had a visit from my friend Robin Muscat, not long before your... arrival, Giovanna. He informed me of all the recent events related to the Black Circle and the Zodiac. I've concluded, in my personal opinion, that the latter is not responsible for these rather dramatic incidents. In this, Muscat and I have divergent opinions because he, the Cartesian cop steeped in logic, never considered you exonerated by the revelations you made to us about Accora. No... I'm pretty sure that a third crony is pulling the strings in the shadows, an enemy who is very likely manipulating the Black Circle in order to cast shame on the Zodiac by passing it off as the instigator of all the problems. A campaign, a... cabal, yes, in a way!"

The Chinese-Italian leaned towards him, scrutinizing him with a look burning with admiration. "You think you're right... and you are right!

"How many Masters are still alive?"

"Besides me, at least two, to my knowledge. Those whom I've had recent contact with, Edward Brown, who lives in London, and Ka'Pholgar, the group's theorist, a person of insatiable curiosity."

"Where is he?"

"In Maakeldar, in the Magistral City of the Arcana of Knowledge..."

"On the planet Mîo in the constellation Aquarius!" Coqdor cut in impulsively. "I had the opportunity to visit this mecca of wisdom in the past. Ah, I should have suspected that... A scholar from this fabulous people as Master of this sign, that's obvious... And the others whom you haven't heard from?"

"The ambiguous Rivu Gaabi from Pisces and the efficient Sansi Screï from Taurus. Troubling rumors connected to the growing powers of the Black Circle make us fear that they've been killed by Luse Borek himself."

"The situation is therefore more than serious, dear," the Star Knight concluded. "Firstly because of the threat hovering over your heads, then because Muscat, given the scale of the affair, has decided to spill the beans about the Zodiac and the inter-world gates. For the first time, he and I parted on a bitter note. Which alone means something. Moreover, before long, the High Council of Interplan will be on the case and they will rush to get a wide police and military involvement. In my opinion, we have to leave as quickly as possible for London in order to protect Brown. And to keep you safe at the same time."

"But how and with whom? I can't go alone..."

"Far be it from me to abandon you, Giovanna. Râx and I are going with you. I'll call immediately to charter my personal helijet. It'll be ready within an hour and will be waiting for us on the terraced part of my roof. Until then, we have time to prepare and equip ourselves with some carefully chosen items. One detail: will you mind being dressed as a boy? Here, women's clothing is conspicuous by its absence..."

The woman got up from her chair and smiled while undoing the fastenings of her silk bathrobe. "Being dressed as a boy sounds just fine to me... provided I've had a few moments to be a woman, beforehand."

A few steps of feline grace and she snuggled up against the Star Knight whose senses ignited in a flash upon contact with a small but ideally proportioned and ever so shapely body. Now, nothing was holding Coqdor back. The barriers of distrust had definitively come crashing down.

"Now that you trust me, Bruno, make me forget that icy slap you once gave me on the *Comet Hyakutake*."

An hour later, most of which felt like a fleeting eternity while the two lovers let bloom an ardent passion that opened views onto infinity, a helijet discreetly lifted off the roof terrace of the Ile Saint-Louis building and rose diagonally into the Paris sky, calm as it usually was on Friday evenings.

The centuries-old customs had hardly changed. When the week was over, many city dwellers fled the city as if they had all its demons on their heels in order to recharge their batteries in more natural, more human settings in the countryside or by the sea.

Facing the pilot control panel, pressed closely together, Giovanna Hi-Ling and Bruno Coqdor monitored the instruments. Dressed identically in very functional suits allowing them, if necessary, to operate comfortably in almost any environment, armed prudently but properly, steeped in worry but infused with the hope of still being able to act in time.

Anticipating a perilous adventure, the Chevalier had brought several of his precious transdim discs, well protected in one of the cases hanging on his belt.

Behind them, on the floor of the passenger compartment, taking up all the space needed for his comfort, lay the little beast born in the rays of the distant sun of Dzo, the Star of Satan from which, thanks to the Earth-lings, the Devil had been chased away for good. Râx, his big topaz eyes riveted on the couple without any hostility or jealousy, brooded with a protective air over the companion whose passionate affections his master had just enjoyed. Perhaps, at this charming sight, he dreamed fervently of Mademoiselle Shô, the adorable female pstôr awaiting him in the leg-endary City of the Doges.

But the road to Venice was starting with a detour via London, and other detours could not be ruled out...

CHAPTER VI

"...From the moment we got back to Earth by inter-world transport from Accora of Capricorn up to the mysterious escape of Cladek Halstar, about six months ago, we haven't heard a peep out of the Zodiac. You'll have to admit that such a long calm should reassure us about the commitment made, that oath of silence that Bruno Coqdor and I had in some way sworn to the Guide of this bewildering organization!"

"Without forgetting the fact," Marc Vérano said diplomatically, "that the famous transdimensional doors had been destroyed or at least heavily damaged very shortly afterwards, as if to say that this transportation system was once and for all out of use."

"An illusion! Deliberate deception!" Councilor Maxan Dao thundered. "A false pretense staged by an occult group of rebels who have never stopped plotting to take over the Galaxy! And who will soon succeed because you have shamefully covered them up, Muscat, by conspiring with *your* Star Knight..."

The Centaurian, one of the five members of the High Council of Interplan whose jurisdiction was not limited to the three planets of the Martervenux, was expressing his hostility towards Bruno Coqdor with the scathing emphasis on the possessive.

It did not date from yesterday. No one knew on what occasion the Terran had managed to offend the citizen of the Empire of Alpha XXI, but there had been a problem.

Furthermore, the animosity had found fertile ground in the pathological distrust shown by the Centaurian towards everything he considered uncontrolled and uncontrollable. A maverick like Coqdor, not part of the Interstellar Militia or any police force, not an agent of any government or of the tri-planetary alliance called the Martervenux, was just a troublemaker who was unacceptable to the conservative Centaurian ethics.

To make matters worse, Robin Muscat had just revealed that the Star Knight and himself were part of a conspiracy of silence protecting the Zodiac!

Suffice it to say that on this Monday morning, at the Parisian head-quarters of Interplan where a special High Council had been convened urgently, the atmosphere was heavy, stormy, electric...

Worthy of the worst seasons of the distant fiery planet over there in the constellation Boötes—where Muscat does not remember having sweated as heavily as in this air-conditioned courtroom.

Facing the accused duo—because how could they have considered themselves otherwise, now that the beans had been spilled?—sat the five High Councilors. In addition to Maxan Dao from Centauri, there were Judge Alice DeWitt from New Amsterdam, acting as president, Chief Magistrate Gil Galin from Mars, Legarch Amahler from Altaïr, and Dr. Tanya Seline of Ozamara.

"I refute the term conspiracy," Muscat countered after a minute of reflection. "The magnitude of what was revealed to us about Accora, the dramatic consequences of improper use of the rotundas and the profound wisdom of the Guide convinced us to swear to stay silent because it was all for the good of the galactic peoples. And I have to admit that we couldn't conspire because we decided on the spot, without even consulting together...

"An admissible argument, in my opinion," the president intervened. "On the other hand, Councilor Dao, your attacks against Bruno Coqdor are unfounded given all the services rendered by the Star Knight to so many races of our cosmos. I will therefore not take them into account."

The Centaurian frowned and looked sullen.

"It is nevertheless true," Alice DeWitt continued, "that Robin Muscat should have revealed the secret of the Zodiac to the Praesidium of the Martervenux and that by not having done so from the beginning he failed in his duty. Of course, he's making up for it today, but it's a little late. I will therefore ask that a sanction be imposed on him with a warning to be put on his record. His record of service justifies, in my opinion, that we go no further."

"I agree with you, President," Gil Galin declared, the mixed-blood Terro-Martian with big sad eyes. "Especially since if I understood correctly, the commissioner is not inactive in the Black Circle affair and that with Inspector Vérano he has come up with a few operational plans on this matter. What exactly is it, Muscat? Do you think you will also strike at the Zodiac by attacking the Black Circle? Because for us, these are two faces of the same threat, you understand that..."

"The data is starting to accumulate," replied the party being questioned. "There are still some gray areas in the overall picture, such as Cladek Halstar's escape, and we're waiting until we've shed some light on them before launching our planned actions."

"We're waiting…" repeated Maxan Dao in a sarcastic tone bordering on offensive insolence. "That's not Muscat! It's Coqdor! Coqdor Cunctator, the procrastinator… This is the perfect nickname that goes far back in the history of your planet, Gentlemen of the Earth! Confound such procrastination, Muscat. By spending too much time with this mesmerist with magnetic eyes, you got caught in his nets and hypnotized by the sneaky spider. You can think only like him now… and be wrong. We have to act, not build castles in the air!"

"I approve of this position," the discreet Altairian interjected. "First, I request action to take control of the Terran Rotunda…in what I believe you call the Hoggar? It's imperative to cut off this strategic route for our enemies. Then, the Black Circle… Tell us what you learned from what was seized at Melun-3!"

It was Marc Vérano, at the heart of the problem, who took the floor.

"The recovered discs have supported the plan of a serious operation on Venus against the headquarters of this new mafia. Most of the data turned out to be unusable, not encrypted but garbled in such a way that it was unreadable. Except what concerns the situation of this HQ, in the underbelly of the city that we all know as Ishtar Terra, and against which we are considering military action."

Alice DeWitt spoke again:

"As president of this high authority, I approve the approach which has just been presented and I therefore declare the special operation named 'Ravenclaw' to be launched. First objective, the Hoggar. Second objective, Ishtar Terra. Commissioner Muscat and Inspector Vérano, you have complete freedom to carry it out successfully. You will benefit from all the resources of Interplan and the Interstellar Militia."

Then, looking Muscat straight in the eyes, she concluded:

"Your misconduct, your… lie by omission will be struck from the record if this operation succeeds, of which I have no doubt. May the Master of the Cosmos be with you, Messieurs!"

Tanya Seline coughed slightly, asking for the floor. She had not spoken since the beginning of the session.

"Commissioner Muscat, do you know where the Star Knight is now?"

"I visited him last Friday, so a little less than three days ago, Doctor, as I mentioned at the start of the session. Since Saturday morning, however, I've tried several times to contact him but have been unsuccessful. Bruno Coqdor left his Parisian home and I don't know where he is at the moment... However, his helijet is in the garage."

"He fled, he's hiding!" Maxan Dao exploded. "You told him you were going to spill the beans about the Zodiac and he hopped away like a whore..."

"A hare, Councilor," Alice DeWitt corrected, having great difficulty holding back a sudden burst of laughter.

"Never mind!" the Centaurian thundered. "It is the attitude of a guilty person, of a conspirator who fears for his freedom. And he's right! I demand that the High Council issue an arrest warrant for him!"

"Objection, Councilor! Refusal, even!" the president countered, seconded by the other councilors. "There's no reason for this. Coqdor is a free citizen—declared innocent and I insist on this point! If, in the future, it appears that his actions deserve punishment, we will then take counsel. But for the moment..."

Turning red, Maxan Dao stood up, gesticulating and puffing out his chest to flaunt all his ire against the entire Universe. Alice DeWitt, even more amused by the appearance of this character who suddenly looked like a moldy bullfrog from Capella VIII, violently hit her desk with her symbolic hammer and made a mighty effort to control herself and declare in a voice as sharp as glass:

"Meeting adjourned! Robot clerk, transfer the minutes to my office, I will sign them immediately. Thank you all, you're free to go!"

Early in the afternoon of that same Monday, phase one of Operation Ravenclaw began when three heavily armed helijets took off from the Interplan Air Base, a vast complex located in what had once been the plain of Saint-Denis, and immediately headed due south towards the African continent.

Aboard Ravenclaw I Muscat and Vérano were prepared to face the Hoggar and its mysteries. During the two hours that the flight lasted, the elder informed the neophyte of what awaited them there and of the path they would have to take to the inter-world rotunda, dubbed in coded language as Ravenclaw Point.

So upon arrival, when the three aircraft landed at the foot of the mountain in question, the young inspector already felt almost at home.

While two armed detachments guarded the helijets, the two Interplan officers and a commando of twelve soldiers advanced to the entrance of the maze they would have to traverse.

Cleverly concealed by two sections of rock which, from a distance, seemed to present no break in continuity, access to the maze of caves looked like the menacing mouth of some monster watching over the solitude of the nearby desert.

Very quickly, the bare stone forming the walls of the tunnel turned into a strange mineral substance glowing with a pale luminosity. Bathed in this weird phosphorescence the men moved forward without fear of physical danger but as if possessed by an unconscious apprehension whose source lay in the most sinister legends of the Earth.

Muscat remembered the discovery of the empire of Queen Antinea, one of the countless versions of Atlantis that the romantic literature of the past had produced. If the fascinating Queen encountered by Captain Morhange and Lieutenant de Saint-Avit had really existed, she must have been initiated into the mysteries of the Zodiac.

He also remembered the strange story told by very young adventurers at the time when an accidental nuclear cataclysm had thrown the planet into a chaos of atomic fire. It was towards the end of the 20th century, shortly before the Third World War. According to them, they had discovered by chance, in a massif of Western Sahara where the simoon caused by the catastrophe had exposed diverse ruins, a mix of different ages and places, an unimaginable stone clock with twelve sectors marked with the twelve signs of the Zodiac and whose pointer, positioned on the absolute midnight of the Universe, marked the opening of a passage to a parallel Earth. Thus, the members of the small group had escaped radioactive death and experienced adventures straight out of the wildest imagination in the world of Mulkis, contemporary with that of Atlantis.[33] Finally, they had earned the right, long after, to return to their original world. Reality or invention? Only a very clever person could have said... The fact remained that their testimony, collected by a writer with a very fertile pen, had given rise to an entertaining little novel which Muscat had greatly enjoyed in his early youth.

Vérano did not see all these things with the same background. In any case, for him, there was no question of thinking about Atlantis! Among the memoirs of his distant 20th century ancestor, Teddy Vérano, the occult detective, was the truly strange narration of a confrontation

---

[33] See *Il est Minuit à l'Univers*.

with creatures straight out of ancient Greek mythology. Cerberus, the three-headed dog, Hercules, the chained giant, the golden apples from the Garden of the Hesperides—unfortunately falling into the possession of an excavator of sunken submarines—were mixed up in a pretty hermetic manner by survivors of Atlantis in order to hide their existence from humans on the surface.[34] There, the legendary sunken continent was clearly located on the side of the Santorini volcano, close to Crete, under the blue waves of the Mediterranean. Absolutely not here, therefore. Here in the Hoggar Mountains, it was definitely something else.

With their imaginations working overtime, the endless descent through the tunnels with luminescent walls did not seem to last forever. And finally the two Interplan men and the Militia commando came to the entrance of a corridor with a flat floor, through a doorway surmounted by a lintel bearing the sign of the lightning eagle. At the end of this corridor, Muscat knew, the phenomenal inter-world rotunda awaited them.

Fascinated as he was, Vérano had not let up his usual vigilance and not a detail had escaped him. It was he who first saw the footprints in the dust on the floor of the gallery.

"Look, boss! People have been here. And it was long after your visit!"

"Indeed," Muscat affirmed. "But... These prints go towards the rotunda and none come back! Let's go!"

They had to go around a fairly large rock that partially blocked access to the fabulous place. Then the two Interplan officers and the soldiers passed through the door marked with the symbol of the Eagle—the constellation where Earth belongs—and entered the rotunda, finding themselves enveloped in a strange pale gold light. On either side of them, the twelve other interdimensional doorways were there, most of them collapsed, blocked by rubble, which prevented them from being used as such.

Muscat and Vérano saw this first before their eyes drifted to the ground and saw the corpse.

Lying in a pool of blood, the chest shredded, the body lacerated with horrible red scars...

"God of the Cosmos..." the commissioner whispered. "It's the Zodiac Guide."

Indeed it was... The small man, dressed in very ordinary planetary attire, wearing thick contact lenses that made even more horrific his my-

---

[34] See *Une Morsure de feu.*

opic gaze forever open to the unknown of the beyond, was certainly the man, both banal and transcendent, whom they had once met on Accora of Capricorn.

A kind of ritual knife with a crystal blade was stuck in his chest. An unusual crystal with a transparency subtly clouded by fleeting, almost unreal colors.

"But it's orichalcum," Vérano stated in surprise. "The crystal of the ancient Atlanteans..."

He leaned over the murdered man and pulled out a small detection device from a holster on his belt.

Muscat, leaving him to work, examined the place again.

"The doors are inaccessible," he confirmed. "No footprints leave here. Where did the murderer escape to?"

"I can't tell you that," announced his young colleague, 'but I can tell you who it is..."

The commissioner turned towards him.

"Well?"

"It's terrible, boss..." Vérano said, standing up. "And the portable scanner is positive. The fingerprints on the dagger belong to..."

He paused, dismayed by the revelation he was about to declare.

"Well?" Muscat urged. "They're not mine, damn it! Speak up!"

The next moment, he felt like a bottomless abyss had just opened under his feet.

"Bruno Coqdor!" Verano sighed. "They're the fingerprints of the Star Knight."

CHAPTER VII

Shortly after takeoff of his private helijet, Coqdor took control from the autopilot and began a series of complicated maneuvers. Several detours, sudden changes of course, dives and ascents followed one after another, as if the Knight was trying hard to not know where he was going.

Obviously, the sole purpose of this false flight plan was to cover his tracks and shake off any potential pursuers.

It was to the south of the Breton peninsula that he reached the sea and changed course again for England, skimming over the relatively calm waves of the Atlantic.

There was no one behind them. On the laseradar screen, not the slightest spot hinted that they might have been followed.

So at dawn on Saturday they were approaching the outer suburbs of London-on-Earth.

In this 23rd century, the former capital of White Albion epitomized more than ever the fundamental values of its inhabitants. If Paris-sur-Terre, the Dazzling City, had focused more on the arts for which it was at the top of the ladder in the Milky Way, even while it also housed the headquarters of Interplan, London, for its part, was thoroughly focused on money, finance and commerce.

It was the center of business not only for the Martervenux, but also for the entire United Star Confederation. The primary icon of this thousand-year-old vocation, the GME or Galactic Mercantile Exchange, with its breathtaking architecture dominated the district that had formerly been called the City and which, spread over seven vertical levels stacked like a wedding cake, buzzed like a frenetic hive where all those whose responsibility it was to crank the cogs of cosmic finance lived and worked.

The GME itself came alive several times a day with apparently uncontrollable excitement during the stock quotation sessions of the biggest interstellar companies.

Chevalier Coqdor felt thousands of light years away from all this agitation around figures whose purpose was the enrichment of some to the detriment of others, the virtual or even fictitious possession of material goods that brought an ephemeral illusion of power and happiness, access to the apparent pinnacle of a pyramid based on money and domination.

For him, it was impossible to find an atom of interest or motivation here. None of this gave security to the living in the face of the unknown and the threats lurking throughout the Universe. None of this gave them the slightest chance of becoming better in themselves so that their soul, once freed from carnal bonds, might take the path of the eternal dawns instead of seeing itself cast into the abyss where the damned wandered.

Finance was perhaps the incarnation of a necessary evil, but he could not help but think that all this energy focused on other purposes would have contributed much more to improving the lives of every person, materially for sure, but especially spiritually.

According to the information provided by Giovanna, the man named Edward Brown was one of the senior analysts of the omnipotent GME and, as such, enjoyed a corporate apartment on the fifth floor of the "wedding cake."

Coqdor therefore merged his helijet into the air traffic network which crisscrossed the foggy sky of London-on-Earth, exactly like the marked lanes set up over Paris.

After getting directions to reach his desired location, he reached the fifth level parking zone and left his vehicle in a temporary slot. Immediately a robot in human form, sparkling with numerous lights on its golden outer shell, rushed towards the visitors and greeted them with a ready-made polite phrase.

An odd detail: the android was wearing a cap like the ones once worn by the drivers of the famous London taxis and on which one could read, in fluorescent holo: O'Neill & O'Neill – London's First Valet Company.

The gleaming machine would take the helijet to the storage box that the central brain had assigned to it and would only bring it out after the call announcing the imminent return of its passengers.

Seeing the pstôr disembark behind the couple, the robot seemed to pause and several colored lights flashed on its front display strip. Conditioned, obviously, by the principles of the stiff upper lip, whose stamp had survived the centuries, he held back from any comment and stood aside for the three characters, before taking a seat in the vehicle.

"Here we are and without any problems. Thanks, Bruno!" Giovanna whispered. "Now follow me, I know the way!"

Fortunately...

Without a plan and without a guide, Coqdor and Râx would never have managed to find their way.

On the heels of the beautiful Sino-Italian woman, they crossed a veritable maze of richly decorated lobbies, common spaces designed for relaxation and informal meetings, and shopping arcades full of the most eclectic merchandise imported from the four corners of the Galaxy. There was an endless supply of pubs, color relief cinemas, swimming pools, fitness centers, restaurants for every imaginable customer, human and non-human.

It had all had been planned so that the employees of the all-powerful GME had everything on site to lead a pleasant life, guaranteeing the best possible productivity and efficiency, without having to leave the premises at any time except during their four weeks of annual paid vacation.

The civil servants working here received healthy salaries of which they were able to save a significant part, in particular because commuting costs were zero and rents were very cheap. So, when retirement came, they had amassed what was needed to buy a luxurious villa on the fantastic beaches of the leisure planets of Altaïr-12, a small farm on the vast plains of Dissixuma-14, a forest ranch deep in the Phocca Woods of Cassiopeia, or a private microasteroid in the belt of the Koar system, that charming collection of wandering rocks at the edge of the constellation Hercules...

As the trio entered one of the lobbies (this one with an almost exclusively plant-based decor) an individual seated in a Betelgeuse leather armchair reacted quickly when he saw that the two humans and the pstôr were going to pass by him.

As if moved by a spring, the man jumped from his seat and hid himself with very effective discretion behind an enormous green plant harvested from the swamps of Venus.

In fact, the Star Knight and even his favorite animal were likely to recognize him...

Veering off to bypass a group of businessmen in the middle of a discussion, Coqdor, Giovanna and Râx walked around thirty feet away from the large flowering bush with fleshy leaves. They were just far enough away for the mysterious person to let out a sigh of relief and contact his no less mysterious associate using a cutting-edge transmitter bracelet still unknown on the worlds of the Martervenux and the United Star Confederation.

Twenty minutes later, Giovanna stopped in front of one of the countless doors lining either side of a long hallway that was indistinguishable from thousands of others.

"It's here," she said, pressing a button and placing her face level with the retinal scan system.

"Welcome, Miss Hi-Ling," a synthetic voice announced. "You can come in."

The panel slid sideways and the three visitors went through the doorway. At the other end of the small entranceway, Edward Brown was waiting for them.

"Dear Giovanna, Chevalier Coqdor... and you, magnificent pstôr," the Zodiac Guide said while petting with sincere kindness the head of Râx who purred with pleasure. "I'm happy to welcome you to my modest home... even if the visit is serious. Follow me and make yourself comfortable, my friends."

"It's an honor and a great pleasure to see you again after such a long time, Master," Bruno replied, a little touched and impressed.

As he walked to the simple but comfortable armchairs in the lounge area of the main room, which also included a tiny built-in kitchen, one part serving as a bedroom with a single bed and another part converted into an office, he glanced out through the bay window that had a breathtaking view of London and its ancient monuments. Or more precisely, the identical reconstructions carried out after the city had been razed almost entirely during the Third World War.

By the time Brown served his guests an assortment of Scottish shortbreads with traditional tea, and not a single one of the many variations from distant worlds that true Englishmen had never been able to stomach, Coqdor recalled memories of the Tower of London museum, the imposing bell tower of Big Ben and the architectural curiosity of the famous London Bridge.

"I'm not surprised to see you here this morning," the little man said, "given recent events. News travels fast among the initiates of the Zodiac... especially as few as we are now. There are only five of us left, maybe three if we admit that Rivu Gaabi and Sansi Screï have been killed. The Cabal has hit hard...and I fear it's not over yet."

"That's why you have to react quickly to get to safety and counterattack," Giovanna said.

"I don't see how to fight back," Brown admitted. "I've never been very keen on combat and violence, in whatever form. But as far as self-protection is concerned, it's already done as far as I'm concerned. As you know, the world of finance is a merciless, no holds barred jungle. I just had to pretend that an industrial company, upset at having been undercut—because of a lack of attention on my part—had sent me graphic death threats and the GME security services were mobilized. Plus, I was given authorization to work from home for a period of one month, renewable if necessary."

"I doubt that conventional security forces would be able to oppose Noa Akatinor," Coqdor objected. "As much as I don't worry about Ka'Pholgar, knowing the Mîos, Maakeldar and the Magistral City, I don't trust any protective measures for you and for Giovanna. That's why I'm here."

"And I am grateful to you, Chevalier," the little man said, handing Râx a piece of shortbread, a gesture which, in the simple mind of the pstôr, classified the kind man in the category of friends. "An ally like you is precious to us. To be honest, I don't understand how Akatinor went about killing our colleagues, even if he is gifted with powers identical to theirs, because these make them almost invulnerable or at least particularly difficult to defeat..."

Bruno Coqdor seized the opportunity.

"By the way, Brown, these powers... The last time we saw each other—the one and only time, in fact—on Accora, you revealed to us the secret of the Zodiac... or what we considered then as such, seeing that we were so stunned by the spectacular information about instantaneous transportation between the thirteen constellations. However, it was only one part. The tip of an iceberg, the visible facet of a much larger mystery of which I'm just starting to glimpse the other aspects. So, I'm also thinking that there's an even greater secret behind all this..."

Edward Brown gave him a genuine smile and his thick contact lenses could not hide the sparkling flame that shone in his eyes. No malice, but collusion and complicity. The Star Knight had guessed right.

"Share your thoughts, my friend! Your vision of things must be very interesting."

"Let's talk about this instant transportation. Certainly, it's practical to be able to move from world to world in such a discreet and rapid way, but it's only ever thirteen worlds and what's more, we leave and arrive at very specific points in each of them!"

The Guide and Giovanna nodded.

"Ultimately, it can be quite useful to a handful of criminals or thugs wishing to carry out very small-scale trafficking," Coqdor continued, "but to go elsewhere and farther while being free to choose starting points and destinations, a spacecraft capable of diving into subspace is much more convenient."

"Therefore," Brown said, "the Zodiac is a rather limited medium, according to you..."

"Absolutely! As it is, it is no cosmic Grail whose quest should set in motion factions like the Black Circle and the Cabal on this scale. That the thirteen rotundas were the only reason for the battle that began would be a heresy to me. In other words, the stakes would not be worth the effort."

Coqdor stopped for a moment to take a sip of tea, then he continued:

"Add to this these powers that you possess, faculties belonging to maybe very advanced mutants... If this is not the result of biogenetic evolution, which is very unlikely in your respective cases, if these gifts are not innate, well... it's because they're acquired. This deduction stems from what Giovanna told me about Noa Akatinor. He stripped the Masters of their attributes and by doing so obtained their powers. Thanks to the medallions, perhaps? You too were careful not to reveal their existence to us! And there you have it, Monsieur Brown. All of this together boils down to one fundamental question..."

The quiet senior analyst of the GME uncrossed his legs and leaned towards his guest, "Which is?"

"What is the real secret of the Zodiac?"

At first, Brown did not answer. He turned to Giovanna and stared straight into her eyes for a moment, as if to confer with her, before turning back to Coqdor.

"If you're here at my house and if you've come this far on your journey, it's because you're ready to hear the answer to your question. And also to fulfill our greatest hopes... You yourself, personally, by becoming one of us!" He paused briefly. "So I'll explain everything to you, Star Knight..."

Among everything that the Zodiac Guide was going to explain to Bruno Coqdor, one important detail was missing. That of the encrypted radio conversation which had taken place an hour earlier, in the lobby with its plant decor, between the mysterious individual who had hidden as the trio approached and his companion located some distance away.

"The foreseen risk has come to pass," the man sheltered behind the giant Venusian plant said. "Halstar's three henchmen failed to remove Giovanna Hi-Ling. Too bad our ex-madman was so set upon his personal revenge... He was too emotionally involved to succeed, especially since he's still unstable. It was easier for him with the Scorpio Master."

"Halstar is inept," his interlocutor thundered in a gravelly voice. "He's a stupid lamb, an easy pigeon to pluck if you know how to make him coo with vanity. The guy won't get very far and if he doesn't screw it all up, we'll take care of it. He's the straw that threatens to make the whole thing come crashing down. On the other hand, as for the Guide and that dirty mongrel..."

"I understand. We have to keep to the plan as it was programmed, therefore eliminate them and get their medallions."

"That's why I'm going to send you Noa Akatinor, my dear D. As the occult leader of the Cabal, I will have no trouble persuading him to act immediately for our desired goal."

The so-called D raised a surprising objection.

"The new problem is Coqdor... He's teaming up with the other two and the members of the Black Circle who have already infiltrated the City will be no match for him. But since it's out of the question to have him killed by Akatinor..."

"We must find another way to neutralize him without killing him. Let us never forget the positive attitude he once showed us and that he was fundamentally against what happened there in the vicinity of..."

"But if he persists in standing in our way, what are we going to do?"

"In that case, we'll figure something out. In the meantime, return to your flat. Signal me as soon as you get there to let me know that you're ready to receive the... transmission."

"Give me five minutes, boss!"

"Okay, D."

After about 300 seconds, Mr. D. had locked himself in his tiny apartment and pressed a button on his special communications bracelet.

Somewhere above London, a transmitting ray of an equally special nature unfamiliar to known galactic civilizations shot out of a giant, utterly black lens. This incredible thing was in the bowels of a rather strange spaceship, anchored in geostationary orbit above the British City. It looked like a baroque machine straight out of a spacecraft cemetery, built from odds and ends of several wrecks thrown together to make a sphere about a hundred feet high, clunky, bulging in its mid-section, everywhere else dinged and dented.

This unsightly masterpiece was, moreover, dirty, as if covered in rust, greasy streaks mixed with remnants of cosmic dust.

And yet, in contrast to its pitiful appearance, the ship was full of devices made from a subtle technology, brilliant in more ways than one, but not up to the usual norms. With a result that it was armed and able to challenge any war unit up to the combat supercruisers, which were the monopoly of the Sagittarians...

A fraction of a second later, like a demon vomited from the dark abysses of outer space, Noa Akatinor rematerialized in Mr. D's flat.

CHAPTER VIII

"The great secret of the Zodiac, Chevalier Coqdor, is what we call the ALEPH... Consciousness, the primordial soul of the Universe, what existed at its beginning and will exist at its end. The Aleph is everywhere and nowhere at the same time, it is simultaneously any point and infinity."

"It's God you're talking about, Mr. Brown," the green-eyed man said. "Not that of one or another of the ancient religions, but this unique principle which includes the cross, the six-pointed star, the crescent and so many other symbols throughout the worlds..."

"Maybe yes, maybe no. It certainly comes close. At the dawn of Creation, in the fraction of the second that followed the Big Bang, it was the Aleph itself that created the thirteen inter-world rotundas and the thirteen medallions. You know now, Chevalier, the use of doors as a means of passage from one planet of the Zodiac to another. What you don't know is that the thirteen rotundas allow you to communicate with the Aleph, to enter into it. For this, each of the thirteen initiates or Masters must have taken their place in the rotunda of their own planet. With all of them, they can then evoke the purely immaterial, virtual fourteenth rotunda which alone gives access to the Aleph.

"It's also what inducts the initiates. Nothing can happen without the agreement and intervention of the Aleph. And since it is the Absolute Whole, it allows the Masters to have certain spiritual and psychic powers as well as the ability to model and remodel matter."

"If I understand correctly, through the Aleph we can control the very substance of the Universe? And it's this gift that it grants you during... the inauguration that makes you shapeshifters, isn't it?" the Star Knight asked.

"Exactly," Edward Brown said.

"I still don't see what's the attraction for dark forces like the Black Circle and the Cabal," Coqdor wondered.

To which the innocuous little man replied sharply, "I haven't finished my speech, my friend. Let me get to the end in logical order and then you'll see!"

A short silence followed while the three humans drank a cup of tea to wash down the cakes, which Râx also enjoyed.

"The Aleph is also a catalyst for evolution," Brown continued. "When the races of our cosmos have reached a certain degree of spiritual maturity, they will be able to use the doors to merge with the Aleph and in turn become Alephs of other Creations, of other universes... This is how the eternal cycle revolves, which must never be broken. It's while waiting for this moment, this transfiguration that the guardians, the thirteen Masters of the Zodiac, are responsible for protecting the doors. But if these thirteen initiates and guardians were to die, then the Zodiac would disappear and with it access to the Aleph. From that moment on, the Universe would begin to slowly but surely wither away, like a living organism whose heart has stopped, and all the races that inhabit it would be deprived of the possibility of fulfilling their destiny, of melding with the Aleph."

Coqdor ran his hand through his hair then petted the pstôr's head while thinking about a point that worried him about his host's explanations.

"Before, on Accora, you led us to believe that it was a man from Earth who had discovered the secret of the Zodiac... What one person could do, why couldn't others do the same later? In other words, since the Zodiac is linked to our Milky Way through the constellations symbolized by its thirteen signs, could it not be that elsewhere, in Andromeda, in one of the mysterious blue galaxies on the confines of the cosmos, among the enigmatic quasars or in another island universe too distant to be visible to us, the same process allows the creation of another Zodiac and another channel of communication with the Aleph?"

The little man smiled.

"That's what I expected of you, Star Knight! Subtle, insightful, ruthless in analysis and logic! Well no, it's impossible. There is, in the divine principle from which the Aleph proceeds, an underlying notion of election, of the chosen. Be careful, don't think about those ridiculous elitist theories that gave rise to most of the religious obscurantism of bygone centuries and allowed dominant minorities to wrap others around their little finger, claw, talon or whatever appendage—because the Earth did not have the exclusivity of these reductive dogmas, far from it!— generations of believers intentionally kept in error and ignorance... I repeat: nothing to do with Man, king of Creation... and the equivalent of this monstrous heresy among the medusoid Skoondzars of Andromeda or the intelligent sperm whales of the Large Magellanic Cloud! This notion of election was reserved, we know not why, for a particular galaxy of this Creation and it was, so to speak, to the first race of said galaxy which would find the secret of building the rest of the network, of binding the contact with twelve other peoples each able to provide an initiate—or already having within it an individual on the path to the fundamental mystery. The reason why the Aleph of our Universe chose the Milky Way, then the Earth to sow the decisive seed, escapes us and will always escape us, I believe deep down inside..."

"Okay, Master... Now that all this is on the table, which certainly clarifies the picture, let's get back to the fusion in the Aleph. If this is the final destiny of all the races of this Universe, in a more or less distant era, could the Cabal not have decided to speed up the process for reasons that are certainly obscure, but very real? Because with the powers that can be vested in an individual who has killed Masters and seized their medallions, I really don't see such a secret society seizing such power just to skirt the law for low-level trafficking or for criminal actions like those that have recently taken place."

Oddly enough, it was Giovanna Hi-Ling who cut in.

"You're absolutely right, Bruno. The Cabal's goals are not so mundane, far from it. But they are neither disinterested nor focused on the spiritual future of the races populating this cosmos. The other face of the Zodiac and the Aleph, the other opening that the fourteenth rotunda gives access to, is the doorway to absolute nothingness... I'll let you continue, Master," she shuddered, "it is too scary for me..."

Edward Brown leaned closer to the green-eyed man and his voice dropped to a whisper, as if suddenly afraid that invisible ears might hear him.

"None of us has ever really verified it, but the stories passed down from Guide to Guide since the dawn of time actually say that the fourteenth rotunda also gives access to Non-Being, to the negation of all matter and all antimatter, to absolute nothingness. There's a term for it and I'm sure a mind as brilliant as yours knows it. MAETH..."

A light lit up in Coqdor's emerald eyes and his lips formed a smile that had no trace of mirth.

"The word written on the forehead of the golem made centuries ago by Rabbi Loew in a dark cellar in the Jewish quarter of Prague... The two syllables that had to be pronounced to break the clay creature animated by a dreadful sapience if it ever escaped its master and became danger-ous..."

"Exactly, Chevalier, Maeth. This is what cosmomancers secretly re-vere. Now, the late Yum Akatinor was one and so is his brother Noa. Hence my intimate fear, my visceral anguish about the objectives that the Cabal has set for itself: I believe that they want to use the fourteenth ro-tunda to access Maeth ... and to uncreate our Universe!"

"Uncreate our Universe!" Coqdor gasped, dismayed, while Giovan-na pressed herself against him and Râx, in harmony with his master's mental vibrations, began to moan gloomily.

"This is the worst threat we can imagine! Let the Zodiac fall into the clutches of the cosmomancers and we will all be blown out like candles by a storm! God of the Cosmos, it's monstrous! But what good will that do them? Because if they do that, it is obvious that afterwards, they..."

A deafening explosion cut him off. As loud as during the worst storms that were so often unleashed on Venus, the thunderclap that re-sounded in the room literally froze the three people and the pstôr whose entire tawny coat bristled.

Then, looking up, they saw the ineffable...

Seeming to burst through the black, swirling cloud which, without them realizing it, had suddenly gathered in the most distant corner of the flat, five dark silhouettes sprang out to pounce on Brown, Giovanna, Coqdor and Râx.

Fit into their customary night-colored jumpsuits, they were four henchmen of the Black Circle, like those who had tracked the beautiful Giovanna to the Star Knight's house.

He jumped to his feet, exclaiming, "These creeps are after us, my pstôr! Go get 'em!"

Already worked up, the bulldog-bat began to flap its wings and roar like a fiend, then it rushed at the first of the four attackers who, from his typical features, must have come from the worlds of Taurus. Coqdor, at the same time, concentrated on parrying the imminent attack of the other three using the Eridanian ooim and on tripping up the closest of them with a partially hypnosuggestive psychic discharge.

Which did not take long since the powers of the green-eyed man were far superior to the abilities of the minions of the Black Circle, to the strength and endurance conferred on them by the link connecting them to their Master through their tattoo. Fortunately, they didn't have the talent for metamorphism which remained the prerogative of the highest-ranking initiates, a trick the Star Knight had seen on Ulmir in the dodgy cabaret called the Bird Woman, then in the surrounding streets during the adventure that ended with him and his companions meeting the Guide of the Zodiac for the first time.

Suddenly believing he saw a monstrous yy from the planets of Orion rising before him, the frightened assailant hesitated for a brief moment and was thrown to the ground by Râx who struck him hard on the back.

The three other henchmen suddenly had to deal with what seemed to them a triple demon with glowing eyes, jumping in all directions and striking them with a thousand subtly chained boots. The Eridanian ooim, of which Coqdor was an expert, once again proved to be the ideal weapon for defeating enemies unprepared to defend themselves against such a combat technique.

During the bizarrely choreographed quadruple duel, which finally only lasted a minute and a half, the Chevalier did not have an instant to focus on what was happening very close to him—a confrontation whose full dramatic scope came as a rude awakening.

The fifth person who had sprung from the dark cloud was none other than Noa Akatinor and he was using the metamorphism which his acolytes lacked. Just like Brown and Giovanna, thrown into an insane battle recalling what it must have been like long ago in a tournament between magicians or sorcerers capable of taking on any form they could imagine.

Coqdor thought he saw one of the accelerated Creations unfolding before his eyes that he had once witnessed on Titan. It looked like a carousel of furious madness, a merry-go-round whose horses could have been monsters dreamt up by demiurges or scientists in the throes of insanity. "A hideous army of vampires and dragons," cephalopods, giant crabs, horned, toothed, clawed and scaly beasts appeared and disappeared in a kaleidoscope of horror, striking violently, biting each other, spraying each other with long jets of flame or acid slime.

It could also have been the sinister flight of the jinns, whose wild procession one of the greatest poets of the Earth, and more precisely of ancient France, had masterfully depicted, a vector of sidereal terror that struck down the unfortunate witnesses of the nocturnal passage.[35]

Gradually, the infernal whirlwind slowed down and a lingering form was tossed from it, groaning, quickly regaining its original appearance.

---

[35] Victor Hugo, "*The Jinns*."

Giovanna, too young and inexperienced to endure, had just given up fighting any longer.

A protoplasmic mass dotted with thousands of eyes soon followed her, sinking to the ground to collapse on itself, twitching. Utilizing an eerie slime effect, Brown had escaped the hold of a pitch-black octopus and was reforming himself, completely exhausted. He was too old and not really cut out for such a fight.

The black octopus transformed into a Venusian vrüülk whose mouth spat electric lightning at the little man lying on the ground. Noa Akatinor, obviously, had not yet lost any of his metamorphic prowess and could take on any transformation he wanted in order to deliver the final blow to his two enemies.

When he saw the final avatar chosen by the cosmomancer, the Zodiac Guide finally understood how all the other Masters were killed by the Persean.

He had returned to his ordinary morphology, but the fingers of one of his hands had taken on the appearance of strange whiskers like those on the sinister mouths of Earth's catfish. And they were a surprising Cerulean color...

"The venomous darts of the blue catfish from the Perseus 5 swamps.," Edward Brown whispered. "Capable of injecting a lethal poison that no one has ever managed to synthesize... This is how this monster did it, thus manufacturing the deadly toxin and injecting it remotely via a psychic discharge with material condensation..."

These were his last conscious thoughts. A fraction of a second later, the little official with the thick glasses stopped breathing.

"Now it's your turn, you beautiful traitor," Noa Akatinor scoffed. "You could have had a different destiny if you had embraced my cause and I would have saved you from that pathetic waste called Halstar. I could have loved you, Giovanna Hi-Ling..."

With bulging eyes, the Sino-Italian woman gazed without moving at her executioner who was walking towards her, looming over her with all his demonic silhouette.

"Bruno... Râx... Help..." she implored.

"Don't count on them, they can't do anything against me and they will die too!" the Persean sneered cynically.

As he stretched out his horribly mutated hand towards his helpless victim, a cold voice sounded behind him.

"Failed, Akatinor! It won't be this time..."

The cosmomancer suddenly had the impression that in front of him, everything was freezing, diluting, changing appearance.

It was as if Brown's body and the statuesque beauty suddenly lost their substance.

The Persian turned around.

Likewise, the Chevalier Coqdor and his pet monster seemed struck by the same inexplicable alteration.

Like flat specters, kinepanorama projections suddenly becoming alive, the four targets of the exterminator slid across the walls like simple two-dimensional images then evaporated one after the other.

A second passed.

Noa Akatinor was alone in the apartment.

Alone except for the four corpses of the Black Circle henchmen.

Wretched remains that he immediately reduced to ashes, unleashing on them all his rage for having failed when so close to the goal.

CHAPTER IX

A little earlier, during the conversation with Brown, Coqdor had taken four transdim discs from the case hanging from his belt, had programmed them by aligning their directional focus on the laseradar microbeacon of his helijet and had tuned three of them on the fourth, which he was going to keep with him. In this way, the Chevalier could at any time, if necessary, activate the dimensional reduction of his three companions.

His precognitive gifts had in fact given him a glimpse that he would *a priori* be the only one capable, at the crucial moment, of triggering the process that might prove to be their salvation.

Brown and Giovanna had each received their disc with instructions to attach it to their belt and Râx had joyfully accepted his pretty necklace of flexible steel-plastic decorated with this new gadget, even if a little weird looking—and not to be eaten, which he had thought at first sight.

Coqdor did not dwell on explanations that would be too hard-to-swallow by the uninitiated, contenting himself with talking about a special micro-transmitter intended to maintain contact whatever happened.

As soon as he saw that the cosmomancer was going to win the metamorphic battle, he activated the call signal of his private vehicle, thus warning the valet robot that he had to get the flying machine out of its garage cell as soon as possible.

It was, therefore, via the two-dimensional singularity that he himself, the Guide, the beautiful woman and the pstôr had just fled Brown's flat, leaving a somewhat stunned Noa Akatinor behind.

The four travelers from the plane universe, which offered a shortcut that also neutralized time, rematerialized next to the helijet, already parked on the takeoff area.

A glance at his transdim disk revealed to Coqdor that the curious little gadgets born of Stewe's genius had been used to their maximum energy potential. Their power was almost exhausted.

It only took half a minute for the valet robot to collect the parking fee and, with typical British politeness, wish its customers a safe flight. The robot had not reacted to their return *ex nihilo* nor did it remark on the alarming state of two of them.

Another thirty seconds and the helijet was hurtling towards the low cloud covering that hung over the city of London.

Brown, whom the Chevalier had just put in a seat tilted back into a lying position, was not far from Giovanna who, under the protective gaze of the pstôr, was recovering quite quickly from the battle. She was waking up and seemed to be regaining a semblance of lucidity.

Brown muttered, "You're really the one we need, Bruno Coqdor... And I will do whatever's necessary..." He gasped and twitched under the onslaught of torturous pain. "I'm going to die, my friends... This demon hit me with a poison that breaks down the biomolecular structure of living organisms... There's no antidote..."

"But the Aleph can save you, Master!" Giovanna protested.

"No, my dear girl... No... The bond that unites me to it is already fraying. There is only one thing left I can do, and for that..."

"Head for the Hoggar, right?" the Chevalier asked the purely rhetorical question.

"Yes, my son..." Brown sighed. "Take me to the Eagle Rotunda... There, it's you who..."

His voice cracked. His mind had just sunk back into the darkness of agony.

Snapping out of the surprise that had literally frozen him in place, Noa Akatinor wasted no time in alerting the mysterious D.

"They escaped but I got Brown!" he announced. "Giovanna's in bad shape. Coqdor and his pet eliminated the four henchmen..."

Standing in front of the bay window of his apartment, D had no difficulty in identifying the helijet which suddenly shot into the sky, straight up into the misty clouds.

"We know where they're going, Noa," he replied. "And also where to find them later. Come back here, I need to send you back before I leave to do what I have to do."

"Famal Maeth! Victory is near!" the cosmomancer exclaimed as he left the flat of the late and reviled Guide of the Zodiac.

The jet was hurtling into the dazzling blue with the full power of its nuclear microturbines.

Another hour and its four passengers would arrive at their destination.

Leaning over Brown, her sensually curved lips almost in contact with those of the Master, Giovanna Hi-Ling was using all her resources to keep the poor man alive.

It was a kind of strange energy transfer. For an observer like Coqdor, literally blessed with a third eye, the ethereal swirls that flowed from the Sino-Italian's mouth and slipped between the little man's barely loosened lips were clearly seen.

It was like the opposite of a vampire kiss. Here, it was a fluid to preserve the vital breath of the dying person that the young woman was offering, drawing on her own reserves, which were already weakened by the battle.

And the transfusion was working.

Giovanna had given the exact coordinates of the terrestrial rotunda in the middle of the Hoggar mountain range, so the Chevalier didn't have to search or hesitate. He set the helijet down as closely as possible to the entrance to the hidden labyrinth.

Having planned ahead, he had on board the necessary first aid equipment and even a small folding stretcher equipped with an anti-gravity microbattery. Thus, Brown could be carried in a horizontal position without too many shocks or jolts.

Before abandoning the vehicle, the Star Knight obeyed a premonitory impulse that whispered that he and his companions would leave here by a completely different means. He therefore programmed the automatic piloting system so that the helijet would head back home. In a few hours, in the middle of this Saturday night, the flying machine would park itself in its garage cell far away in Paris-sur-Terre.

No one would be the wiser.

Coqdor was not surprised to find a scene that was a total mess compared to what he had seen when he and his partners had left this same rotunda of the Eagle that an instantaneous transportation had brought them to starting from the one of Capricorn shortly after their meeting with the Zodiac Guide. How could it have been any different after the earthquakes a few days later that shook the thirteen planets linked by the fabulous system?

On the other hand, it did not take him long to understand that it was all artifice, an illusion, a cleverly discouraging fake.

Giovanna led the way. She knew everything about the place.

The Chevalier was right behind her, pushing the stretcher that was floating four feet above the stone floor.

Râx was the last of the small troop marching solemnly like a funeral procession.

And thanks to the powers of the Masters, to the mental aura with which they were shrouded, all the obstacles that looked so solid turned into smoke, a nebulous and almost supernatural substance that interpenetrated with the atoms and molecules of living organisms to let them pass through their very mass!

Deep in the maze, the rotunda that the Chevalier's gaze finally fell upon was intact. No landslide to block the thirteen doors, no rocks to prevent their approach.

Coqdor remembered the monstrous reptiles which, on an order pronounced by the Guide in an unknown language had once been transformed into seats in the rotunda of Accora.

"The Masters of the Zodiac are masters of matter..." he whispered.

"It's the Aleph that allows us this because it's protecting itself!" Brown replied. "The real rotundas are indeed located on the thirteen planets whose signs they bear but they are tangent to the solid architectures which materialize them. They are superimposed on them, coincide with them in time and space while being elsewhere, therefore indestructible..."

Crossing the Eagle doorway, the small procession entered the extraordinary thirteen-sided room and the Chevalier pushed the stretcher down onto the floor.

"The omnipotent Aleph will also be able to save you, Master," he added. "What must we do to... summon it?"

"Nothing, my friend. Or rather, nothing for me. It's impossible for me to escape death. Impossible and out of the question. It is written thus. Edward Brown is doomed because even if he survived, he would not be able to win the final fight. I'm going to die, Bruno Coqdor. But something else is written, because the Aleph has planned everything. My replacement is here..."

Giovanna Hi-Ling turned around slowly, focusing the fire of her magnetic pupils on her lover's green eyes.

"So it's you who becomes the new Guide, beautiful girl!" the Chevalier whispered.

"No, Bruno... The Aleph's choice fell on you! From the moment you took the oath of silence, then from the moment you welcomed me into your home and saved me, essentially agreeing to embrace our cause... it designated you not only as new Master of the Eagle, as champion of the Earth, but also as the Zodiac Guide for the coming times!"

"The time for your initiation has come, Coqdor!" Brown spoke with renewed energy. "On the sole condition that you freely agree to do it... Because receiving the Aleph in itself cannot be an act consented to under duress..."

The Chevalier did not waste time in useless procrastination. Everything that the little man had revealed to him in his flat in London flashed through his mind. Let the Zodiac die, let it come under the rule of the Cabal and it was the ultimate condemnation of the Universe. His choice was made in advance.

"I freely accept!" he declared in a voice ringing with faith and conviction.

The interior light of the earth's rotunda changed from pale gold to azure, then to an increasingly intense and deep blue.

Coqdor, Brown, Giovanna and Râx were plunged into a night that was not really a night. A night whose darkness shed light.

Suddenly the pstôr seemed to give in to an irresistible wave of sleep. He lay down quietly, silently, and dozed off.

From the body of the little man lying on the stretcher rose a silhouette of cerulean light, his face animated by a peaceful and relaxed smile.

The astral double of the Sino-Italian was then begat in an identical manner, leaving its sculptural plasticity to go and place itself alongside the ethereal twin of the Guide and take his left hand.

The next moment, the Chevalier watched his own frozen, fleshly envelope and he floated up to complete the triangle.

Flooded with a sensation of ineffable plenitude as if he were melting into the Great Whole in an orgasm of eternity, Bruno Coqdor let himself "ascend" with the couple who accompanied him.

Ascend to the highest levels of the Cosmos, the Universe and Creation...

Ascend to "the regions of the highest joy..."[36]

Palace of pure crystal...
Cathedral of light and space-time...
Nave with pillars of hope carved into gossamer spindles...

---

[36] Marcel Landowski, "*Le Fou.*"

Vault from which shimmers a snow of consciousness...

Thirteen thresholds... Thirteen lintels... Thirteen symbols... Thirteen doors...

Thirteen accesses to the inter-world...

Blazing replica of each planetary rotunda...

Superior and transcendent projection of each rotunda of the Zodiac and of all at once...

Passage to the Aleph... but also to the abysses of Non-Being...

I am at the absolute geometric center of the *Fourteenth Rotonda*!

With me, my companion and my guide...

Above me...

Or below or around...

How to know? But what does it matter to know?

The Universe... My Universe... Our Universe...

Creation that must be saved at all costs...

Drift to the farthest blue galaxies.

Graze the photonic magma of the superquasars that mark the confines of the Cosmos.

Spin through the cemeteries where the dead stars end up.

Dive into the abysses of collapsars where titanic cosmic leviathans swarm and mesh.

Spring up in the miraculous conflagration of white fountains, sources of matter whose generous and purified waves give new life to entire zones of nothingness.

Embrace the Universe which loops around in the eternal return of a tireless new beginning.

Fall asleep in the light of the past.

Wake up to the flashes of the future...

Abyss of total darkness at the milky antipodes of the Earth's Sun.

Ineffable flashes of the Great Livid Ray among the groaning complaints uttered by the dark souls of the damned of all peoples.

Billions of paths that lead to the eternal dawns.

Billions of processions of spirits on their way to blend into the Aleph.

With them...

Fusion...

Transfiguration...

Supreme aspiration...

Absolute gift...

I am the Aleph.

The Aleph is me.

I welcome in my bosom a diamond of Universes.

Here I am, Master of the Eagle and Guide of the Zodiac with the thirteen signs.

Fleeting vision of the fourteenth rotunda...

Forever, in me, the engraved image of absolute purity...

Descent... Return...

The rotunda of the Earth...

My petrified body comes alive with unequaled energy.

My lover, the beautiful Giovanna, throws herself into my arms.

Edward Brown lies on his funeral bed.

He is not dead... Not yet...

He beckons me to come closer.

On his chest, a ritual knife that seems to be made of crystal.

"This orichalcum dagger comes from my essence... With it, open my chest and take out the medallion of the Eagle, now yours..."

Do I have the choice to refuse? No! This is not a criminal act... I obey. The little man seems not to feel anything and keeps smiling.

"Well done... Cut your own flesh, deep, over to the heart, and bury the medallion there."

A moment of hesitation. Then I plunge the blade into my left breast. Oh...

No pain! On the contrary, an ineffable heat...

"You have to interact with the medallion and the portion of the Aleph inside you will awaken your powers as a Master... Thank you, Bruno Coqdor. You will succeed me with dignity... To win the battle, to save our Creation…"

Edward Brown breathed his last and I closed his eyelids.

From my gaping chest not a drop of blood flowed. I thought "heal" and instantly, the flesh closed.

Alas, the body of the late Guide did not respond to the same injunction. I was unable to make him whole again as he entered death.

Giovanna grabbed my arm and I took her hand.

"The Aleph refuses to make us false gods, idols or miraculous healers, Bruno. Treating and healing ourselves, yes. But it stops there..."

Râx, who had awakened from his artificial slumber, came to rub against our legs and let out a heartbreaking lament when he realized that Brown was no more.

Unfortunately, we couldn't offer him anything more as a eulogy than the simple and sincere tears of a pstôr born on the distant planet Dzo.

Leaving the dead man on the cold floor of the earthly rotunda, the orichalcum knife stuck straight into his chest gashed by the terrible wound that I myself inflicted, I headed with Giovanna and Râx towards the gate of Aquarius.

"It's the only thing we can still do, isn't it? Join Maakeldar and Master Ka'Pholgar..."

My companion nodded in agreement and we crossed the threshold.

While behind us, no question about it, the Eagle rotunda returned to its ruined and devastated appearance.

CHAPTER X

Venus...

World of contrasts imported by the colonists, mostly men from Earth.

Lush nature in its still virgin parts, its mountains and its swamps haunted by monsters over which a heavy cover of storm clouds permanently loomed and where there still remained a few handfuls of natives, the strange and discreet Tmex'x.

Elsewhere... Raped, desecrated to the depths of her flesh where the predators from the sky had implanted themselves in her and ripped out her most intimate treasures.

The Martians, the majority of whom had fled a dying homeworld, had settled in the southern regions and the Earthlings had never broken their fanatical isolationism. Those who came near civilization did so of their own free will, without constraint.

The city of Ishtar Terra owed its name to the vast highlands close to the north pole of the planet, where the city had been built in the first days of human colonization.

Several distinct geological zones made this region totally asymmetrical. In the center stood the Maxwell Mountains, which plunged steeply to the west and then, further on, rose again to form the broad mesa called Lakshmi Planum.

In the opposite direction, the range gradually died away along a slow but continuous slope down to the immense hollow of Fortuna Tessera, more than 1,200 miles wide.

Ishtar Terra itself nestled in the strange horseshoe that a fissure had carved into the southern slope of the mountains. But was it really a city?

It gathered within it everything that the other worlds of the Martervenux, or even other star systems, no longer wanted for any number of different reasons. A modern equivalent of the mythical Chicago, Marseille or Tangier before the Great Decadence, it was the witch's cauldron where all kind of trafficking simmered, where the underworld thrived, where most of the drugs and illegal drinks passed through.

Its streets and dens, most of them infamous, swarmed with a motley fauna of smugglers, mercenaries, prostitutes, disgraced cosmonauts and inveterate gamblers whom the demon of their passion condemned to be pariahs. In comparison, Ulmir of the green rains and Betelgeuse VI (also called Terminal Despair) were veritable religious institutions...

In the entire United Star Confederation, it was perhaps the place where one could come across the largest sample of galactic peoples practicing space flight.

And in the middle of this turmoil, lurking like an evil spider in the center of its web, sat Luse Borek. Mother of all corruption, nurse of all vices, organizer of the Black Circle and member of the Cabal. For how much longer? It depended on many factors of which Robin Muscat and Marc Vérano were not the most negligible.

The night before, when they had returned to Paris-sur-Terre and Interplan headquarters after the round trip to the Hoggar, the commissioner had issued an interstellar arrest warrant for Bruno Coqdor, guilty of an abominable crime and also for the missing Cladek Halstar.

Councilor Maxan Dao was literally jubilant.

On Tuesday morning, at dawn, an emergency meeting was called and the decision was made to act by following the only trail still likely to lead to these two individuals: the Black Circle. Thus was launched the second phase of Operation Ravenclaw.

Shortly afterward, on board the regular shuttle that took off every day in the middle of the afternoon from the Saint-Jean Cap-Ferrat astrodrome bound for Venus, Muscat and Vérano had left. That same evening (taking into account the time difference) they arrived in Ishtar Terra.

As an old sleuth of the interstellar police, the commissioner had taken on an assumed, foolproof identity, which guaranteed him entry into all the most dubious gambling dens and dive bars in the city: Wolfram Haag, a smuggler notorious for having traveled in all quadrants of the Galaxy, was back.

With him, Terry Reno, a young greenhorn whom he claimed to have rescued incidentally and by chance from the clutches of the formidable Amazons of Qiwâm. A miraculous survivor for whom these winding streets flooded by the colorful lights poured down in torrents from the magnetized neon signs and posters, looked like a march to the gallows. Shy, reserved and prudish, Marc Vérano had never before visited this kind of sanctuary of depravity, debauchery and licentiousness.

And no matter how much he trusted his old boss, he was trembling in his boot...

He only breathed for the first time, so to speak, when he had followed Muscat/Haag, hot on his heels, through the creaking door of the Metalikus Bar.

This was once intended to be avant-garde and modern. Today the decor was so tacky that it made you want to cry. Moreover, there was hardly a customer, apart from three placid Azoa absorbed in the reliefcolor striptease projected by an old box-flugg to the languorous sound of a trendy Martian melody.

Ghar Liett, the manager of the place, was a fat Canopean with yellowish skin and thinning blue hair. Literally placed there by Interplan which had offered a chance of redemption to the unlucky trafficker, "nabbed" for a sordid smuggling of adulterated fluzz in which he was just the fall guy. Now he was the top informant for the police force in Ishtar Terra.

For this, "they" provided him with a shady showcase whose cover had yet to be blown.

With Muscat who, as Wolfram Haag, had pulled him out of the mud and secretly referred him to those who could put him back on the straight and narrow, he had a sincere and unfailing friendship.

After a warm, barely exaggerated reunion, Liett led his two visitors to an office that looked shabby but which was equipped with the most advanced security to protect secrets.

The three men sat down in old and faded yet comfortable armchairs, then a small domestic robot served them a glass of gleaming emerald-green Canopian vurguzz. A rare privilege given the price of this very prized beverage. Wolfram Haag thanked his host warmly and then got straight to the point.

"This is a very serious time, Ghar," he began. "Unprecedented events have occurred very recently and it appears that a large-scale offensive is being planned against the Confederation. We're all going to bite the dust... The haves, the have-nots, the good and the bad. Truth to tell, even Chevalier Coqdor is involved in this... conspiracy."

"Coqdor? No!" Liett said indignantly. "Not him! Impossible!"

"Well, yes, very possible! He's wanted for murder. And behind it all there are plenty of clues pointing to the Black Circle as the one pulling the strings."

The big Canopian huffed several times, took a sip and nodded. "That now... That doesn't surprise me. You know, Wolfram, the Circle is nothing like it once was. Gone is the good old criminal organization that ruled with threats, racketeering, lurid schemes and blood if necessary. Things had already started to change when that bitch Borek got hold of them and now... We're dealing with individuals endowed with superhuman strength, invincible... These new servants are all tattooed, they each got a bizarre mark that kills them if they fail or hesitate to obey. As for this awful harpy, some say that she only looks like a woman. Inside it's different... Monstrous... Well, I didn't go poking my nose around. Just that there are some who'll start shaking just at the sight of her."

Vérano/Reno thought it wise to intervene.

"But the rest of the organization? The older members, in other words? They just let themselves be put on without putting up a fight?"

"Good question, young man... The old ones are foaming with rage because they can't act, even if they're dying to rebel. Before, this bitch held them by the purse strings. Now it's through her henchmen. She silences the disgruntled either by deluding them and buying them off if necessary or by eliminating them. There's only one who's resisting..."

"Who?"

"Larsan. The deadliest of all. He has some followers and they're devoted. I have to say that he's really gained momentum since the Interplan bastards raided the Melun-3 base near Paris..."

Marc Vérano tensed up. A discreet kick from his superior prevented him from making any untimely comments.

"Why?"

Liett thought for a moment. "Word has it that here, on Venus, Larsan is in charge of a depot as important as the one that went up in smoke on Earth. And the Circle has no other. So the guy and his camp are riding high while Borek's star has faded a little. You talk... The invincible warriors were burned like stinking rats in Melun and not a single one escaped. Plus, they weren't able to save the goods. A slap right in the dirty face of that bitch."

"Do you know what they're up to right now?"

"I heard about a meeting of the section heads of the Circle this very night. In two rounds of the dial, to be specific. For sure, they'll take action and this demoness will find herself in trouble. I think it might really be heating up... You want to go, Wolfram, I know you!"

"That would be fun to see!"

"Crap, old man! Even disguised as a gray mouse, you wouldn't pass..."

"Do you have any... relations who will be there?"

Ghar Liett hesitated, then gave him a mischievous smile.

"Of course! If you want news, come back tomorrow morning. Until then, little duckies, hide well. But if you sleep at the Lyre of Orpheus," the Canopean pinched his lips into a grin, "you won't be disappointed... You haven't changed your habits, have you, Wolfram? You're a smart one, you! You won't be bored, they got in a bunch of little Eridanians the day before yesterday...

The manager backed up this announcement with a wide, unambiguous motion of his plump hands.

"Great tip, Ghar! We'll head over there double quick. There's no time to waste given what's in store. Thanks again for your hospitality, old brother!" Muscat/Haag concluded, getting up. "We'll pay you for it."

"You're right to split pronto, friends. The sooner you get to bed, the less you'll have to fear and the more you'll get the kinks worked out. Come on, I'll show you out. See you tomorrow morning for the latest news!"

The path to the front door of Metalikus was peppered with back-patting and good wishes.

"Watch out for this young one, Wolfram! He has a face that reminds me..."

"Don't worry, Ghar. With me and the damsels of Lyre he has nothing to worry about. As if he was still at his mother's..."

Once outside, Vérano let out a whistle, half amused, half indignant. "Well, boss... The underbelly of Venus suits you just fine!"

"Experience, Reno, experience... Sometimes you have to know how to make sacrifices—at least in appearance! That's how we learn interesting things."

"Too bad we can't attend that meeting... We'll have to settle for the guy who heard it from the guy who heard it from someone else and that's no way to get reliable information."

Muscat burst out laughing, "Speak for yourself, Terry! You can't go, but I can."

So saying, he removed from one of his pockets a tiny black crystal with dull facets. Vérano examined the object, perplexed.

"I'm a member of the Black Circle on the planets of Vega, my young friend... This is proof, and the entry ticket to any meeting of this organization."

The young inspector was stunned.

"Of course, I'm a little late in paying my dues," Muscat clarified, "but they're not very particular about that. I just hope they didn't kick me out of the Circle, but I'll find out soon enough."

"You're just going to jump into the lion's den, then?" Vérano asked, continuing to play his character. "And me?"

"You'll spend the night at Lyre. We're headed there right now. Once there, discreetly say your prayers to *Our Mother in Heaven* and beg her to be ready for a Cinemacolorscope haunting."

In their coded language, the pictorial name of the Virgin Mary designated the forces of Interplan whose detachments of the Militia could join up with if necessary.

The young man nodded silently.

"And now, let's go see the girls! You'll be able to work out the kinks a little, kid, as good Ghar Liett said!" Muscat/Haag guffawed and he gave his partner a hard spank on his rear.

No need to ask: the meeting of the Black Circle was held at the famous Palace of Ishtar's Delights.

The huge casino (where all the leading figures of the Martervenux, at one point or another, came slumming) stood on one of the arms of the horseshoe marking the city limits.

Fantastic lighting effects above the building, which looked like a Babylonian ziggurat, lured the customers' aerial vehicles like a magnetized neon projector would have trapped the moths of the Earth or the zlans of the Venusian swamps.

Obviously, the most popular game was priks, a riveting poker game imported from Altaïr. It was enough to add a little euphoria to the drinks and the players, focused on the game, got fleeced without noticing a thing.

The unqualified master of the place was an extremely cautious individual with an ice-cold attitude and very sparing of words. Never one word louder than the other, especially if there was a risk of attracting the wrath of one or another of the gangs operating in the city and in the Confederation. Eko Lamar paid, Eko Lamar remained silent as a grave, Eko Lamar also knew how to strike if necessary. He too had his network.

Starting with the countless security guards who guarded the various doors to the Palace, then the mirrored cabinets in flexible, invisible armor, equipped with all kinds of weapons imaginable in the event that it was necessary to intervene manu more than militari.

Muscat/Haag was not reassured when he approached the first cordon to cross. However, his pass did its job and he was let in. Little by little, some of the guards recognized him and greeted him with a trace of cordiality. The smuggler was, so to speak, in his element.

When he approached the first members of the Black Circle, he was greeted by faces mostly showing surprise.

"Wolfram Haag! Well, I'll be!" a Sirian with a scarred face exclaimed.

"It's been ten years since we last saw you, handsome Earthling," cooed a once attractive Cassiopean woman.

"Ten years? No... Ten months, love of my life!" Muscat replied without getting rattled. "But it's true that when we travel through the Galaxy via subspace, time is hard to keep track of..."

A little Bellatrix homunculus shoved him, laughing, "Where have you been hanging around lately, old vâr?" he asked.

"Around the Polar region, first of all, on the trail of a platinum iridium asteroid. We got it with a net of strong waves but it was already half hollowed out..."

The others chuckled, obviously scoffing.

"As for Qiwâm, on the other hand..." Muscat/Haag continued.

"Did you go and sniff the asses of those devils? Did you dare?" the Sirian said.

"Well yes... And my nose was hollowed out. We set up a short-term barter business, which earned me a few hefty pounds of diamonds as a bonus. They needed weapons, for the Amazons, always fighting... Plus, I saved a young kid they were putting through hell. He's my friend now."

"He's not with you?" the Cassiopean whispered. "Too bad..."

I didn't want to introduce him to the Circle yet," the fake smuggler explained. "He lacks a little grit. But he's in town, where I usually crash."

"The Lyre of Orpheus, with that old madam Tipa Riordan..." the homunculus sneered. "Don't worry, Wolfie, I'll keep it a secret!"

Low and rumbling, the sound of a gong cut short the rest of the discussion.

Then an artificial voice said, "All section leaders are asked to go to the Hall of Supreme Bliss. The meeting will commence in five minutes."

It was now a matter of not being noticed and therefore not being the last to get in. Everyone hurried towards the big door leading to the appointed place.

Muscat/Haag chose to sit next to the Cassiopean. She was so "sloshed" that she was perfectly harmless, except in terms of the advances she was likely to make towards him. But she wouldn't have time to get very far.

Barely had all the guests been seated when Luse Borek appeared, emerging from the left of the platform on which she had her place as head of the organization.

Certainly, Muscat recognized her from various regular and 3-D photos. But they paled in comparison to reality. And light years away from the adjectives which Ghar Liett had showered on her earlier at Metalikus.

The woman was a mixed-race Terro-Venusian. Surely the best that the mixture of the two races could have produced. Tall, thin and svelte, draped in a kind of orange sarong decorated with dark red patterns, her hands and forearms sheathed in black silk gloves, a delicately olive complexion, large almond-shaped eyes with dark mauve pupils, hair forming a sapphire blue helmet. Luse Borek was beautiful.

Beautiful with the devil's beauty. Deadly fascinating. Like a praying mantis.

Her words of welcome were kept to an icy "Good evening", then she declared the session open.

"The goal is to restore order to a system that is not running smoothly," she said as a preamble. "For this, you all can take the floor and everyone will give a detailed report of the dysfunctions affecting them, as well as their comments and objections."

The "rebels" were waiting only for this opportunity. Larsan stood up and attacked without beating around the bush. The account he gave of the events of the last few months, marked by several failures, the most resounding of which was the loss of Melun-3, was more than eloquent.

Those of his colleagues who spoke afterwards painted an equally bleak picture. To finish, the man in charge of the Circle's finances presented an assessment that was certainly not catastrophic, but still troubling. The organization recorded its first losses for rather substantial amounts. The net result was in the red.

A grumbling swelled in the room, discreet but unmistakable. Disapproval was growing.

It was then that Larsan spoke again.

"All this stems from the recent reorganization of trafficking networks," he concluded. "Lady Luse, you wanted to restructure the system on the basis of your inter-world gates, a very beautiful idea in itself, and for this you have drawn heavily from the coffers to pay for the logistical modifications imposed by this reconfiguration... However, what did we get out of it? To date, nothing positive... Quite the contrary! By wanting to move more goods through a supposedly unlimited channel, and instantly, we run up against a too narrow choice of departure and arrival points. Thirteen worlds, thirteen doors! Not one more, not one more..."

Some members did not hesitate to applaud, already knowing what was coming next.

"Let's sum up," Larsan continued. "You organize a traffic between Perseus and Venus for which you have to start from a lost world of Taurus, or wherever, and arrive on Earth in the middle of a desert. Is that direct, in your opinion? Not at all! What you save in time and transportation costs with your doors, you lose through the additional steps before and after the transportation. The same goes for money. Do you have a comparison for a case like this, Lady Luse?"

The questioned woman shook her head in denial.

"She didn't calculate anything!" her accuser exploded. "She didn't plan anything in advance! We're losing money, but her business is doing fine..."

Larsan had achieved his goal.

"You can all see that there's something else going on in this restructuring! And that something is Madame's personal interests! Getting traffic through the doors is a sham. What matters now for Luse Borek is to follow through on her dreams of grandeur, her plans of cosmic machinations—and for that, she had to make us swallow her story of these doors!"

He paused briefly.

"Well, look where that got us: financial losses—and material losses! Plus the risks associated with the too precise location of transit points. The fall has already begun with Melun-3. Proof that your actions, Lady Luse, had to attract the attention of Interplan..."

Despite the increasingly direct attacks, the Terro-Venusian remained impassive. But her face hardened.

"As for your henchmen who seem invulnerable, superhuman and under complete control, let's talk about that!" Larsan went on. "In Melun they were all shot down or burned thanks to those mysterious tattoos. And I lost a lot of drugs there, including tons of extremely rare ionna! Who will reimburse me for this? YOU? With the negative profits that the Circle has just recorded, for example? No! So there you have it, Luse

Borek: today, enough is enough! Stop the massacre, stop your race to the abyss in which we refuse to follow you! I'm done."

The leader of the Black Circle had accepted this cutting accusation without reacting. At least in appearance. In truth, she had listened very little to Larsan's diatribe because his flood of nonsense was of no interest to her. Now she could strike back and settle the issue raised once and for all. As she had planned by calling this assembly of pathetic protesters.

Placing her gloved hands flat on the table, scanning the entire audience with an icy glare, Luse Borek let out all her fury in keeping with the scene that she had carefully staged.

"Criticism... Sarcasm... Reflections of your pitiful personalities, of your basely material aspirations not even worthy of woodlice! Losers! A bunch of numbskulls! You've just shown me that the Black Circle is bound to die... While I was preparing to offer it the Universe! Instead of hiding in your holes like rats, you could have conquered the cosmos and become its masters! The only condition was to follow me and have faith in me. You preferred short-term profits and seeing them dissolve today while they were later going to increase a hundredfold has driven you to stand up against me... Poor little grubs! Well, that's the end of the organization. Too bad..."

She intentionally paused, listening to the silence that answered her statement. Little by little, some dared to fidget and start breathing again, hoping for something to change.

Luse then plucked them with utmost cruelty.

"Too bad for you, not for me! The Black Circle is dissolved, it no longer has a reason to exist... because it has fulfilled its function!... The future belongs to me!... Famal Maeth!"

As if these words spoken in a foreign language had been a signal, an eerie glow trembled in the air around the Terro-Venusian who had stood up. Two discs of darkness suddenly formed, then two silhouettes emerged like angry angels.

Several of the section leaders recognized one of them: Noa Akatinor, whom they considered to be the damned soul of Luse Borek. From the moment he had made his first appearance in the company of the mistress of the Black Circle, the tide had turned... and few had felt it.

The other character was nothing like him. Neither in dress, a simple tight-fitting jumpsuit in sharp contrast to the monk's robe worn by the Persean, nor in his facial expression. Ordinary, quite soft and vague, but lit up by the fanatical fire that gleamed in his wild-eyed gaze. No one knew him. Except...

But Muscat, to whose arm the Cassiopean woman was clinging, uttering little terrified moans, was far from being able to identify him since his attention was focused on everything else.

"Treason!" the participants in this rigged meeting shouted all together. "Borek has summoned her pet demon!"

In total chaos, all the members of the now disbanded Circle jumped up from their seats, some drawing blasters, some inframauve pistols, some paralyzers. The poorer equipped brandished common bladed weapons, swords and sabers very anachronistic in comparison.

With sadistic pleasure, Luse Borek noted that they had all armed themselves for a coup. She would have even fewer scruples about squashing the crawling vermin knowing that the leaders of the rebellion had somewhere planned to turn the meeting into a modernized version of the Ides of March.

Without further ado, she looked at Akatinor and both, using their shapeshifting abilities, transformed themselves into a legion of nightmare monsters. Wings outspread, claws and fangs out, spitting fire, the creatures spawned out of the worst of hells threw themselves on the audience.

The energy rays that met them were useless. And the conference room doors had been locked.

The little chiefs of the Black Circle perished in the teeth of invincible beings. Flames burned, claws gashed, jaws crushed...

And always more arrived in an inexhaustible stream vomited by the most abominable hell.

For a systematic massacre methodical in horror and relentlessness.

"God of the Cosmos..." Muscat gasped when the Cassiopean was pulled away from him by a laughing ghoul. "It's a bloodbath like I've never seen before..."

The man from Interplan had beaten a prudent retreat among pandemonium of apocalypse. But when there was only one left standing in front of a pile of shredded corpses, how could he hope to go unnoticed any longer?

Muscat knew he was lost. Death was imminent.

Luse Borek, once again the inhuman beauty she embodied so well, rushed at him.

The third exterminating angel, who had until then remained in a hieratic pose—probably he did not have the powers of his accomplices—suddenly jumped in between them.

"No! Not him!" he shouted, spreading his arms, a paltry figure of a Christ cast into the depths of the infernal abyss.

The Terro-Venusian held back the deadly blow she was about to deliver with her right hand that still bore sharp claws.

"And why?" she hissed.

"Let's take him with us!" her acolyte tossed out.

For a moment, everything seemed to freeze.

Muscat was able to better scrutinize the face of his savior.

"You..." he whispered in astonishment. "I recognize you! But I thought you were dead..."

CHAPTER XI

In Ishtar Terra, news traveled fast. Faster than anywhere else. The dregs of humanity were much more effective in terms of communication than the most official channels.

In his room at the Lyre of Orpheus where he only slept with one eye open because he expected to have to go into action at any moment, Marc Vérano alias Terry Reno was awakened in the middle of the night by an unbelievable ruckus. The entire dodgy hotel was in turmoil.

Eko Lamar, who was immediately on the scene of the monstrous drama unfolding in his establishment, had the information broadcast near and far.

The young inspector, following orders, hastened to call upon the "Virgin Mary". And this one, much more obedient and available than the real mother of Jesus, immediately answered his prayer.

At the head of four Interplan emergency squadrons, to which a special detachment of the Inter-Stellar Militia lent a hand, the fake Terry Reno entered the sumptuous entrance hall of the Palace of Ishtar's Delights.

Given the situation, Lamar had instructed his security guards to let any law enforcement troops enter. Even if there was not much order left to maintain in the casino...

The talented actor clung to the Earthling like to a branch floating on a raging river, bombarding him with endless groaning and a litany of complaints that would rend the soul of any sensitive individual.

In reality, while he sincerely loathed the quick methods that led to such bloodbaths, Lamar was privately sighing in relief. That Borek and her two acolytes had dissolved into nothingness and the minions of the Black Circle had all been liquidated...

In Ishtar Terra, they would be able to breathe easily for a while and after a lull, business would pick up again.

Vérano shuddered in horror when he saw the horrid spectacle in the Hall of Supreme Bliss. Overcoming his nausea, he discreetly ordered some of the Interplan officers to search the mass grave and find the body of Robin Muscat. The probability that he had escaped the massacre was infinitesimal.

And yet, an hour plus two more later, he had to face the facts. There was not the slightest trace of the commissioner, no corpse, no torn limb, no drop of blood...

In this case, the fake Wolfram Haag had not suffered the dreadful fate of the others.

And if he wasn't dead, his protégé concluded it was because he was still alive.

Why?

How?

Where?

That was a different kettle of fish.

However, there remained one final avenue.

Vérano called over one of the men.

"Take this miniaturized scanner," he pulled out of a case a small flat device that looked like a camera with a display screen. "It's set to the DNA code of the commissioner. Sweep the whole room for me. You're looking for a recording chip..."

The policeman took the device and began his search.

Every Interplan agent, as part of a high-risk mission, was equipped with a tiny biosynthetic disk made from a culture of his own epithelial cells and subjected to a subtle, quite amazing treatment making it capable of biologically recording everything that its wearer could see.

It was the brilliant Moo'N-Reï, a Mercurian scholar, who had developed this true miracle.

Without a doubt, Muscat had certainly not forgotten to leave behind the implant he had equipped himself with.

Less than a quarter of an hour later, the policeman returned, smiling with satisfaction.

"Is this the thing, boss? I picked it up very close to the stage..."

Vérano delicately took the flesh-colored disc and slipped it into a resealable plastic bag.

"Thank you, captain! Thanks to you and this chip, perhaps we will learn the truth. And maybe we'll save the big boss."

The next day, shortly after noon, the young inspector returned to Earth and gave the biological micro-recorder to experts in the Interplan laboratories.

Knowing that it would take them about two hours to decipher the contents of the chip, he treated himself to a frugal lunch and took a few minutes to call the Lyre of Orpheus in Ishtar Terra.

Strangely, although he had been able to stubbornly resist the proposals made to him by the manager of the place, the old witch who was also brave and generous and whom everyone, staff and regulars, affectionately called Aunt Tipa, the fake Terry Reno, at the hotel bar, had met a very charming young lady stranded there as a guest by bad luck.

Angie Russell was coming from a study trip to the Monoceros with all her university classmates. The plan had been to celebrate their graduation at Ishtar's Palace of Delights and accommodations for the group were supposed to be provided at the Cosmostella.

An error in counting, one less room... Curious about everything, Angie took up the challenge and agreed to take on the famous Lyre of Orpheus.

Without risk and with the most honorable intentions. In such cases, Tipa Riordan never played with fire.

This was how Vérano, or rather Terry Reno, met Angie Russell and they promised to meet again.

And a promise is a promise... As she said to him during their brief conversation, the young girl would be in Paris-sur-Terre within a week.

When the inspector finished the call, his eyes shining with fiery passion, the rendezvous had been set.

With a joyful heart, in love for the first time in his life, Vérano went to report to Judge Alice DeWitt who, given the exceptional circumstances, had extended his stay in Paris-sur-Terre. The two then went down to the twentieth basement of the building on the hill of Montmartre where the wisest and best equipped of all researchers had their stronghold.

Ward Philipps, a decoding specialist, greeted them with an encouraging smile and ushered them into the debriefing room.

First, the film from processing the recorded data was projected. The spectators had great difficulty in stomaching the images and the extreme cruelty.

The next step was the most eagerly awaited. Every shot had been scanned, dissected and analyzed by the powerful computers of the Interplan administration. After that, the various individual faces were compared to the pictures of all the suspects registered in the court records as being more or less close to the Black Circle.

This is how the pivotal role played by Luse Borek in the massacre was confirmed and the monstrous participation of the Persean Noa Akatinor was noted.

The voice recording provided more details on the ins and outs of the case. Details that largely corroborated the conclusion drawn formerly by Muscat relating to the mysterious Zodiac with thirteen signs and its no less mysterious Masters.

According to the confidential memorandum that the commissioner had annexed to his official report and to which Vérano had access upon returning from the Hoggar, the assassination of Yum Akatinor on the ship of the Sol-Perseus line and the dementia that had afflicted the Martian financier Cladek Halstar were punitive acts committed by the initiates of the Zodiac in order to punish individuals who had tried to monopolize part of the secret, playing into the hands of a third crooked party lurking in the shadows, the sect of cosmomancers.

Muscat had nevertheless toned down his conclusion by not exonerating the Guide and the other initiates of supreme rank because they had resorted to crime to protect the very instrument of their occult power.

Now the scene had changed. It was very disturbing. After the events that occurred at the Palace of Ishtar's Delights, it appeared that the Terro-Venusian leader of the now defunct Black Circle and the brother of Yum Akatinor had succeeded in taking control of the inter-world rotundas, thus establishing themselves as declared enemies of the "true" Zodiac.

That they relentlessly killed the Masters was a logical deduction.

"The authentic initiates, those whom these monsters surely killed, were therefore innocent," Alice DeWitt stated, somewhat unnerved.

"Bruno Coqdor was right about that, I guess," Vérano couldn't help but comment.

"One to zero against Maxan Dao," the Judge whispered. "Our Centaurian is going to throw a fit..."

The major mystery had yet to be solved.

What was the purpose of this takeover of Zodiac by Luse Borek, Noa Akatinor... and who else?

"There's more to this," Ward Philipps reflected aloud. "The opponents of that evil woman were not wrong, using the rotundas only to restructure trafficking and contraband is really not very smart."

"Play back Luse's megalomaniacal speech just before the appearance of Akatinor and his silent shadow," Alice DeWitt ordered.

Philipps complied.

"They're insubstantial clues, if indeed this crazy woman wasn't delirious," Vérano said after listening a second time to the speech. "Becoming masters of the Universe... Same old song, you might say, but I believe it hides the real goal of the whole operation. The wording is grandiose, certainly, but why wouldn't this be precisely what Luse Borek, Noa Akatinor and others are looking to do?"

"Like the one I call the silent shadow for example?" the Judge said. "He doesn't seem to have any power and yet he's respected. Who is he to deserve such esteem?"

"Someone Muscat recognized, anyway," Philipps said. "Let's see what we might have on this strangely passive fellow..."

The man in question was not a criminal. The research therefore required more time because he was not listed among common law offenders.

A full hour passed and the results finally came.

The individual was classified as dead. Previously, he had been registered for attempted suicide, an act punishable under the law of January 27, 2038, article 8945, volume 2.

His name: Claude Dalbret.

Last place where he was seen alive: in the vicinity of Titan, the largest of Saturn's moons.

As part of the special mission of the cosmaviso *Sterne*.

"Article 723 of the Military Security Code of the Galactic Confederations... I remember it like it was yesterday!" Alice DeWitt exclaimed. "How can we forget one of the extremely rare cases where the Martervenux ordered a total extermination to be coldly carried out? You were both too young at the time. Let me summarize the dramatic story for you...[37]

Originally, there was the suicide attempt by Claude Dalbret, mad with grief after the death of Sylvia, the love of his life.

At the Ménilmontant cemetery, the vast resting field that welcomed the deceased of all faiths, Dalbret wanted to join his deceased wife by diving into a disintegration tank.

Muscat had stopped him in time because the law prohibited suicide.

---

[37] See *Flammes sur Titan*.

And since the desperate man was only looking for death, the inspector had offered him a heroic but equally definitive exit: A mission whose chances of return were minuscule.

It was a matter of going to the ends of the Solar System, to the outskirts of the giant Saturn, where very strange phenomena were manifesting on Titan.

In the company of a few others, in his case Wilfrid and Tchou, Bruno Coqdor and his faithful Râx, Dalbret had embarked on the *Sterne* under the command of Commodore Flood.

Out there, first, a mysterious ghost ship appeared. Tracking it down was one of the objectives of the expedition. The machine, worthy of a spacecraft cemetery as it was dented, dirty and pieced together, was astoundingly proficient. It could emerge suddenly from subspace, blocking the path of any other ship, and then dive back into it with the same lightning speed. Its weaponry was as formidable as it was unusual.

Through its fault, the three suicidal volunteers and Coqdor had crashed onto Enceladus, one of the small moons of Saturn, a world where the atmosphere existed in small traces in the valleys of the terrain.

Oddly enough, it was the ghost ship that saved them from death. Its unknown pilot, who called himself the Marsupial, had generously given them enough to survive. Then incredible energy bubbles appeared, in a fantastic theory that had approached the tiny planet. And the four men had been imprisoned in these unbreakable spheres that shot off into space and carried them to Titan.

Titan, mission number two. For some time now, they had been observing strange flames or lightning springing out of nowhere to crisscross the surface of this planet. Did they have a relation to the spectral craft? No one could have said...

Arriving on the ground, the quartet had been dispersed. Isolated, Claude Dalbret had witnessed the formidable process affecting Titan as a result of the inexplicable fires. An accelerated Creation...

A Genesis that unfolded at an astonishing speed and that, before his eyes, resulted in the appearance of a form of humanoid life.

Human, even. And there, Dalbret had seen the reincarnation of his deceased love. A woman. Magali, that's what he called her. Not Sylvia, no. Certainly, it was her, it could only be her, but in a new form.

Claude had rediscovered the feminine ideal in essence. His feminine ideal...

The Marsupial intervened, once again. Because those who were provoking the Creation on Titan had started the hostilities, using the ruthless snow of fire. Separated from Magali barely glimpsed, Dalbret rejoined his two comrades and Bruno Coqdor aboard the ghost ship.

The pilot was alone there except for four outlandish and ultra-sophisticated robots. Finally, he introduced himself. He was a very disreputable human, an old lout straight out of a bygone age, a child of Earthlings who had emigrated to Mars—hence the contemptuous nickname given to him by his college classmates in Paris—and driven by a misanthropy as extreme as it was incomprehensible. An outstanding scientist, genius tinkerer and adventurer who had perhaps dared to brave the Universe to its limits, the Marsupial had revealed what he knew about the forces at work on Titan.

Those responsible were beings or entities from quasars, blue galaxies, or even from an alternate dimension. They seemed to move in a sort of saucer, generating bubbles of indestructible energy—only vulnerable to the red superlaser that the Marsupial possessed—and their supreme weapon, the snow of fire, was capable of instantly freezing anything to absolute zero.

No one had seen them, no one could see them. But the space pariah seemed to know them. And to know why they were acting on Titan like this.

According to him, the "Others" wanted to make contact with Earth and humans. For this, they decided to create a form of life similar to man on the world that seemed most favorable in the Solar System. They aimed to incarnate on Titan thanks to the flames, the lightning emanating from a distant pulsar that they had somehow managed to control. Beforehand, they had to terraform Saturn's moon and create an accelerated Genesis there.

The purpose of this contact, however, remained unknown. Should they fear an unprecedented attack, an attempted invasion? A mystery…

Coqdor, Wilfrid and Tchou had fled, not without damage to the Marsupial and his robots, then the Sterne had picked them up. Dalbret, however, had remained on the ghost ship with the goal of going back down to Titan and finding Magali there. Even if it doomed him to death.

Unfortunately, as soon as it was informed, the Praesidium of the Martervenux made a sudden, appalling decision, perhaps overestimating the possible threat. The blind application of the famous Article 723 ordering the destruction, by any or all means, of any unknown being or power that cannot be known that might appear in the zone of influence of the worlds of the Confederation.

A huge space fleet had gathered around Titan. Despite repeated calls, the Marsupial did not clear out. When the apocalypse struck, his ship had vanished into thin air.

Had he been destroyed? Not sure, according to Bruno Coqdor. The pariah of space hid many secrets and had extraordinary technology at his disposal, inherited from who knew where.

Perhaps even from the "Others" as the price for his collaboration if he betrayed humanity for their benefit.

The Marsupial had remained an unfathomable, disturbing enigma.

Such a dark character posed a threat, that of the unknown and the unknowable.

But the page had been turned, at the time.

Too quickly, given recent events.

Once again, the Star Knight had been right to doubt...

"If Dalbret survived, it's because the ship on which he had chosen to stay was not destroyed," Vérano said flatly.

"The Marsupial, that pariah of space, the cursed captain of that flying wreck also escaped," the Judge added. "Gentlemen, we are witnessing almost directly the return of an individual capable of making the Galaxy tremble. A misanthrope ready to do anything to satisfy God knows what resentment."

Vérano and Philipps had a hard time grasping the full, dramatic significance of this information.

"We've lost Robin Muscat," Alice De Witt continued. "No leads to where he is. We must therefore find the only man who has proven that he is capable of opposing the Marsupial. All our hopes rest on him...

"Bruno Coqdor..." Vérano and Philipps chimed in together.

"Without the Star Knight, the Milky Way is doomed!" the Judge moaned. "But where should we start looking for him."

CHAPTER XII

Where, if not in the constellation Aquarius?

It would still have been necessary to know that Bruno Coqdor, Giovanna Hi-Ling and Râx had deliberately reached this distant galactic sector through the fantastic intermediary of inter-world portals.

Arriving at his destination, the green-eyed Chevalier had to suffer a great shock of surprise. When he crossed the threshold opening onto Aquarius, he found himself face to face with an old acquaintance.

Zo'Akl, a superior of the Arcana of Science, high official of the Magistral City, center of Maakeldar.

Maakeldar, the capital of the planet Mîo.

In a flash, the Chevalier relived his previous visit to this place. Initially, there was the kidnapping of a couple of Earthlings, Frank and Stella Dusaule. He, a doctor and researcher, had desperately tried to experiment with out-of-body travel to the gates of the dawn but no one among the scientific circles of his home planet, as narrow-minded as always when one skirted the realm of the irrational, had supported him.

The people of Aquarius... Perpetually on the lookout, waiting for any potentially interesting progress thanks to their fabulous radio transmitters of galactic range, the Mîos had kidnapped the Dusaules and Frank had opened the way to interlife for them.[38]

Unfortunately, the incredible voyage had been redirected from its exploratory purpose. A Mîo scholar, Dr. Kowi and his mistress, A'Moon, had attempted to bring about the reincarnation of souls wandering on the border of the afterlife. Strange psychic messages, mental voices picked up by receptive Earthlings, had raised the alarm and made it possible to locate the origin of the problem.

Coqdor and Muscat went to Aquarius. In Maakeldar, the Star Knight had experienced the fantastic plunge into interlife, with other Necronauts. Thanks to his intervention, they put an end to the abomination caused by the demiurges aboard the pirated X-313 satellite.

It was none other than the surge of monstrous creatures driven by the lowest instincts. The masses of synthetic protoplasm intended to re-

---

[38] See *Les Portes de l'Aurore*.

store bodies to the deceased had suddenly been invested by the souls of the damned whose crimes and misdeeds had barred them from the path to eternal light.

It was necessary to mercilessly disintegrate these simulacra of life in order to stem the fateful tide...

Thankfully the wave of horror was not an omen of imminent events!

The august, thin old man with a brown complexion, dressed in a suit whose gold color indicated his position at the top of the Arcane hierarchy, was clearly very moved to see the Earthling again.

"Welcome, Yoo Coqdor, Yooi[39] Hi-Ling!" he declared warmly, but barely showing the shadow of a smile since the situation was so serious. "Welcome to you too, Râx! I've never met you, but your master told me all about you..."

"Thank you for your welcome, Lord Zo'Akl," the Chevalier replied. "You must know that I'm very surprised to see you here in person."

Zo'Akl turned to the other Mîo who stood beside him. Younger, taller, dressed in emerald green—he was therefore a doctor—and with eyes glowing with curiosity, he wore a special badge: The sign of Aquarius. Here, the Masters were not hiding...

"Ka'Pholgar was informed of your arrival," Zo'Akl said, pointing to his companion who offered a distant but courteous greeting to the visitors. "Ah, I forgot: with us, the Zodiac is something that no one is unaware of..."

What was surprising about that? Coqdor thought as the small group went up a tunnel with polished walls to return to the surface. For millennia, the Mîos have been aware in real time of everything that was happening, of everything that was discovered in the Milky Way! And they happily "pumped" it using their radio transmitters.

The old scientist very spontaneously corroborated statement. "It's been more than 2,000 years since we accessed the secret of the interworld rotunda. Ours is located below the Magistral City. Or more precisely, we built the City directly above the building with thirteen doors. But even though we had access to the Zodiac very early on, we almost never used it."

"We still owe to it the creation of the radio transmitters," Ka'Pholgar interjected in a beautiful, well-toned bass voice. "It was the Aleph that put one of the Masters on the right path. Perhaps we were called to play a leading role in the Galaxy through the instantaneous

---

[39] *Yoo* and *Yooi* : Mîo equivalent of Sir and Madam.

knowledge collectors... But the Mîos are a rather contemplative people who are not very prone to action."

"With your transmitters, you surely discovered very early on the Cabal's offensive plan against the Zodiac," Coqdor said.

Ka'Pholgar and Zo'Akl nodded.

"Yes. And yet, will you blame us if we didn't react?"

"We didn't see sufficient reason for it," the Master of Aquarius added. "At least until recently. As long as I myself was in place and Edward Brown was well enough hidden on Earth not to be threatened and with the Sagittarian Y Zeon still alive, the Cabal was powerless. To open true access to the Aleph, which goes far beyond simple initiation, all thirteen medallions must be reunited. With or without the thirteen Masters present, it doesn't matter."

"Furthermore," the Knight added, "how can we envisage an attack against Maakeldar in order to infiltrate it? No one would dare confront you here head-on, in your citadel world armed with all the defenses that you have copied—and improved—by drawing on all the technologies of the Milky Way?"

"Yes, we felt safe," Zo'Akl agreed. "But the power capable of defeating us existed. Without us being able to glean a single clue about it. And that power struck. Look, Yoo Coqdor!"

The two Mîos, the couple of Earthlings and the pstôr came out on the surface of the planet. Leaving a small building in the shape of a truncated pyramid, the entrance lintel of which was marked with the sign of Aquarius, they set foot on the vast metal esplanade that was designated "level zero" of the Magistral City.

And what the visitors saw froze them in place.

The prodigious scientific city was floating in the cosmos.

A cosmos strangely veiled as if by a fine milky mist of a slightly opaline hue. Set out as a perfect sphere, the upper half of which stood out above the City and between its countless buildings, each more bold, each more elevated than the other. A screen of indestructible, hermetic, inviolable energy.

"But what happened?" Giovanna Hi-Ling whispered, suddenly clinging to her lover's arm.

"We were attacked, Yooi," Zo'Akl said. "All our weapons were powerless and nothing could prevent the disaster..."

Ka'Pholgar took up the thread, "The spaceship that suddenly surged out of subspace using a technique unknown to us, looked like a harmless wreck and we thought it was in trouble. We gave it clearance to approach one of our orbital relay stations. And there, without warning, the aggressor initiated an inconceivable attack: it generated a gigantic transparent bubble that not only imprisoned Maakeldar and the Magistral city, but also all the planet's ground below it. The energy used cut through the rock, the earth, the solid crust like what you call butter. Then the sphere rose up into the sky, taking with it what it had just stripped from Mîo."

"And the prison has no means of escape, right?" Bruno Coqdor broke in.

"Correct, Chevalier," Zo'Akl affirmed.

"I myself was captive in one of these bubbles, on Titan, a satellite of a giant planet in our Solar System," the Star Knight added. "I know of only one individual able to create these dreadful things. This ship that attacked you, did you meet anyone on board, pilot or passengers?"

"We were forced to welcome the stranger and accommodate him like a prince, with his retinue," Ka'Pholgar lamented. "He reigns here in a conquered country and demands that we comply with his every whim. He's holding us and the entire Magistral City hostage."

"Who is this monster, since you know him, Bruno?" Giovanna asked, petrified with anxiety.

"It's the Marsupial!" Coqdor declared.

A gravelly, somewhat quivering voice, full of arrogance and sarcasm, rang out at that moment.

"Another woman who will not redeem the others! I am right to hate them! A monster... Nay, empty brain! A monster? No... A demigod, rather!"

And what a demigod... Under other circumstances, it would have been laughable.

The man who had spoken walked towards the small group. He was a redheaded, bearded colossus with huge, old-fashioned sideburns, dirty hair, thick bushy eyebrows and big beady gray-blue eyes. On his weathered face, the thin, tight lips were not likely to smile very often.

For clothing, he wore a suit ready for the disintegration dumpster. Rust colored, filthy, stained. His worn synthetic leather boots were flabby, shapeless.

And his huge hands, gnarled like old alder trees, with fingers as big as sausages, seemed ready to strangle.

Everything about him screamed renegade, outcast. His whole being exuded an indiscriminate misanthropy, a visceral hatred of human beings. There was nothing to rehabilitate him as a brilliant scientist, an unparalleled inventor and handyman, creator of true marvels of subtlety and technique. Nor anything to arouse pity for the desperate person he was, deep down.

The Marsupial, in the end, was just what humans had made him. Unconsciously, involuntarily certainly. But they had done it.

Against the injustice, intolerance, discrimination, the refusal of difference, these negative values defining the narrow minds that his coplanetriots and most so-called intelligent peoples had never succeeded and would never succeed in getting rid of, Coqdor had been inclined to forgive the Marsupial.

"So, pretty little pigeon of Earth, you never would've guessed it, right? And you, fearless, flawless Chevalier, did you think I was dead?"

The person questioned shook his head in denial,

"I never accepted that the attack of the military fleet on Titan had killed you, friend," he admitted honestly. "Given the assets you had and thanks to your friends the 'Others' or whoever, you could only pretend to be destroyed in order to bow out more easily."

The Marsupial burst into mirthless laughter.

"They had to save me, those beings from the distant quasars at the borders of the blue galaxies. It was I who brought them there. Thanks to me, they had achieved what they wanted. My only mistake was leaving you and the other two idiots and that damned Commodore Flood alive. But the 'Others' couldn't blame me for that. That's why they let me go... Also because I was privy to a secret that really interested them."

"The Zodiac?" Coqdor guessed aloud.

"Nice job, Monsieur the green-eyed clairvoyant! Are you reading my black soul or what? Yes, the Zodiac. Some time ago, I had come across the trail of some shady characters who were conniving around this oddity in the name of a nihilist cult that looked pretty good to me. I liked their spiel. Unfortunately, they were complete idiots ready to swallow any nonsense. I gave them the scare of their lives and they were eating out of my hand."

"So it was you who terrorized Cladek Halstar!" Giovanna sighed.

"To serve you, fatal beauty! Good old Marsupial, the phenomenal champion of galactic phantoms and bogeymen! I manipulated those gullible cosmomancers into getting the secret of the Zodiac for me and they failed miserably... They acted so discreetly that they were killed by the initiates themselves. A shame! I felt the storm coming and I sneaked away. The Marsupial Eclipse, it's called. It lasted for years. But now, with the Cabal, I have succeeded and the goal is near. A thriller, boys and girls! You will see it soon..."

He turned around and snapped his fat, stubby fingers.

"Hey, friends, come over here, we've got to keep on eye on the pearl of the islands, the green-eyed monster and his pet vampire dog!"

A strange quartet appeared.

First, three clunky, lanky robots about to fall over at every step. Built in defiance of all laws of aesthetics and kinematics. But they moved forward. Decisively, even. And they were armed.

"Here's the second generation, Chevalier! The new Klym, Avztar and Molyion, brilliant successors to those you loved..."

"There were four," Coqdor recalled.

"There are still four, don't worry," the colossus replied. "The musketeers are indestructible. Zimo has also been revised and corrected. He'll be joining us soon, by the way. I had sent him back into the Solar System for a brief stay to carry out some crucial operations. Teletransportation for discreet, remote parachuting, recovery, re-parachute, re-recovery, and on and on it goes. It will be over in a short time, a few days at most. We will soon be showing 'Zimo 2, the return'. With my good old ghost ship, brrrr... He put on a scared pout, rolled his eyes, made his yellowed teeth chatter and his knees wobble, opened and closed his fists while flapping his arms. The cemetery ship, terror of the captains who crisscross the oceans of the sky... Ah, Richard Wagner, The Flying Dutchman... But the drama's over. The time has come, the reprobate has touched ground and will find salvation. Redemption in the Twilight of Gods, humans, rabbits, pigs, turkeys, sheep, pigeons, idiots, pickles, the whole shebang! The Marsupial gives himself a nasty slap on the wrist. Hey, shut up! Damn chatterbox! You're the only one we hear here! Got it? Make way for His Martian Highness, Cladek the Star!"

Closely following the three robots, stiff as a steel pole, as straight as if he had swallowed a saber, the Master of Scorpio, ex-financier and director of Solexport, approached in turn.

Squeezed into a kind of royal blue ceremonial uniform, a loose cape draped over his thin shoulders, Halstar looked dashing.

In his somewhat fixed gaze no longer gleamed the slightest spark of madness. What shined in his eyes was the cold, gnawing fire of desire for revenge against all those who had betrayed him.

First on the list was Giovanna Hi-Ling.

Without saying a word, ignoring all the others present at the meeting, the Martian threw himself on the Sino-Italian while changing form.

The Marsupial raised his hand and hissed bizarrely. Halstar stopped abruptly, as if he had hit an invisible glass partition head-on and went back to his original appearance.

"Back off, little fly!" the colossus thundered. "And you, divine beauty, put away that ray gun toy that looks as nasty in your hand as a stick of lit dynamite between the lips of a baby... Anyway, you don't need a blaster to defend yourself. And him, the good doggie whose three fried neurons I gave back, watch out for his whiskers if he tries to make you eat your birth certificate!"

During this spat of theatrical ranting, magnificent and ridiculous at the same time, which the space pariah rained down on them, Coqdor gleaned a few precious fragments of a vast mosaic whose lost motif was being completed little by little.

So then, it was the Marsupial who had healed Cladek Halstar, directly or indirectly. The mysterious "clairvoyance device" possessed by the fringe genius had perhaps helped in this.

As for the teletransportation techniques with parachuting then recovery, didn't this explain the disappearance of the Martian from Sainte-Anne hospital, six months earlier?

Furthermore, whatever powers the Masters had, they could not compete with the technological power of the Marsupial. And everyone feared him.

The outcast spoke again, more serious this time.

"I have antennae everywhere, little lambs," he patronized, "so I know that Brown is dead and that you are replacing him now, Chevalier. How does it feel to have access to the Aleph and be the Guide of the Zodiac? Feeling like a big shot, right, Coqdor?"

The green-eyed man didn't answer.

"And you, beautiful one? Queen of Capricorn, that suits you... Halstar went about it all wrong trying to kill you. We can see that he isn't playing with a full deck! Anyway, enough joking around. With the dark-skinned one here, we've got the three Masters whose medallions are missing from the collection of my friend the Persean. We just have to wait for Zimo's return for the series to be complete, because he is obviously bringing with him Noa Akatinor, Luse Borek... and two other acquaintances of yours, my Aldebaran fluozx! Surprise, surprise... I won't tell you any more."

"Whatever happens, whatever your plans, I will never cooperate with you!" Giovanna spat.

"You will have no choice, nor your colleagues either, cute angry wildcat. Have you seen where you are? What you are in? One wave of my hand and I burst the bubble. Halstar and I can each make a small one—but you two, the pstôr and the other burnt toast there, will die like fish out of water when the atmosphere is diluted in the void. A pity... A waste... But we'll get the medallions from your corpses, and presto! The rotunda will be easy pickings. Banco, I win and I hit the jackpot!"

"What will you do with it?" the Star Knight asked casually.

"That's my business, Chevalier! But since it's you asking and because you're the only man in Creation to whom I can show respect, I'll explain it to you. He turned to his three robots. Come on, boys, put all these nice people in the closet for a little while! Well, no, let them stay here, not too close though, while I talk to my friend."

The machines positioned themselves in a triangle, in the center of which stood the two Mîos, Giovanna and Râx. Between Klym, Azvtar and Molyion a barrier of strong waves was created, or at least the equivalent in Marsupial technology. The pstôr let out a series of moans. He was scared. Giovanna put her hand on his head.

"Don't cry, your master will be all right."

The animal seemed to calm down. With a glance, Coqdor also reassured him before turning back to the space pariah who had grabbed his arm and was dragging him away.

"What I want, Chevalier, is to put an end to this monstrosity that is called our Universe... You who have traveled up and down the galaxy, who have flirted with the Great Unknown and the beyond, you can't contradict me: there was something rotten in the State of Denmark for poor Hamlet. Here, everything is rotten... Or almost..."

"So you want to... dissolve Creation, is that it?

"That's it, dear star seer! Before the drama on Titan, I was already an outsider. For what? You will understand when we take the leap together, when everything merges into a single perispirit... You will know what I went through in the past, what they dared to do to me and my poor family... For me, the final blow was the reaction of the Praesidium to the 'Others'. Article 723... The quintessence of xenophobia, of the denial of foreigners. Strike first, think about it later. They coldly annihilated a mini-Creation, a divine process, without trying to know why it had started. After that, since I already knew about the existence of a means to blow away to the four winds of eternity this morass of hatred and abomination called the Universe, all my actions were aimed only at this goal."

"Genocide on a cosmic scale... Monstrous!" Coqdor protested.

"No, not a genocide! Famal Maeth certainly," the Marsupial replied. "Exit the Great All! Long live Non-Being! But afterwards... You read that too: from darkness will come light... Aemaeth! Re-Creation, just like before, minus the negative. And I'll be the one to see to that. Personally. No more tyrants, no more executioners, no more criminals, no more exploiters or profiteers, no more sexual perverts and others... No more pedophiles or rapists... Purification from the start. All of them, all these despicable individualities will be forbidden to be reborn. Melted into the mass of others. Drowned, dissolved. No one will remember being uncreated and recreated anyway. But only the positives will remain..."

The Star Knight thought for a moment before retaliating.

"And it's you who will do the sorting? You who are infused by the breath of universal vengeance? You who are driven by the most primitive negative, by hatred and the craving to satisfy it? This is crazy, Marsupial! Only the mind of the Great Architect can design or redesign a Creation as a whole. Neither you nor any human nor any intelligent being can imagine, at our stage of evolution, being able to replace him to decide, select or direct like him! You are not God and you never will be... Even by plunging into the Aleph! Your second Creation, your new Genesis will inevitably be imperfect!"

Saying this, Coqdor realized in a flash that he had made a huge tactical error.

"Is the present universe perfect? No! Far from it... The next one will be infinitely better and if there remains a handful of negative germs anywhere, then I'll give chase. I'll hunt them down and eradicate them!"

"You yourself will then become what you wanted to eliminate, Marsupial! An executioner, an assassin, an exterminator..."

"Enough!" the space pariah exploded. "You... You... No, you're lying on purpose, you're trying to trick me... Shut up, Bruno Coqdor! I forbid you to say another word..."

The Marsupial was foaming with anger. Beaten at his own game, tangled up in his own words, he had run out of arguments. Dragging the Chevalier, he ran again and huffed like a seal back to the group guarded by the robots near which Halstar stood motionless.

Pressing a button on his big belt covered with various instruments and devices, he created four iridescent bubbles the height of a man.

Instantly, Coqdor, Giovanna, Râx and Ka'Pholgar found themselves prisoners of these unbreakable jails, like young girls who would certainly have surprised and seduced King Louis XI in his time.

"As for you, Zo'Akl, supreme scholar, don't you dare lift even a finger to try to free them or do anything against me!" the Marsupial concluded stonily. "Otherwise, pop! Goodbye to the Magistral City, goodbye to your coplanetriots, I will raze Maakeldar and Mîo to the ground..."

Turning on his heel, he walked away with his three robots and the Scorpio Master.

"See you soon, friends!" he trumpeted in an insolent voice which nevertheless vibrated with a nuance of uncertainty. "Zimo won't be very long. A few hours or days, perhaps? Until then, sleep well..."

With a final wave of his gnarled right hand, each of the prisoners collapsed to the bottom of their bubble.

Before falling into hypnotic sleep, Coqdor had one final thought.

Sinister.

Short of a true miracle, all was lost.

Then nothingness swallowed him up.

All of a sudden, light.

Awakening...

Noise and commotion...

"Get up in there!"

The order was sharp, imperious. Impossible not to obey.

The prisoners opened their eyes.

In front of them were the Marsupial, his three robots and Cladek Halstar. Just like the moment when irresistible sleep had plunged the prisoners into darkness and silence.

"Finally... Here is loyal Zimo! Look, the show's been worth it!"

At the top of the huge, milky bubble enveloping Maakeldar and the fragment torn from the planet Mîo there appeared, as if springing out of nothing, an unsightly and bumpy sphere of dirty rust color. When it came into contact with the energy field, a point glowed and gradually turned into a ring of fire that grew larger as the ghost ship penetrated.

The dazzling ring disappeared as soon as it was big enough for the ship. In fact, it gradually shrank as the ship passed through.

"Supertechnology is a marvel, eh my little lambs!" the Marsupial quivered. "Not a drop of atmosphere escaped!"

Apart from the pstôr whose simple mind could not comprehend such complicated things, the three other captives admired the wonder. Coqdor, however, was not surprised to see the space pariah once again displaying overwhelming superiority.

The cobbled together and unwieldy machine, a real insult to the universal laws of aesthetics, descended to the din of its propellers and landed, as light as a leaf, in the middle of the vast metal-tiled esplanade.

Then a ramp creaked down from its underbelly while the Marsupial, pressing a button on his belt, freed the four staggering prisoners from their energy cells.

Oddly, none of them had suffered hunger or thirst during their term in the bubbles. Subtle, immaterial fluids, rays coming from a science still unknown to them, had fed and watered them as much as necessary.

Five people disembarked from the spheroship that belonged to the genius misanthrope.

A woman, first.

Haughty, of truly infernal beauty, molded in a dark purple jumpsuit that matched perfectly the midnight blue of her hair and the mauve shine of her almond-shaped eyes.

"Luse Borek!" Giovanna Hi-Ling whispered, who had naturally found refuge in the arms of the Star Knight. "And obviously Noa Akatinor..."

Thus, Coqdor was able to identify the Persean with his sinister appearance. The incarnation of absolute black, of the darkness of the underworld, the assassin of seven of the Masters of the Zodiac was frightening. Terribly frightening, like all fanatics.

The one who came after hardly surprised the green-eyed man. Still young, ordinary, his face marked with the infinite sadness of the desperate in whom all optimism had been quashed, the individual had chosen to flee his peers and to remain alongside the Marsupial, once upon a time around Titan.

"Claude Dalbret," the Chevalier said.

"Yes, Claude Dalbret," the outcast immediately confirmed. "My friend Mr. D., my partner in life and in death!"

Coqdor had some difficulty recognizing the next passenger. It must be said that it was hardly Robin Muscat's habit to appear as the shady Wolfram Haag, with makeup and a disguise that made identifying him impossible for anyone not in the know. It was not with enthusiasm that the commissioner walked towards his friend, in whom he still saw the odious criminal who had eliminated Edward Brown.

The last to come down was a robot, Zimo, the fourth musketeer, as his owner called him.

"Glad to see you again, Chevalier!" Dalbret declared with the hint of a smile. "I've never forgotten our shared adventures nor your compassion towards me. Time and time again you saved my life... And thanks to you, even after so long and indirectly, I will finally be able to find Sylvia..."

"How's that?" Coqdor replied, sounding skeptical.

"The Universe will be recreated as it was before. Everyone who has ever lived will live again. Sylvia too. I'll just have to be there to act at the right time and prevent her death..."

"You really believe anything!" Muscat shot back briskly. "Don't you understand? These monsters are manipulating you, keeping you under hypnosis with a smokescreen that not even the most naive person would confuse with a possible reality!"

"No, precious star cop," Coqdor refuted. "In a way, he's not wrong. Creation is about to be remade through an unimaginable process, we don't know what will come out of it, but why not..."

The Marsupial was getting seriously impatient and he thundered in his powerful voice:

"Enough of your yakking and blather! We have better and more urgent things to do. Let's recap: are the thirteen medallions—in the absence of the thirteen Masters, peace to the souls of the deceased!—here? Akatinor, how many?"

"Seven," replied the Persian icily.

"Luse Borek?"

"Two," the former leader of the Black Circle announced.

"One," Cladek Halstar said distantly, before being asked.

"Two with these good folk," the outcast went on. "Capricorn with that pretty Chinese porcelain, Aquarius with that expressionless burnt toast there. In all... Twelve! So, Noa, not quite there? Why not, Monsieur exterminating angel?"

The other glared at him, "As if you didn't know…"

"Ah yes, it wasn't you who got the prize, poor thing," the pariah of the cosmos snickered. "I'd forgotten."

"I killed the Zodiac Guide," the Persean justified himself, "but this Earthling demon, his animal and the girl slipped away I don't know how, taking Brown's corpse..."

"And it is I who wear the thirteenth medallion," Coqdor cut in. "Before dying, because we managed to keep him alive until the Hoggar, he and Giovanna opened the way to the Aleph for me and I became the Master of the Eagle..."

"God of the Cosmos!" Muscat sighed loudly, as if suddenly relieved of an enormous weight. "You weren't the murderer, Bruno! But... your fingerprints?"

"I had to take the medallion myself, Brown no longer had enough strength to take it out. A barbaric act, true, but something that I had to do."

"How could we have known?" Muscat said.

"By remembering that the Chevalier is a good person, you blind man!" the Marsupial chided. "In all this Creation, he's the only one who can be judged as such... Come on, to hell with these useless speeches, it's time! To the rotunda of Aquarius and quickly! Otherwise, I'll burst the bubble."

The threat was final. The six owners of medallions had to head to the bowels of Maakeldar.

As he passed Muscat, Coqdor whispered a few words to him:

"I'm entrusting Râx to you, keep him well. I don't know what's going to happen... If I don't come back, take care of him."

"Hurry up, hurry up! No more goodbyes!" the renegade scholar barked.

A few minutes later, in the rotunda of Aquarius, the thirteen medallions of the Zodiac were all together.

The last phase, the one in which the annihilation and then the supposedly corrected reconstruction of the Universe would result, was imminent...

Bruno Coqdor, Giovanna Hi-Ling, Luse Borek, Cladek Halstar and Ka'Pholgar were placed at the tops of an equal hexagon in the middle of the system with thirteen portals. Occupying the center of this unique pentacle was Noa Akatinor—and the Marsupial.

It was obviously the Persean who began the process with ritual words used only for total access to the Aleph.

"Famal Aleph!" his deep voice resounded with the unfamiliar syllables.

As in the Hoggar caverns, Coqdor first saw the superdimensional image of the fourteenth rotunda forming, erasing the rocky vault that surrounded them with its dense mass.

Ghostly, immaterial.

The next moment, the projection of the corresponding rotunda appeared behind each of the thirteen inter-world doorways. Luminous, ethereal, impalpable figures, they formed a wondrous geometric pattern reminiscent of the structure of an extraordinary ice crystal, arranged around the spectral copy of the fourteenth rotunda coming down.

Slowly, inevitably.

Suddenly, the fourteen "doubles" of light merged into a single intangible artifact.

At the same time, all materiality vanished. That of the stone constituting the room buried under the Magistral City, that of the fleshly envelopes of the seven gathered people of whom only the astral bodies remained, hovering in the middle of an unreal setting.

Seven silhouettes of light shining with a different aura, surrounded by the wave projection of the thirteen thresholds.

They were now in the fourteenth rotunda.

Then, in a titanic blaze, the entire Universe revealed itself to them.

The Universe and more.

The Aleph in the absolute of its breadth transcending all times and all space.

CHAPTER XIII

Here, infinity...

Zenith and nadir of Creation.

Four cardinal points multiplied to the eternity of duration and distance.

Slow, continuous and rhythmic bass pulsation of an immeasurable living organism.

To the beats of a heart-spirit embracing all dimensions, from Alpha to Omega, from the initial explosion to the ultimate coalescence.

Infinity?

No... The transfinite...

Facing the Universe, facing what a reductive vision would have hastily assimilated to the spherical projection of an unimaginable planetarium, a silhouette.

Packed, thick, unsightly despite its contours of clarity.

All light but a morbid and sad light, not very reassuring.

The ethereal double of the Marsupial.

Ready to dive, to blend into the Universe, finally within reach of his twisted arms and his knotted hands which would reshape it as it pleased.

In the minds of everyone else, a dazzling thought...

Do not be afraid... Do not tremble... This will not affect you, you will not be recreated. You are outside the Universe—so am I until I merge with it...

Last-minute response, final attempt to return to reason.

Don't go there, Marsupial! You aspire to the pure and absolute positive but you carry within you the germ of the negative that you want to banish forever... The Aleph will reject you—or you will reject yourself! What awaits you is death. No—even worse! Eternal wandering in the limbo of interlife... Listen to me, I know what I'm talking about!

Sarcastic, mocking laughter.

Ha! Ha! Ha! My dear Chevalier, do you fear for yourself? What nonsense... I will save you. We see ourselves as the gods of this new cosmos. And it will be beautiful, in our image, in the image of the goodness that is in us. Come with me!

Bruno Coqdor had fought often, on many levels, in many realms, up to the two-dimensional continuum and the infinitely small world of intelligent snow crystals. He had braved nothingness, the void, the seven chromatic lights in a formidable photon labyrinth, crisscrossed the roads of the afterlife to the gates of the eternal dawns. Material or immaterial, battling was familiar to him.

Currently, he did not have to rely on any physical resources. Only the soul could act, only the spirit could prevail against the spirit.

And although the Star Knight had repeatedly resisted it, it was the weapon of psychic suggestion that he would have to use.

Stop this sick man... Stop this madman before he effected a cure worse than the disease itself...

Coqdor discreetly deployed a net of mental waves, made it grow to a size able to envelope the Marsupial's ego, tortured and bloated though it might be. Then he sent the hypnosuggestion network towards his potential adversary.

The outcast had not forgotten. Formerly, in the space suburbs of the giant Saturn, Coqdor had done likewise in order to neutralize the master of the ghost spaceship so that Claude Dalbret, Wilfrid and Tchou could escape. In a flash, the Marsupial remembered and prepared a suitable defense for the assault. In doing so, he called for help or, more precisely, he summoned Noa Akatinor to intervene and block the Star Knight.

The dark fluidic form of the Persean broke away from the group of six astral doubles and moved towards...

Bruno Coqdor?

No!

The Marsupial himself...

And he struck him with a tremendous burst of mental energy, literally laying him out for the count. Easy, for those who combine the powers of seven Masters...

Poor fool... Akatinor's psychic voice burst out in the minds of the others. *Uncreate and recreate the Universe? So it was the cosmomancers who won the game? Well, we fooled him, that idiot Marsupial, my brother and I—from the start! We were barely past childhood when a forgotten sect of our home planet introduced us to Chaos of which we became followers. From the day Yum got in contact with the Zodiac, we understood that we had finally found our way, the solution to ultimately establish the reign of Non-Being!*

Yum recruited Cladek Halstar and Luse Borek. We got two of the most faithful followers. Through the involuntary intervention of Giovanna, then Cladek's mistress, the infiltration of the Zodiac could begin.

The first time, it didn't go very far. Lack of discretion, subtlety and patience. And despite the help of the Marsupial, who already believed he was manipulating us when it was the opposite... The Masters were powerful, their Guide cunning, we made mistakes...

But Non-Being has time, Chaos knows how to wait... Now, the moment has come.

Famal Maeth!

Moving away from the fluidic form of the space pariah, which lay on an immaterial and invisible ground, the black Persean advanced towards the fascinating hypersphere that was the Great Absolute Whole.

Suddenly, between the Universe and the cosmomancer, another silhouette stepped in.

All haloed in emerald, like the eyes of its original...

The astral double of the Star Knight...

Then began a mind-boggling fight, an out-of-this-world and common confrontation between two spirit-entities having only their psychic resources to strike the most terrible blows.

As if on cue, Giovanna Hi-Ling pounced on Cladek Halstar and Ka'Pholgar leapt like a mad beast at Luse Borek.

Jealousy, hatred and desire for revenge of the abandoned lover were unleashed against the rediscovered purity, the resplendent redemption radiated by the aura of the Sino-Italian. The Martian was no match for his opponent. His mind, once already deconstructed and reconstructed by artificial means, could not endure the icy determination of the Master of Capricorn.

You tried to kill me, Cladek! screamed the young woman telepathically. *Don't count on my pity anymore...*

Halstar's spirit shattered into a myriad of diamond fragments against the barrier put up by Giovanna. Then the astral body of the ex-financier faded away forever, to the sound of the final thought he uttered before passing away:

It's snowing on Syrtis Major.

And the last Martian is no more...

Almost at the same second, if time still had a meaning in this place beyond all others, Ka'Pholgar fell under the enormous negative shock with which Luse Borek struck him.

Between Coqdor and Akatinor, the fight was not yet over. The metamorphism of the Masters also taking place on the fluidic level, the two silhouettes had launched into a Dantesque ballet in which their forms changed smoothly.

The bolts of superdimensional energy they bombarded each other with streamed off their defensive shields, also of pure energy.

Tremendous lightning flashed, breaking into millions of blinding streaks that snaked their way up to the Universe-sphere.

The very fabric of Creation absorbed their final dissolution. From one end of the cosmos to the other, unprecedented phenomena were occurring, plunging into perplexity and worry those who had sufficient means to observe and record them.

The "Others," those superentities populating quasars or blue galaxies, began to fear for the metastructure of the Universe, the complex eleven-dimensional edifice whose inconceivable architecture they were the only ones to have glimpsed.

Deep in a pre-world of amorphous darkness where confused currents of thought seethed, the shadows of the Uncreated came to life little by little having glimpsed the light of the bordering cosmos, with the hope that materialization could be authorized for them there.

Around Aldebaran, an immense stellar whirlwind which would later sow desolation on the space routes crossing this sector took shape then started spinning faster and faster, generating microspheres of absolute nothingness.

In Southern Pisces, the strange organomineral people of the Prismoids became aware of a pervasive threat of unknown origin and began to take an interest in the rest of the Milky Way. In a few centuries, the encounter with humans would lead to a terrible war...

Near the Magellanic Clouds, the rival races of Urizz and K'Toon suddenly saw the formidable cemetery of stars (the secret of which they had not yet unlocked) ablaze with countless torches when dead stars torn from their bodies were resurrected for a few seconds in their cosmic tomb of eternity.

Over in the Monoceros, an extraordinarily advanced race developed the model of the Mechanicosmos based on the paradimensional measurements carried out by its incredibly gifted mediums, and embarked on the construction of plans of conquest on the scale of the Universe.

The giants inhabiting a very distant blue galaxy were gripped with irrepressible fear, starting to believe in the imminence of a cataclysm which would sweep them away, and they began preparations for a mass migration. Much later, their cosmic movements would reach the Milky Way and give birth to fearful legends about the night threatening to fall on worlds condemned by their progress...

Inside the immaterial super-rotunda, while the Terran and the Persean were still fighting, a vortex of absolute darkness sprouted under their insubstantial feet. A lens of unfathomable darkness, condensate of total nothingness, eye of Non-Being slowly opening...

Famal Maeth!

Noa Akatinor repeated the incantation with wilder and wilder fervor.

Famal Aemaeth!

Tirelessly, at each pause, Bruno Coqdor counterattacked with the creative Word to counter the call to eternal Chaos.

The disk of darkness grew, throwing black flashes of light which streaked the ambient luminosity, cracked the virtual super-rotunda, coiled in the astral bodies of the protagonists and in the Universe-sphere.

Little by little, the Aleph seemed to ebb, to move away, and the Non-Being to come closer.

Suddenly, a long shape moved slowly. With a final burst of energy and will, the Marsupial stood up again... And jumped on the Persean.

Forgive me, Great Architect of all cosmos... Forgive me, for I did not know what I was doing...

The pariah of space and the zealot of Chaos sank at the same time into the abyss of Non-Being.

As if an invisible link had bound her to the two missing people, Luse Borek was also swallowed up. Then the eye of darkness slowly closed, like the mouth of a sated monster.

As the Aleph continued to move away, the astral remains of Ka'Pholgar and Cladek Halstar faded away.

In the center of the super-rotunda, two silhouettes of light melted into an ephemeral embrace, for a brief intimacy with touches of eternity and infinity.

Giovanna Hi-Ling.

Bruno Coqdor.

Lovers on the magnificent scale of the Universe.

Little by little, the phantasmagorical process took place in reverse.

The fourteenth rotunda separated itself from the others, then they all separated while materiality regained its imperious rights.

Very close to the two lovers, hovering in the void, eleven small objects of an unknown metal, eleven medallions stamped with eleven distinctive signs.

The Star Knight grabbed them one by one and gave them to his companion.

Then, just before reentering his fleshly envelope, he tore the Eagle medallion from his chest and stuck it under the left breast of the Sino-Italian woman.

Giovanna shuddered throughout her being as if a new orgasm was making her vibrate and she scrutinized her companion with a questioning look.

"A man like me cannot be the Zodiac Guide," Coqdor declared. "Either I would be forced to disappear in order to protect the secret, to prevent it from falling into the hands of the leaders of the Martervenux or other powers, or I would be forced to reveal everything so that humanity and its allied peoples could benefit. I refuse both, darling. You, on the other hand, will be able to perform the task very well."

"Wherever I am, Bruno, wherever you are, you can contact me anytime. Don't forget that you carry within you the indelible imprint of the Aleph."

"And don't forget that the Star Knight loves you, beautiful Zodiac Guide," Coqdor replied, happy and terribly sad at the same time. "He will always be there for you, no matter what. May the God of the Cosmos help you in the reconstruction of the circle of Masters, beloved Giovanna."

"Tell Râx that I will miss him too, Bruno. See you soon..."

The beautiful woman had recovered her body in its perfect, so alluring plasticity. Moved, the Chevalier watched her walk away towards the

Capricorn doorway after they had exchanged one last kiss, long and passionate.

He gave her a final wave goodbye, then headed towards the portal of Aquarius.

Apart from him, the rotunda was empty. With the dissolution of the immaterial doubles, the physical remains of the pitiful corpses had also vanished.

The Universe was saved—this time.

As he returned to the surface, Coqdor had the strange feeling of being resurrected. As if he had been given the opportunity to die, the better to come back to life and emerge from the tomb.

In his heart the cold of the interstellar void had settled. Parting with Giovanna was a terrible heartbreak. But somewhere, the flame of hope continued to burn.

Wherever he was, whatever the moment, the Star Knight could see the new Zodiac Guide again.

And he vowed not to wait another eternity.

Râx, Robin Muscat, Claude Dalbret, the four motley robots of the late Marsupial, the old scientist Zo'Akl and a group of other Mîos surrounded Bruno Coqdor as soon as he stepped out of the small building in the shape of a truncated pyramid. They all looked a little dazed, as if they had suffered a shock whose cause they could not explain.

Rushing to his master, the pstôr welcomed him with a great display of joy.

Seeing his long-time friend reappear alone, the commissioner opened his eyes wide in astonishment.

"Where are the others, Coqdor? Did you kill them, or what? Here we didn't understand what was happening, but it was as if the cosmos had been struck by an earthquake. The bubble vibrated, was streaked with black scars... But fortunately, it held up!"

"Almost all the others dropped into... nothingness, an irreversible fall. Only Giovanna survived and she left... The crucial problem is resolved, rest assured. Neither the cosmomancers nor the Zodiac will cause you trouble in the future. I'll tell you everything in detail later and you'd better be sitting down to hear the whole story."

Dalbret, who was listening, came up to the Chevalier.

"The Marsupial?"

"Exit the space pariah... In the end, he realized his mistake and the plot of the Perseans. His death, his suicide rather, is a kind of redemption. I'm sure the Great Architect will receive him with mercy."

"I hope so too," said the young man. "Deep down he was a misunderstood person who suffered from the stupidity and indignity of his peers. And a scientific genius whose services humanity could have been proud of if it had not forced him to turn his back on it and make some serious mistakes. If one day I can tell you everything he revealed to me about himself and if it serves to rehabilitate him, I'll be happy to."

"What will you do without him?" Muscat asked.

"I'm now the new Flying Dutchman of the cosmos, the captain of the ghost ship... You remember, Chevalier, the strange clairvoyance device that you saw on board the ship, that armchair crowned with a helmet bristling inside with very thin little spikes? It's also a knowledge transfer machine, as long as it functions first as a recorder with a subject who 'gives' then as a transmitter with the person to be taught. I went through it, the Marsupial wanted it. He said that one day it might be useful to me if he disappeared or hung up his hat... Here I am, his equal in terms of knowledge. But I didn't inherit his creative faculties and I won't invent anything beyond what he bequeathed to me."

"So? Are you staying with us?"

"No... I'm setting off again through the cosmos, a bit like the cursed sailor of the legend... Perhaps one day I'll reach one of these distant sidereal lands where the saving angel will incarnate for me in my feminine ideal—Sylvia, whom death stole from me, Magali, ephemeral resurrection whom my peers swept away as soon as she was reborn, or another..."

"You're fleeing , you're fleeing the Confederation and that's good," Coqdor concluded. "The secrets hoarded by the Marsupial will never fall into their hands and I trust you to guard them so that they don't leak to any other people. Thank you and good luck, Mr D."

"But I'm not taking off just yet, my friends. I still have a big job to finish. Let's call it a... repair job. Lord Zo'Akl, Master of Aquarius, your world will recover its initial integrity right away!"

Dalbret swung around, made a sign to his four robots who started off and followed them in the direction of the big round spacecraft so unsightly, so ugly and stained from all its cosmic wanderings.

Before disappearing into the belly of the craft that now belonged to him, he made a final farewell gesture to the Mîos, to the two Earthlings and obviously to the pstôr.

The ramp folded up and three minutes later the ghost ship soared off. It passed through the bell of opaline energy in the same way it had arrived, then headed toward a fixed point in the distance.

All of a sudden, a great big azure cone of radiance shot out of its equatorial ring and flowed over the spherical surface of the bubble enveloping the Magistral City and the parcel of planetary soil under it. The bubble, slowly but steadily, started descending towards the surface of the homeworld of the Aquarian scholars.

For the spectators of this marvel beyond all imagination, the refusing process took place with incredible and also very thorough gentleness.

An hour after the start of the operation, the milky veil which blurred the view of the surrounding cosmos had vanished silently.

With it, the rusty and dented ship evaporated in a fraction of a second, in one of those instantaneous subspace dives of which only the Marsupial possessed the secret.

The fragment torn from Mîo had returned to its place, looking as natural as before.

Once again, Maakeldar stood where his first stone had been laid, millennia before.

In the Magistral City, seat of the Arcana of Science, an enormous sigh of relief escaped everyone's chest.

Then a celebration fitting the narrowly avoided universal cataclysm was hastily organized before Coqdor, Muscat and Râx set off again for distant Earth.

EPILOGUE

It was in the Saharan desert at the foot of the Hoggar Mountains.

More precisely, at the base of the massif in which access to the labyrinth leading to the Eagle rotunda opened.

For Robin Muscat, verification accomplished: the places had the ruined and off-putting appearance that they usually had.

For a moment, Bruno Coqdor had seen the virtual mirages fade away to let him glimpse the real inter-world rotunda, intact, immutable, eternal.

This passage through which later, whenever he wanted, he would be able to join Giovanna Hi-Ling, the new Zodiac Guide whose circle of Masters would soon be re- established.

The Star Knight smiled at the thought of the beautiful Sino-Italian woman, whose enchanting image he unconsciously projected into the pstôr's brain. Râx raised his head, riveted his big golden eyes onto Coqdor's emerald pupils and made a very soft sound, a cuddly purr mixed with affectionate harmonics.

High in the clear night sky, stretched like a canopy of black velvet over the solitude of sand and rock, a bright point of azure color was visibly shrinking.

It was the great spaceship of the Mîos, wrapped in one of those blue spheres making subspace dives possible while ensuring maximum undetectability, which had brought the two men and the bulldog-bat from Aquarius back to the Solar System and had dropped them off at the requested location on their home planet which they were very impatient to get back to.

While the machine, having crossed the upper limits of the atmosphere, vanished into the fourth dimension, Muscat tapped on the keyboard of the microcommunicator hidden in his space smuggler's harness and established a connection with Marc Vérano.

"Wolfram Haag calling Terry Reno! Wolfram Haag calling Terry Reno! I know, it's nighttime but wake yourself up, lazybones, this is no time for napping!"

An indistinct noise answered him, half yawn, half annoyed grunt. Then two words, barely better articulated: "Yes Boss…?"

"I'm at Ravenclaw Point with two old friends," Muscat said. "A medium of the stars and a pstôr of Dzo. Come and rescue us right away, kid. Got it? Don't worry, all's well. Get here as fast as you can. We've come a long way..."

He paused briefly.

"And we even saved the Universe..."